HELLO, YOU

HELLO, YOU

Rebecca Gregson

Severn House Large Print
London & New York

This first large print edition published 2009
in Great Britain and the USA by
SEVERN HOUSE PUBLISHERS LTD of
9-15 High Street, Sutton, Surrey, SM1 1DF.
First world regular print edition published 2007 by
Severn House Publishers Ltd., London and New York.

British Library Cataloguing in Publication Data

Gregson, Rebecca
  Hello, you. - Large print ed.
  1. Middle-aged mothers - Fiction 2. Sisters - Fiction
  3. Domestic fiction 4. Large type books
  I. Title
  823.9'2[F]

ISBN-13: 978-0-7278-7762-8

Printed and bound in Great Britain by
MPG Books Ltd, Bodmin, Cornwall.

To my boy

Prologue

August 1968

In retrospect, the day the cat was let out of its bag dawned auspiciously. As the sunlight, already tinged with a sense of what hadn't yet happened, seeped through the tent's faded orange canvas, Maggie slipped her chewed fingers under her pillow, pulled out her diary and turned down the top right-hand corner of the day's page. Marking Keep Days was normally a bedtime decision, but for the mere fact that she had company, August the eleventh 1968 deserved the accolade before it had even begun. She yawned but neither of the twins stirred. It was impossible to tell which cousin was which, because only their tangled dark hair showed above the nest of old blankets. At a guess, the one in the coveted middle position was still Diana. There had been a violent midnight struggle for the privilege and Jane, as always, had lost.

Maggie was impressed by their unbridled thumping but she was puzzled by it too. How could they beat each other to a pulp at bedtime and still manage to wake as friends in the morning? If Maggie so much as scowled

7

at her mother, she paid for it for days.

She whispered their names but there was no reply. When her cousins were asleep, especially if the older two were there as well, they reminded Maggie of puppies, oblivious to someone else's foot in their face, resigned to being pinned down by an outflung arm. Their mouths would be so close, they'd share breath. If she watched them closely enough she could see them twitch in sequence, as if the same dream were passing through each of them in turn. If ever she joined the litter, she stayed awake all night, too frightened to move in case she disturbed them.

For all their pugilism, the Barton girls never thumped *her*. Jane sometimes called her a cry-baby and had twice accused her of being spoilt, but the others jumped to her defence so quickly that Maggie suspected they were on orders from above. And their mother – her Aunt Bronwen, who was not a fusspot by nature – checked she was all right at least five times a day.

Why? Maggie's favourite theory was that they were all keeping a tragic truth from her, that she had an incurable condition that was going to snuff her out like a candle before she reached adulthood. But no. Her after-bath routine, where her daddy refused to read her a story until she had sworn to look after him when he was an old man, made it unfeasible. 'Precious Papa,' she'd have to say, 'I give you my solemn word.' If she was going to die before he did, he would not have been able to keep up the charade. He cried too easily. Sadly, the most likely reason for Aunt Bronwen keeping such a careful eye on her was that she felt sorry for her for being stuck in such a small and tidy life.

She yawned another loud, hopeful yawn. This time, Jane (if it was Jane on the far side) pulled a blanket over her head. Maggie sat watch for further movement. She would have liked to have been in the nest of blankets too, but her new sleeping bag made it impossible. She was a giant caterpillar wishing she had been born a puppy.

She imagined herself in there and someone (not her mother, the image didn't work) untying the tent flap and peeping in, trying to work out whose head was whose. Blurring her vision to force the optical illusion that would turn Diana's head into her own took a while because Diana's hair hadn't the same gloss that came with being brushed a hundred times and nor was it plaited or ribboned like hers, but the trick worked eventually. When it did, it was like an article she'd read in her mother's weekly magazine about a woman who died for two minutes on an operating table and had been able to look down at herself from the ceiling.

Too quickly, Diana's head became Diana's again and Maggie flopped back on to her pillow. Her stupid sleeping bag smelt of polythene. She was angry with her father for rushing out and buying it yesterday afternoon. The speed at which her sudden needs were

9

catered for annoyed her. If blankets were good enough for Diana and Jane, why weren't they good enough for her? *Did* she have a hole in her heart like the new girl at school who had to sleep in the sick bay with Matron?

There was movement! She coughed loudly, desperate now for the twins to come into the orchard with her so she could feel the dew between her toes. They didn't know she'd never been outside at this time of the morning without shoes on before.

When she touched the mouldy tent canvas, her finger made the material darken and, with the rubber end of her diary pencil, she wrote 'Maggie Barton' on it in tiny letters. The name sounded so much more exciting to her than Maggie Wetherham. She started to draw too, but quickly remembered her daddy had warned her not to make contact with the sides if she wanted the tent to stay waterproof. So she put her pencil back into its holder and her hands back into her sleeping bag. She was a good girl, mostly. Diana and Jane were mostly bad.

'Dear darling favourite Aunt Grace,' Diana had bargained insincerely with Maggie's mother yesterday as Grace lay on the morning-room sofa with a towel underneath her, 'if we put it up and promise to pack it away just as we found it, can we sleep out in the tent tonight?'

Through the crack in the door, Maggie had seen Grace nod weakly and wave her niece away.

10

'Never underestimate the usefulness of the mummy's curse,' Diana had told her later as they hammered in the pegs with a mallet and two bricks, and Jane had laughed like a drain. That was the other difference between them. Diana and Jane understood stuff that she did not.

In the house, where the day always broke early, Grace Wetherham slowly became vertical. Her long body slid from under the bedclothes and moved into the sitting position with barely a disturbance to the mattress springs. Then, with an inelegant clutch of the wadding between her legs, she stood up. She felt the rush of blood immediately and imagined the slivers of her disintegrating womb slipping like dead fish from a net into her ugly night-time knickers. Menorrhagia, the doctor had written in his notes, but all Grace could read from upside down was the 'hag'.

'Dysfunctional uterine bleeding. I'm afraid it's your age, Mrs Wetherham. Try and eat more spinach, more liver, more prune juice.'

A hysterectomy would be preferable. She would be delighted to see the back of the monthly mockery she'd had to put up with for thirty years. How dare the doctor only now bestow upon her uterus the kudos of being officially dysfunctional when it had never functioned properly in the first place.

She crept to the tired white bathroom that her daughter Margaret wanted to paint bright yellow 'like the Bartons' and leaned over the enamel roll-top bath to retrieve the ointment-pink, cracked rubber shower hose. It was still wet from the girls' stupidity the night before, making it difficult to force on to the taps. She turned on the hot tap but the water pressure blew the hose straight off. She pushed it back, and again it slid off. Not being the sort of woman to rise to a challenge, she walked to the basin instead, where she stood patiently with her hand in a stream of water until it ran warm.

Grace opened the white wooden cupboard with the painted green cross on its door, took a pair of surgical gloves from the box on the top shelf and snapped them on. Washing herself standing up was an awkward operation but the idea of sitting in bath water in her state was unthinkable.

She took the stiff brown flannel from its neat position on the porcelain rim and dipped it in, feeling the lukewarm water seep under the plastic cuffs of the gloves. Needs must. Arthur would be up and about in a minute and she preferred to greet him once she had this beastly business under control. She was proud of the fact that in all their twenty-one years of marriage, she had never subjected him to the sight of any menstrual nastiness. Every four weeks, his folded pyjamas would discreetly appear on the pillow of the iron bed in the guest room and seven days later, they would be returned to the far-side twin bed in the marital bedroom, no questions asked. This time, his brushed cotton nightshirt had been in exile for nine days already and thankfully, there had been no queries as to an expected return date. The way the water in the basin had turned vermilion suggested it was anybody's guess.

If only she could avoid the intrusive enquiries from her daughter too. Sending Margaret to her bedroom after the business with the sanitary towel last week was undoubtedly asking for trouble, but the child had no need for answers yet. The fact that Margaret had wanted to use it for a hammock for her teddy bear surely proved that she was not ready, and her stocky body showed no signs of the sort of pubescent change that Rex and Bronwen's hormonally charged twins were displaying.

The muscles around Grace's mouth tightened involuntarily. She made a mental note to suggest to Bronwen that both Diana and Jane wear something under their Aertex shirts the next time they came to stay.

Her nieces' brazen parade of their budding breasts on the beach yesterday morning had irritated her and even, quite possibly, brought on her afternoon's cramps. The way the two of them had pulled off their tops, climbed out of their knickers and changed into their swimsuits without so much as holding a towel up for each other was verging on exhibitionism. She had offered them the opportunity to cover themselves under Margaret's towelling robe but it had been refused.

'There isn't anyone here to see us,' Diana

had protested.

There is *me*, Grace had wanted to snap. I don't wish to have my eyes drawn to the promising curves of your new waists. I don't need to *see* the advantage of youth, it is bad enough to *feel* it. And there was Margaret to think of too, whose assessing glances had made her head pound with nerves.

It had been a relief to get the twins out of the house and into the tent, to know that she would not run the danger of bumping into them half naked on the landing or catch them looking at themselves in the full-length mirror in her dressing room as she knew they did. She would ask them not to go in there but Rex and Bronwen's girls did not understand boundaries. They had access to everywhere and everything in their own home and such freedom led to a total lack of awareness of appropriate behaviour. She dreaded to think what kind of women they would make.

Grace blamed the careless Bronwen. Understanding her brother's choice of wife had always been a challenge, and these days her misgivings carried some substance. What used to be curvy was now heavyset, what was once bohemian was now plain untidy, what was originally an emotional nature was now prone to such highs and lows that Bronwen's mental state stole the summer every year. Why Margaret wanted to spend so much time in such an unsettled household was beyond Grace's comprehension. A yellow bathroom didn't fool *her*.

It would certainly not have been the choice of her dear brother Rex to raise four daughters as such feral creatures either, but then it was not his choice to have four daughters at all. Each time Bronwen fell pregnant, Rex had referred to the bump as Henry. A boy was all he had ever wanted. Of course, when a boy *had* finally arrived, the poor child hadn't needed a name at all, but there was no need to hark back to that now.

She rinsed the brown flannel until the water ran clear. Her body might now be ready to meet the day but her mood was not. The twins would be invading the house in a moment, asking for things before they were offered and refusing things that they were. As if it weren't difficult enough accommodating such wilful conduct, she would have to put up with the change in Margaret's behaviour too; under such influence, she became as unbiddable as they were.

She wrung out the flannel and placed it back in its position on the side of the basin. It would be safe there, no one would use it. Margaret's facecloth lived in the wire bath rack with the loofah and pumice stone. As for her nieces picking it up, that was as unlikely as finding a hairbrush in their suitcase. She doubted if they washed at all. There was no danger of Arthur mistaking it either. He had his own bathroom at the other end of the house, which (much to her fury) he had indulgently promised Margaret she *could* paint yellow.

15

A shriek of laughter made her open the metal latch of the frosted bathroom window and look across the lawn through to the orchard. One of the twins – it was too far away to tell which – was facing a tree with her nightdress hitched to her waist and her legs wide open. Grace couldn't actually see the stream of urine hit the bark as the girl thrust her hips forward but she didn't need the confirmation. They were relieving themselves like they had seen the village boys doing against the upturned rowing boats on the beach yesterday. Then there was another scream and she saw Margaret run into view. She too bunched her nightdress and bared her chunky buttocks but judging from the shout of dismay, she was less successful in hitting her target.

The revulsion that swept through Grace set her dysfunctional uterus off again and she turned from one indecency to deal with another. Having Rex and Bronwen's girls to stay was becoming an arrangement she was less and less inclined to encourage, although there was nothing she could do about it today. The eleventh of August was a non-negotiable date.

Arthur Wetherham lifted his rake into the apple tree and hooked down his daughter's polyester nightdress, which was still not completely dry. Bless Maggie and her temperamental bladder control. Like chopping the logs and putting petrol in the car, cleaning up

16

after her little accidents was something he was expected to do. He didn't mind. Bed wetting at ten years of age was just the sort of thing to tip his wife over the edge, and she had been teetering on the brink for days.

'Why is it that I am short with dark hair, and Mother is tall with light hair?' Maggie had asked them at the supper table last week, as if she already knew.

'You take after your father,' Grace had said, collecting his plate as his fork had still been in his mouth. There was no such thing as a leisurely meal in Grace's book.

'Daddy isn't short.'

'He has dark hair.'

'But why am I short? You were the tallest girl in your class. I've seen your school photograph. You're nearly as tall as the teacher.'

'Where have you seen that?'

'Uncle Rex has got one in his study.'

'You're not allowed in Uncle Rex's study!'

'He was the tallest boy as well. You were the tallest two children in your school.'

'Perhaps you'll grow.'

'And will my hair change colour as well?'

'Don't be silly, Margaret!' Grace had snapped, snatching the child's plate too. 'That's enough nonsense. Now run along!'

Later, when the child was in bed, he'd dared to question his wife's evasiveness.

'We agreed,' was all Grace would say.

'Yes, ten years ago.'

'We agreed.'

'But she...'

17

'The more you pander to her wheedling, the more she will keep on asking.'

'I do think Maggie is old enough to know the truth.'

'Oh? And where do you suggest we start with "*the truth*"?'

'We could take our lead from Maggie.'

'Her name is Margaret.'

'She wants to be called Maggie.'

'Since when did "I want" get?' his wife had retorted tersely, which quite frankly was a bit rich. So far, Grace had got everything she wanted, even the one thing that had once seemed impossible.

Oh well, Arthur thought, raising the rake into the tree. She appeared to have banished him to the guest room for good for his gall, which made little difference really. If he was honest, he preferred the arrangement.

He wiggled the branches to try and hook the nightdress. The nylon fibres made a tearing noise as they detached themselves from the bark but nothing had ripped, which was just as well since even he drew the line at clandestine sewing. He rolled the nightie up, put it into the empty trug that he had taken out there for the charade and walked back to the house. He could quite easily put the item into the linen basket in his own bathroom without Grace seeing. Mrs Sacks was the only woman who sorted his laundry and if she was puzzled by the frequent appearance of urine-stained sheets on his bathroom floor, that would at least give her something to tut about. It was a shame that Grace was such a disappointing mother, but it boosted his paternal role and so he was selfishly grateful. He liked the kind of father he had turned into, and when he compared himself to the kind of father Rex had turned into, he liked himself even more.

'Do you wish Maggie had been a boy?' his niece Diana had asked him yesterday as she'd helped him put up the tent. She had a knack for getting straight to the point, did Diana.

'No, of course not!'

'But if you had another baby, would you like it to be another girl?'

'Boys are made of slugs and snails and puppy dogs' tails but girls are made of sugar and spice and...'

'No, *really* Uncle Arthur, I'm being serious. Would you?'

'I'd be happy with a hundred Maggies,' he'd told her and the hurt had spread across her feisty face like a rash.

All three of them – Maggie, Diana and Jane – were digging away for some truth or other. They knew it was in there somewhere, and he was becoming increasingly committed to helping them find it.

The hand bell that his wife ludicrously rang each meal time interrupted his thoughts. She even rang the damn thing during term time when it was just the two of them and the meal she was heralding was a curled sandwich left alone on the kitchen table. If he had his way he would eat when and where he liked, but he didn't have his way. Grace had her way and that was the way it was.

As he slunk back to the house, he saw the girls emerge from Maggie's Wendy house. One, two, three little gypsies. Together, his chiselled brother-in-law Rex and Rex's preoccupied wife Bronwen had created a strong look. Freckled, athletic, sparky. His own potato-face features would die with him, an iniquity that he had come to terms with a long time ago. He had never felt the injustice of infertility that Grace struggled with. He waved. It pleased him that the sturdy wooden hut he had built by customizing a large garden shed was being used at last. It had gingham curtains made by Mrs Sacks and its final lick of paint had been dry for a month, and yet Maggie had to be actively encouraged to show it off to her friends. He knew why. He had made the same mistake with the sleeping bag yesterday afternoon. It would be his epitaph. Here lies Arthur Wetherham, who tried too hard.

It was lunchtime when it finally happened. Maggie would remember the mood in the kitchen just beforehand as one of false calm. The blue vinyl table was not big enough to seat a normal family and usually when the twins came to stay, the three of them were allowed to eat separately, but today her mother had laid out five embarrassing portions of sliced tomato, cucumber and bought ham and was arranging triangles of buttered bread into a fan. At each place setting a plastic beaker of orange squash had been positioned at the top right hand of the blue-bordered plate. It looked to Maggie like a pretend meal, something you might make out of Plasticine, and she thought it funny that her mother had been inside playing more or less the same game as they had been playing outside in the Wendy house.

Grace sent the twins upstairs to change their Aertex shirts for something 'more suitable'.

'More suitable for what?' Diana asked.

'More suitable for your uncle,' Grace hissed.

While they were gone, Maggie was given an oblique lecture, something about not troubling her father with silly questions that he couldn't answer.

'Why? Is he ill?'

'Not yet, although if you carry on with your...'

'Are these more suitable, Aunt Grace?'

The twins reappeared in matching striped T-shirts. Maggie looked away. She hated it when they wore identical clothing.

'A little more so.'

Diana and Jane looked at each other and shrugged.

'Now look what you've gone and done,' Maggie said hotly under her breath to Grace's back. At least the Aertex shirts had been different colours.

'Have you washed your hands?' her mother

asked, spinning round, the disapproval in her voice louder than ever.

'They're not dirty,' Jane answered, flipping her palms up to prove it.

'Oh, I think they are. From what I have seen this morning, I think they will have all sorts of nasty germs on them. Don't you?'

Jane put her hand to her nose and sniffed.

'No, they're fine.'

'In this house, Jane dear,' Grace told her too evenly, 'we do things properly. Now run along to the utility and use the soap.'

Perhaps if Jane hadn't shouted that there *was* no soap, Grace wouldn't have bustled in there and caught Arthur bundling the nightdress into the laundry sack as if it were stolen goods. Perhaps if Grace hadn't ordered Arthur out, and perhaps if Arthur hadn't told her in reply that he had had enough of her treating him like a child, there wouldn't have been what Maggie called 'an atmosphere'. But because all these things had happened, the cat was indeed let out of its bag.

'What have you been playing this morning then, girls?' her father asked them in strained cheeriness over the thin ham.

'Sisters!' Maggie smiled. And that was when her mother dropped the plate.

That night, back in her own bedroom, with Diana and Jane on an early train home in some ambiguous disgrace, Maggie reopened her diary. Taking her time, she drew a picture of five girls with varying lengths of black hair.

Under it, with a great deal of pleasure, she wrote 'The Barton Sisters'. Before hiding it back under her pillow, she ran her nail along the folded edge of its page to confirm its status as the Keep Day of all Keep Days.

One

Forty years later

Jamie stopped digging, took his phone out of his back pocket, lined it up and pressed the button to capture another grainy image of his young son. He did the same thing at least once a day. Although he had learned to resist the temptation of then sending them on to everyone on his contacts list, he had yet to tire of showing off to himself.

He cupped his roughened hand around the phone to shield it from the sun and squinted into the screen. The picture wasn't really worth storing but he couldn't bring himself to delete it. At the back of his mind, superstition lurked. What if it turned out to be the very last image taken? It was the same fear that had led to his rescuing Ben's soft-soled red leather booties from the bedroom bin last week. They were currently in hiding in the pocket of his gardening jacket that was hanging from the wheelbarrow handle, acting like a comforter when his hand came across them from time to time. He would rather Jess didn't find them. Not only because she had been the one to throw them out, but because she confused love with sentimentality, which embarrassed her.

'Nice one,' Jamie said, putting a thumb up to his son.

And it was. He suspected that, even before he'd got Jess pregnant, he'd subconsciously wanted to be a dad. This was odd on a few counts. His age for one, and his own father's non-performance for another. Don – which was how he now publicly referred to him – had made considerable efforts to strip the role of its appeal. He'd been a decent enough parent for the first fourteen and a half years but the last five had been a dwindling charade of expensive presents and awkward meals. How his father's separation from his mother had also come to mean a separation from *him* was still unclear, but it was all water under the bridge now. In fact, Don had kept such a low profile lately that Jamie no longer had a number for him, although to be fair, it wasn't quite the dramatic estrangement his mum was trying to make out. His older brother Rob maintained contact, so it wasn't like the old man was on the missing persons list or anything.

No, he thought as he uprooted a stump of something long gone and dumped it in the wheelbarrow, all in all, there was a lot to be grateful for. As far as he was concerned, fatherhood had come along just in time to save him from a university degree in Procrastination. He had been much less committed contemplating three years studying English

26

and Politics than he was now. He'd only gone down the uni route to please his mum anyway, which, thinking about it, was the same reason he'd finally given up on his dad. He was more than happy being a part-time gardener and full-time father, and on the whole couldn't give a toss that the general consensus was otherwise. Maybe nineteen had been a tender age to achieve one's aspiration, but someone had to peak early. He no longer cared what other people wanted for him, nor indeed what they thought of him. What he wanted was right here, making mud pies.

Every single thing his son did amazed him. The way Ben was squatting now on his nappy-clad haunches, scooping and tipping with such coordination, seemed to Jamie some kind of miracle. Time after time, the spadeful of mud slid on to Mrs Bertoli's lawn instead of into the bucket, but the lack of achievement didn't seem to bother the boy in the slightest. Like father, like son then, Jamie thought. He had grown so used to foreseeing the usual criticism, he countered it even when he was on his own.

'Bad luck,' he said.

'Bad luck,' Ben echoed, shovelling another tiny load.

Jamie felt most valid when it was just the two of them. The incessant female correction that came in stereo at home from his mother and Jess – don't give him those, that's too high, they're too small, less than that – had

27

the effect of relegating him to the status of Ben's incompetent older brother. With his slight frame and smooth cheeks, he looked enough the part without being made to feel it as well. He continually tried to counteract the impression – 'I'm his dad, all right?' – but his objection was lost in all the other role-related grievances that hung in their fragile domestic air.

It was no wonder the air at home was so delicate. It had barely recovered from the traffic-control chaos of the divorce when it had been disturbed by a maternal tug-of-war between his mum and Jess. The kitchen-based power struggle was sometimes so tangible, it was tricky to know on which side of Ben's high chair it was best to stand. Only Ben's position was clear, sitting aloft in the eye of the storm.

The trouble was, no one really understood the pecking order. It had undergone so many changes in the last few years that the old four-tiered system with his father at the top and himself at the bottom now seemed medieval. He supposed he was now living in a classic twenty-first-century household, but there was still no room for him as alpha male!

When Don had walked out – or been banished, depending on whose view you took – Rob, being the eldest son, had become the man of the house. You'd think, therefore, that when Rob had left too, Jamie's own status might then have been elevated, but for one reason or another he was still stuck on the bottom rung.

Rob's 'jokes' didn't help. Sticking a 'Little Weed Gardening Services' sign on the side of Jamie's old red van might have been funny for everyone else, but it was hard to laugh off on its twentieth telling. It was simpler just to resign himself to ridicule until Rob went travelling, as he kept threatening to.

Jamie heard a sharp knock on glass from the house behind him. Mrs Bertoli was at the window, gesturing to him to get on by tapping her wristwatch. Jamie lifted an arm to acknowledge her. He had been anticipating the surveillance. The old woman hadn't hidden her displeasure at the sight of him turning up with a toddler on his shoulders, but he was no one's slave, not at the price per hour she was paying him anyway.

'He's yours?' she had asked him disbelievingly as he had introduced his pride and joy.

'He is.'

'But you're only a boy yourself.'

'Got the vote two years ago, Mrs Bertoli.'

'Where's his mother?'

'At school.'

'What does she teach?'

'Nothing, she's a pupil. How far would you like me to cut this rosemary back?'

It gave him pleasure to tell people like Mrs Bertoli how it was. He wished she could have seen Jess two years ago, feeding Ben through her school shirt, her striped tie trailing over his downy head. That would have polarized the old woman's views. She would either have

29

seen the beauty in it or spontaneously combusted.

Right now, watching her sprightly form crossing the lawn with quick little steps, he favoured the latter.

'I'm not running a crèche, James. The child is clearly distracting you, so I would rather you come back when you aren't minding him.'

'I can't guarantee when that would be, Mrs Bertoli.'

'Do you not have a back-up for such emergencies? A nanny or...'

'This isn't an emergency, this is the way we do things. If you have a problem with Ben being here, perhaps you should look for another gardener.'

He took hold of the wheelbarrow handles and tipped it on to its wheel. A porous stalk of fennel slipped from the top of the precarious heap on to the floor and she bent down in a conciliatory gesture to pick it up.

'I don't wish to be taken advantage of just because I am an elderly...'

'No one likes being taken advantage of, Mrs Bertoli.'

She let out a little cough.

'Quite. How long are you expecting to look after him for?'

Jamie thought about saying, *Until he leaves home.*

'I have him all day.'

'So you've time to clear the pond weed as I asked?'

'I won't leave until I've done everything on your list.'

'Well, in that case, I'm in the house should you need me.'

Jamie nodded, smiling victoriously at her retreating back. Parenthood gave him a confidence he had hankered for all his life. It no longer mattered if he got asked his age (nearly twenty-one, thank you very much, Mrs Bertoli) in pubs or was called 'sonny' by market traders, and as for prejudiced old biddies who only paid him six pounds an hour and expected him to do the work of two men on not so much as a cup of tea...

'Let's go and see the fish,' he said, taking Ben's muddy hand and leading him to the pond. It turned out to be a murky affair with slimy concrete sides and a plastic heron keeling over into a clump of oriental grass. They peered into its darkness.

'Fish all gone,' Ben said sadly.

Jamie poked the algae with a stick. 'Dirty old pond.'

'Dirty o' pon'.'

'I don't think there's much life in there, do you, mate?'

Ben mimicked his father's head shake.

'Tell you what,' Jamie said, 'I'll take you to Big Pool one day. There are fish in Big Pool, loads of them. We'll sleep in a tent and cook sausages and I'll teach you how to climb an old oak tree and let yourself drop ten feet into the water. Splash!'

''plash!' Ben laughed.

31

The confrontation with Mrs Bertoli had warmed Jamie up and he took off his fleece-lined overshirt, exposing his sinewy arms. The freedom was good, and he bent to unzip Ben's winter quilt.

'You can't move in this thing.'

'Can't move,' Ben said.

'That's better.'

'That's better.'

The repetition made them laugh. Ben's use of language was still a novelty.

'You show off with him,' Jess had accused after they'd bumped into their mate Gatesy in the park on Sunday. She was always accusing him of something or other. 'You don't have to make him perform like a circus monkey...'

'I'm proud of him...'

'You're proud of you, you mean.'

'What's wrong with a bit of pride? You want to try it sometime.'

He shouldn't have said that. It wasn't Jess's fault she was ashamed of what had happened. Her upbringing propelled her across roads, into shops and out of sorts when she spotted people from her parents' church.

'Anyway,' he'd added quickly, 'why should I show off to Gatesy?'

'I don't know. Because he got body hair before you?'

'Oh, you three make a beautiful couple,' Gatesy had slurred, hanging on to a swing frame, whacking the helium balloon tied to the pushchair handle too hard for Jamie's liking. He'd been in the pub, celebrating booking an open ticket to Bali.

'You're just jealous, mate.'

'That's it, man, me and Rob wish we were staying here in this shit town in this shit weather all summer changing nappies with you instead of—'

'Rob's going?'

'If he sells his Transit in time.'

'Big Pool is better than Bali, isn't it, Ben?'

The April wind was whipping their faces.

'Big Poo' better 'an Bali.'

'Say Bali sucks.'

'Bali suck...'

'He's not a parrot,' Jess had snapped. 'Stop treating him like a wind-up toy.'

'You're mixing your metaphors, Jessica.'

'What would I know? You're the English student, not me.'

Mrs Bertoli was nowhere to be seen, so Jamie rested his clogged spade against the barrow and briefly wondered about sending Jess the picture of Ben. The last time he'd sent her one, she'd been in the middle of a chemistry practical and he'd got a sharp text back, but the time before that, she'd been pleased. That was the problem. How she reacted depended entirely on the day, on whether she was in the mood to see her fall from grace as a stumble or a dive.

He clearly *wasn't* an English student any more, nor likely to be one ever again, but he knew Jess needed to keep up the pretence. 'I don't want anyone ever saying you gave up

33

your studies for me,' she used to say when Ben had been the size of a strawberry in her schoolgirl womb.

No one could ever say Jess had given up her studies for *him*. The book under the baby monitor on her bedside table was *Energetics, Kinetics and Equilibrium*, which she read, he suspected, for pleasure. He sometimes accused her of wanting a university place more than she wanted him.

'Who says I can't have both?' she would answer.

Jamie assessed Mrs Bertoli's denuded herb bed. The branches of a brutally pruned rosemary looked to be putting two fingers up to him and he felt some sympathy for it. An argument with his mum the evening before had left him feeling a bit on the pruned side himself. They never used to argue – neither of them enjoyed conflict – and all he'd said was that gardening was a perfectly good way to earn a living.

'You don't know the meaning of the words,' his mother had scoffed. 'It might be a perfectly good way to earn some beer money, but as for a living...'

'But, but, but, but! That's every woman's favourite word!'

'It's called being realistic...'

'So how am I supposed to find out what realistic is when you refuse to accept any financial contribution from me?'

'It's not a question of refusing, Jamie. You

don't have anything to give me.'

'Gardening fits in with Ben.'

'You're too bright for manual labour, it's a waste of a good brain.'

'Oh right! It must be genetic then.'

'What do you mean?'

But she knew what he meant.

'Your father is a cabinet maker, Jamie, not a kitchen fitter. And anyway, we're not talking about him.'

'No, we never do.'

His mother's face tightened, which made him even more defensive.

'You don't give Rob this grief, do you? He's about to chuck in his job to go travelling, but no one has a go at him.'

'Rob doesn't have a child, Jamie. Nor does he have your brains.'

'Then credit me for having enough intelligence to know what I want.'

'Ben will be at school in three years.'

'By which time Jess will be in her final year at university. I need to be flexible.'

'My very own house husband,' Jess had purred unhelpfully.

'And he doesn't qualify on either count yet. I can't see how you can even begin to imagine you can bring up a child on a part-time gardener's wage.'

'Your problem is,' Jamie had finally shouted, 'you can't see how I can bring up a child at all!'

No one really believed he could do it. It wasn't just Mrs Bertoli who thought he was

35

too young to be a father. It was his mother, his brother, his mates, possibly even Jess. For two years now he'd been trying to prove his point, but everyone was too obsessed with the idea that fathering was about putting bread on the table to listen.

'You won't even let me buy Ben's nappies, for God's sake!' he'd thundered at his mother, his frustration out of control.

'Buy them with what? With the golden egg your goose is going to lay any minute now?'

'So if we're costing you too much, we'll move out.'

It was his trump card, and in the cold light of day he was ashamed of himself for using it. Ever since he'd been Ben's age, he'd known that all he had to do to get his mother's attention was to take a little of himself away. He and Rob were the centre of her universe and suffocating though that could be, Jamie accepted it. There were worse ways of mothering – or 'smothering' as Rob called it – and everyone knew she was only trying to give her children something better than she'd had. He understood that desire completely. He was going to be a better father than Don, wasn't he?

He took his phone out of his pocket again and sent her the grainy photo of Ben. There was never a more appreciative recipient of a grainy photo of Ben than his mum, which was why he forgave her everything. Then he collected up the last of the cut rosemary, sat the delighted boy on top and pushed the barrow down the narrow suburban garden towards the compost heap. Rob and Gatesy could keep Bali. His life was right here.

Two

As Jess ran from the bus stop, late again, her heavy school bag bounced off the bruise on her hip where Ben had kicked her that morning. She had been on the point of kicking him back when Jamie had appeared, all calm voiced and matey, and taken him downstairs. An apology would have been nice, but the blissful ten minutes in the bedroom all to herself was better.

Jamie and Ben's exclusive love-in had ceased to hurt. In fact, it had become her godsend. The words 'You take him, Jamie, you're so good with him' had a magic touch and they were leaving her lips more and more often. Maybe she could train Ben to throw his tantrum at the same time every morning. That way, she might manage a whole shower without him banging on the glass with his bloody metal train. 'Leave me alone!' she would scream through the door. 'No!' he'd holler back – God's penance, she supposed, for all that longing for company she'd done as a child.

It was drizzling. Her hair that was once so perfectly groomed fell forward and stuck to her face as she bent to retrieve the door key from its unoriginal hiding place.

'Shit,' she muttered as she let the plant pot fall back on to the empty terracotta dish. 'Shit, shit, shit.'

She had come late to swearing but was more than making up for it in her nineteenth year. If people were going to paint her as a scarlet woman, then her language might as well be colourful too.

She pressed her finger on and off the bell, although her sense of urgency was entirely self-imposed. The leaflet had been lying, ignored and crumpled, in the bottom of her school bag for months. 'Yes, I see, thank you, yes, I'll look into it...' she'd promised the health visitor without any real intention. She only half listened to anything the woman ever said, her other ear on the tick-tick-tick of the clock on the surgery wall telling her she was late for double chemistry, or for the nursery pick-up, or for Ben's lunch or his supper or any of the other thankless tasks that separated her life from her friends'. It was like being trapped in a never-ending PE lesson. When the whistle blew once, you had to run to the red circle. Twice meant green, three times blue. Peep, peep, peep. Get it wrong and you were out.

She was about to be out any minute, unless she got into the house soon. This appointment with the organization calling itself '2Feet' had started to really matter, ever since she'd finally bothered to read the leaflet and discover, only last week, that it wasn't about

Ben's two feet, it was about her own. Nothing to do with teaching babies to walk or count as she'd assumed – she had too much help in those departments – but about helping young people like her and Jamie become independent. *'Are you a parent living with parents?'* it asked. *'We are a government funded initiative to help you stand on your own two feet.'*

Jess had almost crumpled under the relief of knowing that somewhere, someone actually cared. She was desperate to prove, not least to herself, that there was life after pregnancy at sixteen. She was sick of reading articles that told her teenage mothers were less likely to finish their education, less likely to find a good job and more likely to bring up their child alone and in poverty, or that teenage birth rates in the UK were the highest in Western Europe, or that six per cent of women between the ages of sixteen and nineteen were mothers, and so on. If she couldn't now be the high achiever that everyone had once assumed she'd be, then she damn well wanted to make a good job of being a statistic.

Please someone be in, please someone be in, please someone be in, she prayed as she pressed the bell again. Her own door key was in her coat, which, when she peered through the letterbox, she could see hanging in the hall. When she thought about how much she had to remember, and how much she therefore managed to forget, she wanted to cry, but Ben did all the crying round here. No one came to let her in.

She let her bag – a lucky dip of nappies and textbooks, toy trains and revision sheets – drop from her aching shoulder.

'Bloody great!'

Calm, Jess, calm, she told herself with the same rhythm she used on Ben sometimes. There was still time. One o'clock, she'd told Jamie she'd be back, and it was only five minutes to. The home visit wasn't until quarter past. She pulled her phone from her blazer pocket and called Jamie's number only to be told that the Vodafone she had called was switched off.

Sprinting, even in the rain, had made her hot. Her legs were prickling under her grey wool regulation trousers and a trickle of sweat ran between her small breasts that for an embarrassing few months had given her such a motherly bosom. Four minutes to. Bloody hell, Jamie, Ben would be needing his lunch.

Then she remembered. She walked quickly to the back of the house, over the paving stones, past the drain and through the arched creosoted wooden gate, just as she had done three years ago during all those covert lunch-time sessions. Sneaking out of school as the bell went, Jamie with one hand on the steering wheel of his rusty red Fiat, the other under the hem of her kilt as she rested her feet on the dashboard. She hadn't been allowed to wear trousers to school in those days. Trousers, at her co-educational independent school, were a privilege for sixth-form girls only and she'd been in the fifth. It was tempting to blame the whole saga on school uniform policy.

Jamie maintained there was nothing shocking about it at all. She'd been over the age of consent, hadn't she? But Jessica Morley up the duff! Jessica Morley kicked out of home by her parents! Jessica Morley an unmarried mother! Not Jessica Morley? Some days she could have curled up and died.

The shed was unlocked, for which small mercy she felt like falling to her knees and giving thanks. Not to God – the recent lack of interest was mutual. She swung the faded floral peg basket that hung from a rusty nail to one side and unhooked the single steel key that would let her into Jamie's mum's house. It was continually pointed out to her that she was perfectly entitled, after two years, to call it *her* house too, but the words wouldn't come. Something stopped her from forming them every time.

The smell of the shed brought back the memory of his bed sheets against her naked skin, the anxiety of his mother coming home early, the frantic race to get dressed and back to school for the afternoon register, the delicious secret trickle running back out of her during maths. The one thing she couldn't remember *ever* thinking was that pregnancy was a possibility. And she was supposed to be an A-star student?

She turned the key in the back door lock and pushed her body against the wood to give it the extra force it needed. If she couldn't call Jamie's mum's house 'home', at least knowing its little ways reinforced her flimsy status as a putative member of the household. But that had its downside too. The more she allowed herself to be sucked into Jamie's family, the more it enhanced the exclusion from her own.

What were her parents doing now? Did that shiny image of her former self still smile beatifically down on them from their marble mantelpiece, or had it been packed away along with all the other things they liked to show off about at church, like forgiveness and understanding? And if she had married Jamie as they had tried to insist, would they now be holding Ben's hot baby hand on the way to the altar rails for a blessing? In what way would that be any more honest than this?

Jess boiled with indignation over the way they had cast her out – and yet she still couldn't quell the childish voice in her head that sometimes wailed 'Why haven't you come to get me yet?'

Inside, the kitchen smelt of stale toast. Ben's green beaker with the chewed drinking spout was on its side on his high-chair tray, leaking a dark red juice into the remnants of his breakfast. Jess put it to her lips and sipped. Jamie's mum called her The Sugar Police, but by the taste of it, the concentration was eighty per cent Ribena, so she tipped it down the sink.

She put the beaker in the dishwasher, the

bread in the crock, the lid on the Marmite and the milk in the fridge. Then she scooped up the soggy bread, wiped the high chair and tossed four metal trains, a lift-the-flap board book and a plastic phone into the toy tub by the fridge. She could tell just by looking at the state of the place that the last person to have been in it was Jamie.

Easing her school tie with one hand, she picked up a handwritten note from Jamie's mum with the other. *I gave Ben a dose of cough medicine at 8.30 a.m. and think he should be seen so have booked a doctor's appointment for him at 5 p.m. There's a Shepherd's Pie in the fridge which he'll eat with some broccoli. See you later, M x*.

Jess wanted to scream. She pulled open the fridge door, took one look at the homemade individual pie with clever little criss-cross fork marks on its fluffy mashed potato topping and slammed it shut again. The price she paid for a roof over her head seemed to be getting higher and higher. 'Mum's just trying to help,' Jamie would say, but Jess smelled manipulation. The easier life was for them here, the harder it would be for them to leave. And the longer they stayed, the more pride she would lose – not that she had much left.

Last night, after that stupid row about money, Jamie's mum had got all guilty and given them twenty pounds. Go on, I'll baby-sit, take advantage of it, you're only young once, she'd insisted. But the pub was hardly fun. Free alcohol had changed Jamie's tune and he'd spent the whole time telling anyone who would listen what a saint his mother was, how they'd never manage without her. After her fourth vodka, Jess had had enough. 'Well, your mum isn't stupid, is she? Twenty pounds is a good investment.'

'What are you on about, investment?'

'If it keeps us where she wants us...'

'What do you mean, where she wants us?'

'In the palm of her hand?'

'God, Jess,' Jamie had said, 'that's a bit ungrateful, even for you.'

She knew she *ought* to be thankful, she'd been brought up to give thanks on a daily basis, but she didn't *feel* thankful. If anything, people's kindnesses made it worse. She felt like an effing charity some days.

'Tell you what,' their mate Gatesy had suggested over his free beer, 'next time your mum gives you twenty quid to get pissed, you can give it to me. I need all the money I can get if I'm going round the world. I'm chucking it all in, man! I'm going to see the sights! Do you know how to milk a cow, Mr Day? 'Cos if you do, the job and the house are yours, mate.'

Of course Jamie knew how to milk a cow, Jess thought as she drank straight from the juice carton. How hard could it be? She checked the clock on the cooker. Five past one. Jamie had ten minutes to get Ben back here, feed him, change him and have him ready to charm the woman from 2Feet into believing that here was a family in need of standing on their own.

'Jamie, where the hell are you?' she barked into her phone when it rang.

'At Mrs Bertoli's.'

'How far's that?'

'I dunno, ten minutes' drive?'

'So you're on your way?'

'I promised her I'd clear the pond before I left.'

'But I need Ben here. I told you this morning, the woman from 2Feet is coming...'

'You don't need Ben for that.'

'I do, Jamie. I'm a mother, asking for help. I need a baby if I'm going to pretend to be a mother...'

'What do you mean, pretend? You *are* a bloody mother!'

'And I don't feel like one living here! Have you told your mum yet?'

'Not yet...'

'You know what she's like ... she'll think it's her fault we want to move out.'

'So it's *not* her fault now, then?'

'It's not normal to live with your parents when you're a parent yourself. It's...'

'We've got all the support we need here.'

'There's such a thing as too much support.'

'Christ, Jess, I don't understand you. One minute you're saying you're so tired you want to stop the world and get off and the next, you're refusing help as if...'

'She's *too* helpful...'

'That's just who Mum is, Jess. Get used to it.'

'No, Jamie, it's what she *does*, for a living. She's blurring the boundaries between work and home. We're not two of her special needs kids.'

'I know that...'

'I feel like another one of her projects.'

'Jess, please—'

'Look, I've got to go. But quickly, tell me, I need to know, how's Ben's cough?'

'What cough?'

'Exactly,' Jess said triumphantly before ending the call more abruptly than she'd meant to.

She took a tin of spaghetti hoops from her blazer pocket, put it down with a bang on top of the note and called the doctor's surgery.

'Hello, this is Jessica Morley, Ben Day's mum? He has an appointment to see a doctor at five p.m.? Yes, could you cancel it please? He's fine. I don't want to waste your time.'

Ben's health was a constant issue between her and Jamie's mum, inextricably linked, Jess felt, to her decision to give up breast-feeding at six weeks. He'll get more colds, Jamie's mum had warned a hundred times. Jamie never had colds. Yes, well, Jamie had been fed until he was three years old, when he was old enough to ask for 'mummy milk' himself, and that was just weird.

A pile of ironed clothes sat on the dresser. She flicked quickly through it, reclaiming the odd small-boy item to take upstairs to the bedroom she and Jamie tried to pretend was their own. Its middle-aged decor made her miss the lime green and silver walls of her old room. Had her parents redecorated, she wondered? They had painted her out of their lives in every other way. Did she miss them? Did she wish *her* mum made Ben mini shepherd's pies and phoned the doctor? It wasn't worth thinking about.

So, Jess thought, as she rolled two T-shirts and a pair of Thomas the Tank Engine pyjamas into a sausage, here I am, Jessica Morley, set for Oxford but pregnant at sixteen, living in the spare room in Jamie Day's mum's house. How close was *that* to a Department of Health statistic? But things were looking up. There was the woman from 2Feet and there was Gatesy.

Ten past. On her way upstairs, she noticed a child's red-checked brushed cotton shirt she hadn't seen before hanging over the banister. Pulling it off and putting it to her nose, she could detect the tenacious whiff of a charity shop. For God's sake! Ben didn't need any more clothes – or not ones she hadn't chosen anyway.

Her room in Jamie's mum's house was really no more than a holding space. It would help if Jamie could stop referring to it as the 'spare room', but old habits clearly died hard. His room would always be the box room across the landing, where Ben had been conceived, where his computer and CD player still sat on the desk and where his mother continued to put away his clean underwear, despite the fact that the Jennifer Aniston posters had long been replaced by an alphabet frieze running at cot height around its walls.

Ignoring the clutter, she whipped off her flat black lace-up shoes, grey trousers, white blouse and striped tie and pulled on the button-fly jeans and long-sleeved T-shirt that were lying on the chair where she had left them last night. She brushed her hair, put on some mascara, slid her tiny hand through three silver bracelets and tugged on her battered trainers. With a quick glance in the long mirror, she wondered if she should perhaps try a skirt, but it was too late, the bell was ringing.

'That's mine, I'm so sorry,' Jess said as she opened the door.

But the apology was wasted on her caller, a girl not much younger than herself who was pushing the dumped school bag to one side with her foot. The zip of the bag was open and a pot of nappy rash cream rolled out, but all Jess noticed was the mottled blueness of the girl's bare legs and her dirty black shoes. One of these was twisting on a newly discarded cigarette butt, yet it was stale smoke Jess smelt.

'Is Mrs Day in?'

'No, she's ... er ... she's out.'

Jess wondered what had caused the two crusted scabs on the girl's left cheek.

'Oh.' The girl bit off a hangnail from one of her fingers and started to suck on the trickle of blood. Her nails were painted with chipped black polish.

'She should be back about five.'

The girl made no attempt to move. Her voice, when she spoke, was rough. 'Is she your mum then?'

Jess looked down the road in the vain hope of seeing Jamie. 'Sorry?'

'Are you Mrs Day's daughter?' She didn't pronounce the 't'.

'No.'

'Her daughter-in-law then?'

'No.'

The girl scratched one of the scabs on her face and it too started to bleed. It wasn't eczema, Jess decided.

'What are you then?'

'I'm sorry?'

'Why do you keep saying sorry?'

'I...'

'What are you if you isn't her daughter?'

'Just a friend of the family,' Jess said.

The girl turned her mouth down, like she'd never heard the phrase before. Which one of us, Jess wondered, would a stranger pick out as the statistic, the unmarried teenage mother?

'Well, when she gets back, tell her it weren't my fault what happened this morning, will you? She's told them they shouldn't leave sharp stuff lying around when I'm there, but they don't listen to her so...'

'OK...'

'I got a detention, that's all. I'm not excluded nor nothing.'

'OK.' Jess started to close the door. The girl continued talking.

'She won't mind me coming round. She's all right is Mrs Day. Tell her I don't know what I'd do without her, will you? She's the only one I'll have anything to do with up there. Tell her if I *am* excluded...'

'I'll tell her.'

But from the kitchen window, as she watched the girl stumble back down the drive, she decided she would tell Maggie no such thing. For one thing, she didn't have the girl's name, and for another, telling Jamie's mum someone needed her would be as stupid as giving a dirty needle to a drug user.

Three

Maggie scrubbed at the ancient scorch on the unfamiliar kitchen work top like a woman with an anxiety disorder.

'Bloody stubborn...' she muttered to herself, 'stupid bloody stubborn...'

It was no good swearing, it was time to face it. If the sibling rivalry wasn't going to stop now, it never would. The sand in the egg timer was all but run through and yet the Barton sisters were *still* vying for position. Was that the female race for you? she wondered as she scoured obsessively away. Or was five sisters just one sister too many? Would it have been any different if there had been a brother in their midst? If Rex had had his damn boy?

After one last wipe at the singed laminate, she stood up, easing her back. Oh, what did it matter? Whatever she thought would be misconstrued anyway.

She looked around for further distraction but her frustration had whipped every corner. There was nothing more to do. She felt like an intruder without Diana in some sort of executive role at the sink, but Di hadn't negotiated the steep tiled steps down to the basement since Tuesday and already the room had reacted to her absence. Even with other people in it, it seemed laid up, like a ship in dry dock.

As Maggie tossed the cloth in the direction of the taps, she caught sight of her magnified face in a small double-sided circular mirror on the windowsill. She flipped it round and her image shrank. With wet fingers, she massaged the bridge of her nose and the two permanent vertical grooves either side of it. She didn't think she was a frowner but the deep furrows on her face suggested differently.

'A penny for them?' her brother-in-law Stefan asked gently.

'Uh? Oh, I was just wondering if wrinkles were genetic.'

'Liar,' he said, his Welsh lilt coming through. 'Your scowl of disapproval has been hanging in the air ever since Jane's phone call from Spain.'

'Has it?'

'Like a rogue Cheshire Cat.'

She managed a laugh. If anyone knew how to make her feel better, it was Stefan. Perhaps she should let it all out.

'It's just that Jane is always *so...*'

Stefan raised a single bushy eyebrow.

'Well, she *is...*' Maggie protested. 'She's always been the difficult one.'

It was an unhelpful habit of hers, seeing her sisters in such over-defined roles, but it was too late to shake it now. Since forever,

Amanda had been the bossy one, Judy her weak deputy, Di the speaker of truths. Jane (the bitchy one) had once suggested that Maggie only did it so she could define herself as the extra one.

I can't just get on a plane like that, Jane had huffed down the phone earlier as if she'd been asked to pop back for a coffee morning. Di will understand that I'll come when I can. But I'm asking you to come now, Maggie had replied. And I'm telling you I can't, Jane had snapped back.

'She'll regret it,' Maggie said into a silence.

'Who will?' Stefan's mind had returned to its default position, preoccupied by the inevitability that was staring him in the face upstairs.

Jane. If she doesn't get here until it's too late, she'll have to live with it for the rest of her life. I tried not to be alarmist but she was in one of her belligerent moods ... she can be really quite aggressive when...'

'She'll come,' Stefan said calmly, heaping spoonfuls of fortified powder into his wife's cup of tea as if a few extra vitamins and minerals might make a difference. Trays and trays of high energy drinks had been up and down the same steps for weeks and weeks. 'I've been married to the two of them long enough to know how these things work.'

Maggie's furrows dug in deeper. For a split second, she braced herself to be the last yet again to hear a family secret.

'What do you mean?'

She knew what he meant, but the day had been too intense. At this hour, everything needed clarifying.

'Your mother once told me...' he said.

She blanked. Her mother? Who was that then? The conversation was flickering like a computer on the blink. It might have been a better idea to switch it off. Stefan reddened.

'Sorry love, I always forget. I mean Bronwen...'

Maggie nodded. Of course he'd mean Bronwen. Everyone always meant Bronwen. It wasn't just Grace's early death that was responsible for her barely registering on the family radar. Her adoptive mother's fifty-three years on this planet had left no imprint whatsoever, not even on Maggie, whose eighteen-year-old self had recovered from the news of Grace's fatal hysterectomy indecently quickly. She could still remember the relief, exhilaration even, of being able to use the phrase *my sister* whenever she liked. Arthur had been just as bad. 'Your sister is on the phone!' he'd shout as loudly as he could up the garden. 'Don't speak like that to your sister!' 'Don't ask *me*, ask your sister!'

Stefan was burbling, almost talking to himself.

'Bronwen told me, you see, on my wedding day, that in marrying Di I had taken Jane on too. Twins and all that...'

'Was she right?'

His eloquent eyebrow went up again.

'You picked the right one to live with then,'

she said, silently chalking up a point.

Stefan dropped the box of build-up dust back in its white chemist's bag. Each time he did it, he both feared and prayed for the need of a repeat prescription.

'It's complicated,' he said reasonably. 'If Jane dropped everything and came rushing over here just because you'd told her to, she wouldn't be here because she wanted to be, she'd be here because she'd been ordered to, wouldn't she?'

'By me?'

He shrugged.

'So keeping me in my position in the pecking order is more important to her than saying goodbye to Di?'

'Those two can probably say their goodbyes by thought transference.'

It was a generous attempt at levity but Maggie was no good at being flippant around the subject of the twins. She had never been able to emulate their mix of love and blithe unconcern.

'Don't cry now,' Stefan said.

'I'm sorry, it's been a long day.'

And so it had. One that had started with a pupil in Year Eleven locking herself in the staff lavatory and cutting up her arms with a compass, and now seemed to be ending with a deathbed row.

'So if *Di* had asked Jane to come?' Maggie sniffed.

'Di's not going to ask her! You know that as well as I do!'

'All right then, if *you* had asked her?'

'It's not me Jane's jealous of.'

'For God's sake. Can't she just ... what's her problem?'

'Bronwen loved you,' Stefan stated baldly.

'She loved us all.'

'But she loved you unconditionally.'

'No, she loved me *guiltily*.'

Stefan acknowledged the truth with a quick glance. Bronwen had spent years of precious maternal energy trying to assuage her guilt over Maggie. Diana had been able to cope with the discrimination and Jane hadn't. It was as simple – or as complicated – as that.

'We can't really be talking forty years of resentment here, can we?' Maggie asked. 'Shouldn't I be the one who ... I mean, what about the effect it had on *me*?'

Stefan smiled a very tired smile.

'I don't know. You girls, you're all as bad as each other.'

It was meant gently, but the observation was just too harsh with Di upstairs in the sitting room struggling to let go.

'But I don't *feel* bad. I do my best to...'

'Look, love, we can't do this now,' Stefan said, putting his arm round her. The maleness of his hug was welcome. 'We're all saying things we don't mean.'

'Did Di mean what she said to me this afternoon, do you think?'

'She's angry at dying, Mags. She's having a pop at everyone.'

'Has she had one at you?'

'More than one.'

'But was she right? *Am* I needy?'

'You know what Di and Jane are like. You can't put a cigarette paper between them. They've always stuck up for each other, bad behaviour or not. All that lather Di gave you, it was more to do with Jane not flying back from Spain than anything else.'

'And I shouldn't have reacted?'

Once again, his eyebrow answered for him.

'You mean I should be used to it by now?'

'It's all about to change anyway,' Stefan said heavily.

Maggie suddenly felt utterly drained. Di's assault had soaked up her last reserves. Was she needy? Was she ever! A wife sat dying in another room and here she was, dragging reassurance out of the widower-in-waiting who had nothing left to give. Maybe what Di had told her this afternoon was true. Maybe she *did* carry around a load of unresolved baggage, and her marriage *had* failed as a result.

'You take the tea up,' she said. 'I'll finish off down here.'

Maggie folded a tea towel and hung it neatly over the oven rail. The work surfaces were devoid of clutter, the taps gleamed, the potatoes were already peeled and sitting in a saucepan of water. It really didn't look like Diana's kitchen any more. The mistress might have left the building, but her recent verbal attack still ran on a loop in Maggie's head, like an audio track of a Tate Modern

58

installation.

You exhaust us all with your need to be needed. You can't let go, can you? You've let your childhood shape your entire life! You let it take your marriage and if you're not careful it will take your children too. Even your job is about emotional dependence! You're the one with special needs, Maggie. Turn over some stones, Maggie, stop being a bloody ostrich, Maggie, do us all a favour, Maggie!

She put a hand on the back of Stefan's carver chair to steady herself. The room swayed and an overwhelming desire to close her eyes came over her. The crash as the carver fell on to the quarry tiles drowned her feeble cry but the sharp knock of eighteenth-century oak against her shin was enough to bring her back from wherever she thought she was going.

'You all right down there?' Stefan called as he guided a mug to his wife's dry lips.

'Everything's under control,' Maggie quavered back. But it wasn't. Suddenly, her whole highly-strung life was unravelling at speed.

The 2Feet woman clipped down the gravel drive clutching her empty folder, trying not to feel as if she had been taken advantage of. It was what she was paid for whether she approved of the set-up or not.

Really though! She had spent her lunchtime telling an intelligent girl who went to a private school and lived in a comfortable house how best to extract money out of a mishandled

59

government scheme that could ill afford to support the poor, let alone the rich.

She had gritted her teeth through the tale of middle-class woe but to her credit, she had advised the girl on what she, her absent boyfriend and missing two-year-old son might or might not be entitled to without so much as a change in her deadpan expression. She had passed on the addresses of local parent-toddler groups. She had stressed the importance of weighing up the pros and cons of moving out. The rest was up to the couple themselves. But as she got into her nondescript car that still smelt of the manufacturers' fabric protector and pulled away from the desirable detached family home, her prejudice started to erupt.

She knew privilege when she saw it. She would have liked to have put the young lady into her car and driven her to the other side of town where the real statistics lived. Then perhaps the girl would have understood the difference between need and want. They could have given Kelly-Ann Drew a lift while they were at it.

Truancy was not her field, so it made no difference to her what Kelly-Ann had been doing clumping down the girl's drive as she'd arrived, but it had certainly not helped her warm to the spoilt little madam inside. What a lottery birthright was!

She rammed her car into third gear. In her rear-view mirror, she saw Jessica Morley shut the front door, pick up a bag and run. The woman from 2Feet hadn't worked all these years in social security not to realize the girl was up to something – and it wasn't double chemistry. Perhaps the girl had something in common with Kelly-Ann after all. Working the benefits system was clearly an activity that crossed the class divide.

Jess escaped down the road with a let-out-of-lessons feeling. She had been able to tell two things halfway through the disastrous meeting. One, that Jamie was not going to get back with Ben in time, and the other, that the woman from 2Feet thought she was an unappreciative princess. She could have put money on both of them.

Her two text messages to Gatesy – or more accurately his two replies – as she had made the coffee were the only reason she had been able to resist throwing herself at the woman's sensible court shoes, begging to be taken seriously. But people only saw what they wanted to see. She knew that so well these days, she could write a paper on it.

Gatesy's van was already at the corner, full of promise, and she picked up her run. He smiled his tobacco-stained smile at her as she climbed in.

'You're mad, you are,' he said, pushing chocolate bar wrappers, dirty socks and God knows what else off the passenger seat.

'I will be soon,' she said, and leaned over to give him a kiss on his unshaven cheek. He smelt of the cow shed.

Jess had to kick straw and muddy cigarette packets out of the way to find somewhere to put her feet. A beige woollen hat caked in brown organic matter lay by her suede boot like a giant crisp and she had the sensation of something large and damp lurking behind her head, but the back of the van was and would always be a mystery.

'Is your house any cleaner than this?'

'Nothing wrong with a bit of muck,' he laughed. 'You can't live on a farm without a bit of muck.'

'So it's mank then?'

'Probably needs a woman's touch,' Gatesy said truthfully. 'But beggars can't be choosers.'

'I'm not begging anyone.'

'No, you're too posh to beg, you are.'

'Oh bugger off, Gatesy.'

'Give me a couple of weeks and I'll be in the crystal clear waters of Nusa Dua!'

'And I'll be...'

'Like a pig in muck!'

She giggled. He fancied her, she knew it.

'I'm not a sty kind of girl, actually.'

He gave her a quick, wicked glance. 'What sort of a girl *are* you then, Jess?'

'To be honest, I don't know any more.'

'Lost your way, have you, babe?'

He slapped his hand down on her leg.

'Ow!'

'You need a bit more fat on you, you do. You'll be all right once you start living off all that full-cream milk straight from the udder...'

'No thanks. But seriously, Gatesy, do you think this is going to work out?'

'If it doesn't, you can come over to Bali.'

'No, I mean, is Jamie really a suitable replacement for you?'

'I don't know about *him*, but *you* are just what Mrs House is looking for. A little home-maker, that's what she wants, although why you want to be one of them is fucking beyond me, babe. You're on to a good thing living with Jamie's mum...'

'Did you tell Mrs House I was coming?'

'She's put the kettle on for you. You've missed the boss but there's no point fluttering your eyes at him, he can't see a thing, one eye goes one way and one the other. Make a bloody good sheepdog, he would.'

'When can Jamie go and see him?'

'As soon as he's ready.'

'Tomorrow?'

'So you've told him what you're up to now, have you?'

'Not exactly.'

Gatesy started scrabbling in the tray for a cigarette lighter.

'Better hurry up. If he leaves it much longer, the boss will find someone else. He's a good bloke, Mr House is. There aren't many farmers who'd keep your job open for you like he's doing for me.'

'Are you definitely coming back then?' Jess asked carefully, pulling a corrugated card-board cup out from under her thigh. There was a soggy coke-stained fag end in it.

'I've only got enough money to last me six months.'

'So if you're leaving in April, that gives us till October.' Jess saw the months stretch out before her. Exams, results, university. The timescale fitted perfectly.

'That should be long enough to get the bath clean again,' Gatesy said, turning the wheel sharply left on to an unmade road.

The van clanked over the potholes and came to a stop outside a narrow red-bricked house with four windows and a door. If there had been smoke curling out of the chimney pot and flowers of primary colours in the garden, Jess might have thought she had drawn it for Ben. She tried to imagine them-selves there as a family – Jamie and Ben at the threshold, waving her goodbye as she left for her lectures. The vision wouldn't come.

Gatesy switched off the engine and turned to face her.

'Had your tetanus jab have you? Because I'm warning you, it's not a pretty sight.'

Four

Two days later, even the sitting room was no longer an option for Diana. The cancer, having no more than dawdled its way round her tissue for a whole year, had saved its energy for the final sprint. The bedroom, they all knew, was the finishing line.

Maggie lay next to her sister on the double bed, holding her cold bony hand between her own warm ones and wondering if it would be appropriate to check her phone. Its text message had warbled its alert a good five minutes ago and Diana had been still for ten.

Her hip settled into the dip in the mattress made by years of Stefan's sleeping body. It comforted her, even though the dip was a similar shape to the one her ex-husband Don had once left in her own marital bed. His departure had come four years and nine months ago and although she was hoping to have stopped counting by the time it got to a round five, he had been on her mind almost constantly during this last week. Her thoughts had been so much in the past, sucking up crumbs of comfort from the good times she and Di had shared – holidays when the children were little, Christmases, barbecues in back gardens, Easters. And of course

Don had been at them all, organizing the beach cricket, filling glasses, flipping burgers on the grill.

At least Death would be robbed of any pleasure in destroying such memories. Don and his mistress had got there first, and the devastation his infidelity had caused was still visible, a great big crater in the family where there used to be such solid ground. And he'd *promised* her, he'd *promised* her, that if she allowed herself to love him, he wouldn't let her down.

Well, Maggie thought, shifting slightly, she had a new mattress now, a soft pocket-sprung queen size, layered with Egyptian cotton and dusky pink cashmere, which knew nothing but the contours of her own body.

The rasp of Di's breathing was oddly reassuring. Listening to it was not unlike watching over a newborn baby. There was that same lack of faith that the next breath would come, then the grateful relief when it did. This ghastly rattle was at least something to hang on to.

'Jane?' Di asked suddenly, pulling her pitiful head off the pillow. 'Did you get the flight?'

'Not Jane, darling,' Maggie told her. 'Just Maggie.'

'Just Maggie?'

'Just Maggie. Jane will be here soon.'

Village noises drifted in through the open window. Bell-ringing practice, random and discordant, cars slowing down for the blind corner, children calling to each other, their

66

skateboards rattling on the pitted tarmac of the playground. Maggie thought of Melwood School's gates, double locked, its perimeter fence alarmed. She should be there now, at a meeting with the head. It was thought that Kelly-Ann Drew had formed an 'abnormally dependent attachment' to her. So what? A troubled child needed security, attention. If a teaching assistant was willing to give it in the absence of anyone else, what *was* the problem?

A ripple of carefree laughter rose from the playground below, a sound she had quite forgotten. Laughter at Melwood was manic, confrontational and confused. She didn't know why some children spent their school-days cutting their own flesh in the toilets when others spent theirs playing tag any more than why some sisters died at fifty-one and others lived till they were a hundred.

She shivered. It wasn't a warm day but with the window shut, the room took on a sickly smell that quite frankly terrified her. With all four parents buried, death was hardly new territory for her, but she had never had the – was the word privilege? – of watching the process quite so closely before.

Di seemed to be sleeping, although her strained expression was not undisturbed. There was a concentration behind the eyes, a determination to either hurry it up or fight it to the last. But was dying *ever* the peaceful passing away that the death notices claimed?

A macabre register began to play out in her

head. First Grace, then Arthur, then Bronwen and, finally, Rex. She would have tweaked the order if she could. Grace's death had been so remote, it hardly counted. She had just disappeared into thin air. One day, Maggie had been sitting on the end of her dormitory bed, reading her weekly letter from home – *Your father thinks I should let you know that I shall shortly be going into hospital for a personal procedure (you do not need the details)* – and the next, she had been called to the headmistress's study to be told that her mother was dead. Very neat and tidy, very typical, but then Arthur's death had more than made up the dramatic deficit.

Wonderful Arthur, the only one of them who had ever attempted to make sense of it all for her. 'Your mother and I were desperate for you,' he would say. 'We begged and we begged for you. We put terrible pressure on them, it was emotional blackmail, really.' Sweet of him to try, but it had never made any sense. Why would any mother give up her baby? What was lacking in her that hadn't been lacking in the other four? With Bronwen's death she had lost her last chance to ask, because for certain sure, Rex had never been going to throw any light on it.

Down in the sitting room, Di's plain-speaking husband was talking quietly to another male voice. The vicar perhaps, or the doctor. There were no random well-wishers any more, it was now by appointment only. Stefan had grown protective around the peep show that accompanied his wife's terminal illness. He could no longer tolerate people forgetting to hide their shock at her wastage or pressing their hands into his and saying 'If there is anything I can do...'

Di grasped weakly at the bedcovers to pull them up.

'Would you like me to shut the window?' Maggie asked.

'Will we hear Jane's car?'

'Jane's not coming today, darling. She couldn't get a flight. She'll be here tomorrow.'

'If it's too late...'

'It won't be too late. You'll see her, I promise.'

It had to be worth the risk. Maggie shut her eyes too. She had looked at her sister's papery skin long enough. It was hard to believe that the skeletal form next to her was the same woman who had spent last week ranting like a banshee. 'I'm not ready to die! I've got things to do! It's spring for God's sake, the bloody bluebells are coming out! I wanted grandchildren! I wanted old age!' How sweet the haranguing seemed now.

Half of Maggie was not lying next to Diana at all. It was rummaging in her handbag, trying to find her phone, waiting for the bleep of the next text and attempting to establish the source of the first. Even in this dire room her mind couldn't give up its sheepdog mentality, herding in her own flock.

She imagined her phone flashing frantically inside the zipped leather sack. *Help cum kwik s'thing awful hs happend.* Like there could be something more awful than this. Maggie rolled gently away, hung over the edge of the bed and fumbled in her bag. Her fingers found the cold casing quickly among the tissues and pens. The message read *Ben says thanx 4 gingerbread man xxx.* It had the magical effect of a swig of brandy.

'Jamie,' she told Di quietly.

'Mmm?'

'That text was from Jamie ... to send his love.'

'Uncle Arthur...' Di murmured.

Maggie stroked her sister's brittle hair, the grey roots of which had reached the tips of her ears. That Di had given up colouring her hair two months ago should have been a warning to them all.

'No, not Arthur,' Maggie said, 'Jamie.'

If Di's morphine-fuelled imagination was assembling a farewell party with the people, dead or alive, she loved best, Arthur would be among them for sure.

'Jamie...' Di croaked, 'he reminds me of Arthur, the way he is with Ben...'

Maggie understood it as an apology for any accidental hurt. Arthur had been their joint hero.

'He's turning out to be a good dad.'

'Not like Rex.'

'Forget Rex.'

'He despised my girls. They weren't boys. Like us, we weren't boys either. Not good enough...'

'Ssshhh...'

'Not good enough, like his son...'

Maggie rested the backs of her fingers on Di's cheek. Rex had never had a son. That had been half the problem.

'...his only son and heir...' Di was mumbling.

'Come on, darling, forget Rex.'

'The baby that didn't come home...'

'What baby?'

'Ask Amanda...'

But their eldest sister was the last person Maggie could quiz on such matters. Amanda was superb on material that was already archived. She could produce a great-great-uncle or a second cousin twice removed out of the family hat just like that, but ask her to validate a rumour or offer an opinion on a scandal and she clammed up like a shellfish.

Maggie put her hand to Di's forehead.

'Mummy's empty cot...'

The delirium frightened Maggie. She wasn't sure where it was going, where Di was going.

'In the box,' Di said, raising her head. 'It's in the box.'

'Stefan?' Maggie called anxiously, settling Di's head back on the pillow. 'Ssssh, your girls will be here soon. And Jane. Jane will be here soon.'

Di fell silent and Maggie, her heart thumping, pressed her cheek against her phone. Its communication from the outside world soothed her – the defusing of stress was something she could write a thesis on. Most of her pupils – she had a struggle not to call them her children – had their own technique. Josh in Year Eleven would put his head on the desk and drum his fingers loudly on the wood underneath. Ashlee in Year Nine would sit with one eye shut and draw with her forefinger around the outline of furniture, people, windows. Danny hummed, Kayleigh rocked, Lee moaned. And what did Maggie do? Maggie summoned proof that she was loved. It was just a question of discovering what worked for you.

Her eyes chased around the room but nothing diverted her. Stefan's attempt to recreate a sense of normality in the room that had once been the hub of their marriage had only served to accentuate what he'd been trying to avoid. This bedroom, with its outdated floral-sprig wallpaper, white paper prescription bags, stripped pine furniture and Macmillan commode, was the very end of the line.

All of a sudden, she couldn't bear the silence. Even the delirium would have been welcome so she began, of all things, to hum a lullaby.

Di, exhausted with the effort of conversing, made a strange, involuntary grunt.

'Nngg...'

She let her head fall to one side of the plump pillow, opened her eyes wide and then shut them again. But they didn't quite shut. A glassy slit between her dark lashes remained and for one dreadful moment, Maggie thought the time had come.

'Di? ... Di?'

'I'm trying,' Di murmured.

The joke was too much for Maggie and her laugh turned into a choke as she stroked her thumb gently over the back of Di's hand. She could feel a little scab where three days ago a hospital drip had been inserted. This human activity was liquid gold, dripping through an hourglass.

Her sister's parched mouth was slightly open. Maggie reached over her emaciated body, which barely made a shape under the bedclothes, and took a lolly stick from a glass of melting lemonade ice on the bedside table like she had seen the district nurse do. She ran the stick along Di's mouth, whose parched tongue pressed itself against shrinking lips. Maggie put the lolly stick back in the glass again.

'You're going to leave a huge hole in my life,' she whispered.

'I am ... not ... the hole,' Di said, before drifting to a world where Maggie could no longer reach her.

Kelly-Ann Drew was the only girl in Melwood Special School who knew why the art work that had only just been put up in the main corridor was now on the floor. A handful of drawing pins in the pocket of her trousers were burning holes into her mottled thigh. It was so easy to get them out of the wall without anyone seeing. You needed to get your longest nail underneath the flat bit and flick. If it didn't come out quickly, you just left it and went on to the next one.

There were two things she did with drawing pins and she hadn't yet decided which one to go for. If she put them in her mouth and moved them around with her tongue, she could dribble blood, which was good because it always looked worse than it actually was. Scratching her face with them hurt a lot more but at least the mark stayed for a while, particularly if she picked it, in which case it came with the added bonus of making her look as ugly on the outside as she felt inside.

Disfiguring yourself, Kelly-Ann had come to realize, was a much more effective way of getting someone to take notice of you than swearing or hitting or shouting. The rest of her class, apart from Marcus, was too stupid to get it.

Marcus was the only other pupil in 11H who had earned himself a label. She was a 'self-harmer', and Marcus was a 'runner' – just not the sort that trained on racetracks. Last term he'd ended up in a river and now Melwood had a new expensive wire fence right round it which made it look like a prison camp. Secretly, Kelly-Ann liked it behind the wire, but she only had fifty-two days left. Fifty-one and a half after lunch.

Mrs Day wasn't in school again and nobody would tell her why. They would only say it was for 'personal reasons', which made Kelly-Ann angry because Mrs Day always told

74

her everything, private things, like she'd been given away as a baby by her mum, like she was split up from her husband, like her boy had got a girl pregnant and never had no contact with his dad. Mrs Day had even given Kelly-Ann the number of her mobile phone 'for emergencies', whereas Mrs Andrews wouldn't even come to the staff-room door. And now Kelly-Ann knew where Mrs Day lived too, she could go round whenever she liked. Next time, maybe that stuck-up bitch wouldn't answer the door.

Some of the teachers, as far as Kelly-Ann was concerned, should be sacked, or shot. They didn't have any idea what it was like to be fucked up. They smelled of shaving foam and hair spray and they hadn't got a clue about the stench of stale fags, or needles by the bathroom sink, or smashed TV screens or empty food cupboards and fridges with cartons of curdled milk. They had no right to tell her what to do.

It was the third time in as many weeks that Kelly-Ann had had to put up with Mrs Andrews. 'Miss?' she'd asked her a couple of days ago. 'Do you earn the same amount as Mrs Day? 'Cos if you do, that's a rip-off, Miss.'

Mrs Day and Mrs Andrews were 'one-to-ones', but sometimes they were called 'velcro assistants' because of the way they had to stick close to their self-harmer or their runner, so close they were practically attached. Well, if anyone had to put their hooks into

75

her, Kelly-Ann wanted it to be Mrs Day. Mrs Day made her feel safe. She said things like 'What does it feel like?' and 'Make sure the pins are clean' when the other teachers said 'Take those out' and 'I'm giving you one last chance.' Mrs Day was kind to her even though it made her unpopular. Once, when Kelly-Ann had locked herself in the staff toilets and made a right mess of her arms with a compass, she'd heard Mrs Andrews having a go at Mrs Day.

'You're not doing anyone any favours with all this touchy-feely stuff, Maggie.'

'I prefer to call it being supportive,' Mrs Day had said.

'Letting Kelly-Ann believe it's normal to eat pins is hardly preparing her for life in the big wide world, is it?'

'She's not *eating* pins. She's holding them in her mouth and that *is* normal for her at the moment. And in any case, I'm not preparing her for life in the big wide world just now, I'm preparing her for life outside the lavatory door, if that is OK with you.'

Go Mrs Day! Kelly-Ann wished Mrs Day was with her now. The RE lesson was boring. Mr Warren had a posh voice and he wore ties and Kelly-Ann didn't care what each Hindu god was holding or wearing on their heads, and she was definitely not going to colour them in.

She slid one pin into her mouth, found its round flat head and pressed her tongue against it until the sharp point sank into her

76

cheek. It was true what she had told Mrs Day about the scratching pain taking over from the other sort of pain that went on inside her all the time. Her blood sometimes tasted of metal and sometimes of fresh raspberries but today it was mild, like slightly flavoured water. She sucked on the pin for a while, as if it were a boiled sweet, until she had collected enough spit in her mouth.

Next to her, Danny stopped humming, lifted his head off the desk and said, 'Kelly-Ann's gob is all over the table, sir!'

The teacher looked at the classroom assistant. Spit wasn't his thing.

'Kelly-Ann, what did you do that for?' Mrs Andrews asked calmly.

'Personal reasons,' Kelly-Ann said, her palm squeezing itself round the rest of the pins in her pocket.

'Go and get some paper towel from the toilets and clear it up.'

Kelly-Ann grinned, showing her red teeth. The toilets? Silly cow! How were pupils supposed to learn at Melwood School if the teachers didn't? Mrs Day would have to come into school now, personal reasons or not.

Five

Jamie was drunk. He wanted to be even drunker. He wanted to be so drunk that he wouldn't have to worry about one single sodding thing. Not Jess and her ambitions for him as breadwinner, not Ben and his persistent cough and – if he could reach intoxication nirvana – not even his mum and what she was going to do when he told her the news.

Gatesy's house, which was soon going to be *his* house, was trashed. The party was supposed to be a double whammy – a farewell and a housewarming in one – but both causes had been lost hours ago. There were bodies everywhere. One bedroom reminded him of a snake pit, there was so much writhing.

He stumbled into the kitchen to find some more alcohol. Any alcohol would do. It wasn't the taste he was after. He saw his hand shuffling through a random collection of opened bottles and marvelled at its ability to detect the one with the most left. His fingers wrapped themselves around something with a kangaroo on its label and before he knew it, his lips were around the glass neck and a tepid chardonnay was pouring down his throat.

'Gatesy my man!' he shouted to the figure leaning over a female form, pinning her against a wall. 'The world is your oyster!'

'You going to look after my little shell for me then?' Gatesy said, his arms moving knowledgeably under the blue top of a girl Jamie had never seen before. Gatesy was still in his sarong and flip-flops and Jamie's blurred vision couldn't tell whose skirt was whose.

'Like it was my own, Gatesy, like it was my own.'

He staggered into the sitting room to find Jess. His girlfriend was the most beautiful of all girlfriends ever. He had fallen in love with a speccy scientist who spent her days in a school lab that smelt of bad eggs, and now she was the mother of his child. She was a bit like a chemical experiment herself. When he'd first started going out with her, she was shy and good and tidy, but then she'd gone near a flame and crackled into life. Sparks of shame and anger and determination came off her if you got close enough. He understood. She knew what she wanted and she was making sure she got it. Well, he wanted what she wanted too. She had given him the most wonderful gift in the whole world, hadn't she?

'The whole bloody world!' he proclaimed, falling against the door frame.

'Bali,' someone yelled back. 'He's only going to bloody Bali.'

'No mate, I'm talking about my son...'

79

'You're always talking about your son, man, but we forgive you, yeah?'

'Bless you, Father.'

Where was Jess? Jess was always up for a chat about Ben, except when she had her nose in a book called Practical Skills in Organic Doo Daa, or when she was with her new friends, or when she was tired, or when she was pretending she wasn't interested. He fought his way through the narrow hall lined with tall people – or people taller than him anyway. Rob was one of them.

'Hey, bruv!'

'Hey, short-arse!'

Jamie knocked a pint glass and the beer sloshed down someone's sleeve.

'Sorry mate, sorry...'

I say sorry a lot, I do, he realized as he lurched on. I say sorry to Jess for letting Ben out without a coat, I say sorry to Mrs Bertoli for not finishing her list, I say sorry to Mum for asking her for a fiver. How am I going to make this next sorry sound sorry enough?

'Sorry!' he shouted as he found himself in the room where Gatesy kept his pushbike and his dog's bed. He raised his arm in the air and waved his bottle.

'I'm sorry everyone, all right?'

'You will be tomorrow,' Jess said from a low sofa covered in a hairy grey blanket patterned with black doggy bones. 'You've got to help me clear this place up.'

She was wedged between Amy and Carl, as she so often was. They were like the unholy trinity, those three. Carl called her his 'fallen angel', which Jess loved and Jamie hated. If Ben had been christened, Carl and Amy would have been his godparents. Gatesy would have been the other.

'As rale mole ruddles go...' he started.

'What?'

He had another go. 'As male mole roddels go, you couldn't get two more different—'

'*What?*'

'Role muddles ... male ones...'

Carl had his arm around Jess and Jess's hand was playing with Carl's fingers, but Carl might as well have been the Tressy doll Maggie still had (in its original triangular box complete with comb and ribbons) for all the sexual threat he posed.

'*What?*'

'Forget it.'

'Don't worry, we already have,' Amy squeaked. She was like a cartoon girl, Amy was, all pink and glittery and she didn't talk, she just made short high-pitched noises. He'd once asked Jess why she liked her so much and apparently it was because Amy had no expectations of her.

'What are you lot doing down there anyway?' Jamie slurred. 'Choosing curtain material or something?'

'Planning our makeover,' Carl declared, pulling off the dog blanket. 'This is going for a start. And so are those.'

He pointed theatrically to two large, cheaply framed prints on the woodchip-papered

81

wall. One was a Lamborghini Diablo against a fiery sunset, the other a Shelby Mustang against the American flag.

'In fact,' said Carl, hauling himself up and pushing the sleeves of his carefully ruched shirt up to mid arm, 'they're going to have to come down right now. I can't look at them a minute longer.'

Jamie was still not quite drunk enough. 'Leave it out, mate,' he said, reeling towards him. 'Leave them there, yeah?'

'No, go on, Carl!' Jess egged on from the sofa. 'They're gross.'

'But they're Gatesy's. He's proud of them, man.'

'Well, he can take them to Bali with him then.'

Carl lifted the Diablo off its single nail and propped it against a beige gas heater on wheels.

'No, mate...' Jamie tried again.

'Go for it, Carl!'

'Jess, babe...'

'Don't give me Jess babe, you haven't even told your mum yet! Listen everyone! We're moving in next week and he hasn't even told his mum!'

'I'm waiting for the right—'

'There isn't going to *be* a right time, Jamie! Just tell her, will you?'

Carl stood back from the wall with his hands on his hips.

'Neutral emulsion, a big canvas here in earthy colours, a terracotta something, and pebbles and candles ... I like candles...'

Jamie suddenly felt sick. He fell out into the hall again and ploughed his way through the tunnel of bodies. Rob was nowhere to be seen. That was his older brother all over. Flitting in and out, gracing other people's lives with his presence when he felt like it, cherry picking his moments to be there and to not be there, whereas Jamie had to give notice, apply for leave, photocopy his diary.

'How come?' he slurred to a girl whose breasts scared him. He belched and stale alcohol rose again in his throat. The front door was already open and he launched himself into the night air.

A few straggly daffodils waved at him. They looked fed up with having to herald spring when it was still so cold and twiggy but that was better than being thrown up on, which was their current, most likely, fate. He concentrated on the tree trunk behind them, which wasn't moving quite so much, and he found a bit of wall to rest against.

'King of all I survey,' he said out loud. It wasn't much, was it? A concrete path from the metal gate to the front door, two rectangles of scrubby looking grass either side, and plenty of dog shit. Jess didn't yet know about Stanley the Jack Russell being part of the deal. She hadn't done her homework as thoroughly as she should have.

'Could do better,' he mumbled to Stanley. The log he was talking to didn't reply and he pushed it with his foot. It rolled lazily on to the lawn and he emptied the wine bottle on to it to see if it moved again.

He looked up. The full moon was like a huge cordless lamp from Ikea. Carl would love one of those for the bedroom. It floodlit the whole yard, and Jamie thought the tractor shed beyond the gate seemed like a good place to go next.

He was right. It was quiet in there and smelt of hay and oil. There weren't any car posters or pebbles or writhing bodies to make him feel guilty or skint or tired. Tractors didn't ask anything of him. Tractors didn't care if he stayed or left. They didn't cough or say things he didn't want to hear about his mum and they didn't know the difference between tall and short.

This one looked bloody big though, a lot bigger than the one he'd driven on his two-day course. One hundred and fifty quid to learn how to drive a tractor! And use a front end loader, fit an attachment, take it down a slope, reverse a two-wheeled trailer, change the oil, check the fluid levels, do all that greasing. Money well spent, although he still felt crap about having to sell Jess's iPod. Not all *that* crap. She was the one who'd talked him up, told Mr House he had farm experience, forgetting to say it was selling ice-creams at Dairyworld.

He pulled himself up into the cab. Sitting in the enclosed space with his hands on the thin cold wheel gave him a jolt. When he was a kid, his favourite place was in the garage, sitting on his dad's red sit-on lawnmower pretending it was his. Here I am, in my tractor, about to go and plough a field. It is a big tractor and it takes some handling but although I am small, I am strong.

The memory made him feel safe and connected, as if his crazy future was a logical extension of his past. Maybe his mum would find that connection too. Put the right way, she might even want to take a little maternal credit. She had helped him get here, helped make him what he was. He was small but he was strong. And at least he wasn't buggering off to Bali.

Hope sunned him like the first warmth of spring. He could tell her how he planned to take Ben out in the tractor with him, how Mrs House had said Ben could help her collect the eggs and feed the lambs, how Ben's cough stood a better chance of clearing up with all that fresh air. Ben, Ben, Ben, Ben, Ben. The boy was their shared language.

The sealed cab was a sanctuary, particularly now he could read the three dials on the dash. Rev counter, oil pressure, electrics. There wasn't so much to learn. Life was as simple or as complicated as you wanted it to be.

Tonight was the night then. Everything was all right. His mum loved having Ben all to herself, she was never happier than when she was being indispensable. Who cared what came first, the special needs of the kids she taught or the special needs of the teacher who

85

taught them? Her heart was as big as the Ikea moon and the stars were the people she surrounded herself with.

He pulled his phone out of his shirt pocket and imagined Jess peeling herself away from Carl and his touchy-feely fingers and putting her arms round him instead. 'Jamie, you did it! You did it for me! Thank you, Jamie, kiss me, Jamie!'

Love was in the air. He spun the jog dial, found his contacts book and selected Home. He was going to tell his wonderful mum the good news. The time, not that he noticed, was 2.40 a.m.

Maggie supported herself on one elbow and reached over with her other arm to put a hand on the forehead next to her. Ben's thin fringe was still wet, both from the flannel she had just wiped him with and from his earlier temperature, but at least his skin was cool clammy rather than hot clammy now.

Despite his fever, she felt less anxious tonight than she had for ages. Night after night lately she had been woken by his terrible hacking through the wall. Prop him up, she wanted to call out to his young parents. Rub some Vicks on his chest. Open a window. No one acknowledged the effort it took to remain tactfully behind her shut door, lying there as stiff as a board listening for Jess's footsteps, Jamie's low reassurances, Ben's barking to stop. She worried in the darkness alone these days.

Her grandson's cot was stripped of its sick-covered bedclothes, which were already in the wash. She could hear the spin of the drum through the floorboards, the only noise in the house now his coughing had subsided. In a while, she would go down and pop his Thomas the Tank Engine duvet cover in the tumble dryer so that it would be ready for him if he wanted a morning nap. If she had time, she would make the cot up before Jamie and Jess got home to avoid the inevitable 'you didn't need to do that' conversation, which, when it came out of Jess's mouth, took on a less grateful, more literal form than when it came out of Jamie's.

The nurse on the helpline had been almost offhand about the vomiting. Catarrh, she'd said, quite normal for a child with a heavy cold. Give him liquid paracetamol and make sure he has enough to drink. The same age-old advice. Some things never changed, but they were not often the things you wished could stay constant for ever.

Rob and Jamie had never been prone to the number of illnesses Ben managed to pick up. They'd been robust babies, fed on their mother's milk until they themselves had chosen to stop. For a while, she had fed a toddler and a newborn at the same time. She used to have to leave Jamie crying in his crib while Rob, one victorious eye on his mother's anxious face, would help himself to a few proprietorial sucks. 'Robbie have the first sips,' Rob would insist, tugging at her blouse every time Jamie so much as squealed. And then one day, Rob had, thank God, declared himself 'full'. 'No more baby milk for Robbie,' he'd announced at the age of two and a half. But Jamie had been almost four before he had stopped sneaking the occasional night-time suck. It was their little secret. No wonder he was such a secure person, such a good father, such a—

Maggie stopped the thought in its tracks. This self-congratulatory reminiscing was becoming her version of comfort eating. She ought to give credit where credit was due. Jess had done well at her age to breastfeed at all, given the statistics. Six weeks was better than nothing.

She put the pot of menthol rub inside her bedside cabinet, along with the rest of her stash of infant cures, hidden behind a box of tampons that struck her as looking truly redundant. It was possible she had had her last period without realizing its significance. Perhaps her constant proximity to tears was more to do with the menopause than anything else. If she hadn't been bobbing around in the sea change of life, then Di's words might not still be whispering, like emotional tinnitus, in her ear. But wasn't everyone needy to some extent?

Her grandson coughed again and Maggie stiffened. She had bitten her tongue to bleeding point over the decision not to have Ben immunized, and after the last outburst, all discussion about the five-in-one vaccination had been banned.

'Just entertain the possibility that the dangers of Ben *not* having his jabs might be more than if he *did.*'

'No. I'm not putting my baby at risk.'

'It's not a *new* vaccine. It's been used in other countries for years.'

'I don't care.'

'I thought you were a chemist...'

'I'm a chemistry *student.* That means I am learning, that I am open to the idea of failure just as much as the idea of success.'

'But—'

'I'm not having my baby used as a guinea pig and that's that.'

Her baby? What about *his* baby, *their* baby, *our* baby? Well, one further bout of this abnormal hacking and Maggie didn't care what Jess might say, she would put the boy in the car and take him to the doctor's herself.

From the kitchen, she heard the washing machine come to rest after its frantic rotation. She felt a certain empathy – she was at least as wrung out as the bed sheets themselves. With one more assessment of Ben's forehead, which was no longer on fire, she crept downstairs for a spot of midnight laundry.

Once upon a time, there had been great plans to bring the tumble dryer in from the shed, to extend the back of the house to create a utility and add a conservatory. But then, with the application for planning permission still sitting on a council office desk,

Don, her husband of twenty-one years, had admitted – in front of the children – his doorstep adultery. 'It just happened,' he told them. 'I didn't mean it to.' A day later, he'd been gone, and Maggie had wanted the house to shrink, not grow. Besides, the conservatory plans had involved knocking down the shed, and that would have been verging on the sacrilegious.

Her beloved Arthur had built – or rather reconstructed – it for her twelve years ago, from the timber of her old Wendy house, but it wasn't just the wood that made it special. Poor Jamie, aged only eight, had come home from school one day to find his grandfather everlastingly asleep in it, stone cold to the touch in a garden chair, the radio on and half a cup of tea by his feet.

Maggie unlocked the back door and slipped out. The three paving stones between the back door and Arthur's final resting place were freezing to her bare feet, and the bundle of wet bedclothes made damp patterns on her cotton nightdress as she hurried across the path.

With a full moon beaming in through the window, there was no need to turn on the light. She shoved the covers into the dryer and gave the door a positive push shut. The loud hum of its motor and soft thud of its cargo being tossed in its twenty-year-old barrel was reassuring and if it weren't for Ben upstairs, she would have stayed for a while. 'Goodnight Dad,' she whispered on her way out.

She could still feel his presence as she climbed carefully back into bed. Ben was wheezing in and out, and she found herself breathing the same rhythm, taking deep lungfuls through her clear nose and exhaling slowly through her pursed mouth. The last person she'd tried to breathe for had been Di.

Her sister's outburst of a fortnight ago still came to her at odd times of the day, in the middle of a brain gym session at school, peeling potatoes at the sink, in the queue at the supermarket, while trying to coax an autistic fourteen-year-old down from a Portakabin roof. *You exhaust us all with your need to be needed, you let your childhood shape your life, you let it take your marriage and it will take your children too. You're the one with special needs, Maggie. Turn over some stones, Maggie, stop being a bloody ostrich, Maggie, sort it, Maggie.*

She could feel a truth in there somewhere, but *Don* had taken her marriage, and tossed it away, with his infidelity. And how could her needs take her children? Where were the stones Di wanted her to turn over? What did she think was underneath them?

Sometimes, as she told the children at school, we have to accept that our actions and words will be misunderstood. So Di thought she was a taker, when really she was a giver. She would have to live with that.

Maggie sank into less coherent thoughts. A familiar drama, half memory, half dream, flickered on her closed eyelids. Three girls peeing against a tree, a woman in an apron dropping a plate, a cat leaping out of a drawstring sack.

'Maggie is our sister!' a young Diana was shouting like 'Eureka!' into a silence. 'She's the baby that never came home!'

A man scrabbling among shards of china on the lino floor, a female gasp.

'Maggie, you're our sister! Ask Amanda, ask Judy! You're the baby that never came home!'

The baby who never came home, a phrase guaranteed to prick the sleep bubble. Maggie took a sip of water from the glass next to her bed and wished it was dawn. The details of August the eleventh 1968 were still so firmly logged that they felt more like a scene from a favourite film than something that had actually happened. Hard though it was to believe, Diana's 'Eureka!' had come to nothing much. Despite great hopes for a brave new world, the old order had remained. Unbelievably, Maggie had been kept, like a princess in a tower, away from her sister-cousins, closeted in her own singular fortress. Pony camps and boarding school, trips to Paris and London, friends, daughters of Grace's wittering cronies, chosen for her and forced upon her to create the illusion of a full childhood. And all the while, under the bed sheets with a torch that Arthur sneaked batteries for, she drew pages and pages of families, all of them five sisters with long dark hair.

Maggie groped in the dim light for more water, tipping a little down her chin. Her family's dysfunction still shocked her. Had nobody really ever explained anything? It was a miracle she had turned out as sane as she was!

As she turned her head to check Ben again, it could almost have been Jamie next to her. Ben, Jamie, Arthur, Arthur, Jamie, Ben ... Maggie was too tired to sort it all out. Real sleep was creeping upon her, her rationality blurring again. The rise and fall of the baby next to her became the rise and fall of Di's laboured death breath. Her bed became Di's. Ben became Jamie, whimpering in his sleep.

'Ssshhh...' she murmured. 'Sssshhhh...'

And in her drowsy semi-conscious state, she was saying 'Sssshhh' to Di.

'His only son and heir...' Di had rambled. *'...the baby that didn't come home ... look in the box.'*

And then suddenly, as if at the click of a hypnotist's fingers, Maggie was back in the conscious world yet again. Di's voice was as clear as if she were in the room with her.

She's dead, Maggie thought, sitting upright as the blood in her veins turned to dry ice. *My sister is dead.* It was no surprise at all when the phone next to her rang. She snatched it up.

'Stefan?'

'No, Mum, it's Jamie. Hey listen, I've got some good news...'

Six

Di left strict instructions for her funeral. According to her handwritten note, she did not want to be carried into a full church like a bride of death; rather, she wished to be put in place beforehand so guests (who should not be referred to as mourners and therefore should not dress in black) could get used to the sight of her coffin gently. She did not wish to lie in state to music she had never heard before, but to songs from an acoustic cassette she and Stefan had compiled years ago for a drive through France, featuring Eric Clapton (of course) and the favourite family singalong 'You're So Vain'. Nor did she want her daughters Leyla or Carly to have to sit right at the front where there was nothing else to look at other than her wooden casket, nor should they be the first to follow it back down the aisle so that the congregation could rubberneck at their grief. There should be no earth throwing at the grave side, no cellophane-wrapped lilies, no display of In Sympathy cards in the cottage, no cucumber sandwiches and no half measures of wine. Di had gone almost as far as banning tears.

So far, however, tradition had the upper

hand. The church had been packed a good half hour before the service began, so most of the 'guests' had seen the coffin arrive anyway. The congregation was not the riot of colour she'd wanted but a sea of aubergine, charcoal and slate, and there in the front pew within reaching distance of the simple oak bier was Stefan, with his arms around his girls who had their young heads bowed.

Maggie's body burned with self-conscious-ness as she took her seat in the third pew back. Her eldest three sisters, Amanda, Judy and Jane, sat with their feeble entourage in the second row, and then, behind as usual, there *she* was. She couldn't help thinking bitterly what a familiar representation of the Barton hierarchy it had turned out to be.

Her face was as red as her jacket. She was one of the few to have followed Di's instruc-tions to dress brightly, but it wasn't her choice of outfit that she minded. It had taken courage to lead her boys to the front to join Stefan and the girls as she had promised Di she would, but she hadn't banked on the wind of disapproval that had blown in from the pew behind. At the hissing of her name, Maggie had turned to see her eldest sister Amanda beckoning her like a school prefect to come back. Beside her, Judy had been shaking her head and tut-tutting.

'But Di didn't want...' Maggie had tried to tell this wall of sibling authority.

'Leave Stefan be,' Amanda had command-ed, starting an ordered shuffling of bums to

95

make room.

'Di asked ... the girls weren't to...'

'It's not your place.'

But nor was pew number two as it turned out, so she had taken her 'place' behind them, on pew number three, as a hundred sympathetic eyes averted their gaze.

'Don't take any notice of them,' Jamie whispered, squeezing her hand. 'You were doing what Auntie Di wanted you to.'

She gave him a small nod, worried that the bob of her head would set a tear loose.

'You know what they're like,' he mouthed. 'I mean, what's with the black veil?'

His support nearly tipped her over the edge. Struggling to remain calm, Maggie focused on the backs of the heads in front. Amanda's hair, under a pretentious black pillar box hat, was entirely grey now, cropped to her neck. Judy's was still the same light copper it had been for years, shoulder length and pulled off her face with the inevitable velvet hair band. Jane's was her usual boyish cut, that from the back made her look twenty years younger than she was and from the front made her look like, well, Di with short hair. Her bronzed shoulders peeked seductively from her Madrid-bought pashmina, cutting an intentional contrast with the outmoded blazers of the other two.

So there they were in all their sadness – the three surviving Barton girls. Did she love them in the way other people loved their sisters? Did they love her likewise? What was

96

sisterly love anyway, and where on the scale did it belong? It was hard to believe this post-menopausal line-up was once an indistinguishable tangle of sleeping limbs that twitched in sequence as the collective dream passed through them. Distance had forced them apart and yet Maggie still thought of them as a club she would never have full membership of.

The last funeral to pull off such a family turnout had been their father Rex's six years ago, which had been a miserable, difficult day with too much both said and unsaid. As always, Di had been the most vocal. 'Bloody misogynist' and 'vain bastard' were the two phrases Maggie had particularly enjoyed. Today, though, there would be no desecrating the dead. It wasn't just that they were burying the most likely desecrator. Despite, or maybe because of her propensity for blunt truths, Di had been universally adored.

Maggie suddenly needed oxygen – the pull of the coffin was strong. She took in a sharp breath and concentrated this time on the two men in front of her. In the aisle seat sat Amanda's husband Peter, his back army-straight as always. His attentive hand had steered Amanda into pews and cars and restaurant doorways in its unemotional way for years. Was her eldest sister aware that she had married such an obvious version of Rex? What relationship did Peter, a shining example of an upright conservative disciplinarian if ever there was one, have with *his* three girls? Did he wish, like Rex, that he had sired a boy to carry on the male line?

And what about the latest partner of Judy's – Clive, was it, or Cliff or Clifford? What did this bespectacled intellectual make of his new woman's three failed marriages and long-term estrangement from *her* daughter? Had he yet wondered if Judy's inability to stem the flow of bad feeling might have repercussions one day for him too?

Three sisters in the pew, but only two men. Jane liked to defend herself on this, telling anyone who cared to listen that it had been a teenage decision not to marry or have children, and that she was glad she had stuck to it. She had 'no desire to screw up another human being', she claimed, although up until now of course, Di had filled any gap.

Maggie sneaked a glance at her own sons. She wore her pride in them like a flak jacket. Clever me, she thought, to have produced boys in a family where girls are two a penny. Jane, flushed under her Spanish tan, swivelled round as if she had felt the scrutiny.

'Good to see your father here, boys,' she said loudly.

Jamie immediately dropped his head. Rob shifted and rubbed his clasped hands nervously. Every muscle in Maggie's body contracted.

'Still the same old Don, I see.'

Jane's voice seemed to bounce off the stone-cold pillars.

'Sshh!' Amanda directed.

'Dad's here,' Maggie whispered stiffly to Jamie, the fight-or-flight hormone rampaging through her blood. Her neck locked itself into position and her heart thumped against the pillar-box red linen.

'He's not staying,' Jamie said quickly, his jaw rigid. 'He just wanted to come and say...'

'You knew?'

'Yes.'

Maggie gripped the pew shelf.

'Where is he?' She sensed him right behind her, piggy-backing her space, ready to drill a hole into her with his eyes the moment she turned round.

'At the back, by the door ... he wanted ... he asked if...'

'When did he...?'

'Rob gave him a lift down yesterday.'

Rob leaned forward.

'I was going to say something but...'

'You gave him a lift? Where did he stay last night?'

'I don't know. Some B&B.'

'Jamie?'

'Sssh!' Amanda warned again.

Jamie stared at the cold church floor.

'Why didn't you say something?'

'You know why.'

'Leave it, Mum.'

Rob shook his head and took up a position of avoidance, resting his elbows on his long open legs, his gaze fixed on the faded green kneeler as if it were the Bayeux Tapestry. He shouldn't be here. He should be in Bali.

People died at such inconvenient times...

'Did you really think,' Maggie hissed to Jamie as the vicar passed her in his solitary procession to the pulpit, 'that it would be easier for me if—'

'Maggie, please...' Amanda said from under her veil.

'I'm sorry,' Jamie said. And, his mother had to admit, he looked it.

Weeping is acceptable behaviour at a funeral, so for once, Maggie made no further effort to control herself. Di's coffin became a source of immense comfort. As she stared at it, forcing herself not to think of the cold stiff shell inside, she allowed herself to cry for all the things she had tried hard not to cry about for as long as she could remember. And when those sobs subsided, she cried some more, for all the other things that had only just happened.

Even though Don Day was standing at the very back of the largest parish church in England, he could clearly identify the convulsing figure of his ex-wife. She wasn't a woman who normally showed her emotions in public, but he knew just how much Di had shored up Maggie's relationship with her other sisters: 'She's the glue that holds us all together,' she used to say. Di's death made Don feel genuinely sorry for Maggie, much sorrier than he'd felt during their divorce, when he'd been feeling far too sorry for himself to have any sympathy going spare.

Maggie's need for glue was dangerous. It had made their marriage so sticky that eventually, for his own survival, he'd had to pull himself free. Grubby adultery with a neighbour hadn't been the best method of escape but it had been a means to an end. A clean break, the severing of all that stretchy marital adhesive, had been the only way. Maggie's desire to bond was so strong, he'd still be there now, pulling its glutinous agent off the tips of his fingers, making great long gummy strings, lifting his foot and finding it still attached by viscous tendrils to the bedroom carpet. And yet now, free of all that, in this cavernous house of God that he could walk out of whenever he liked, he felt unusually stuck. Earlier, from the discreet distance of Rob's Transit van – the same van he had just agreed to buy in order to fund the boy's travels – he had watched Maggie emerge from Stefan's cottage into the village square. Her russet hair had fallen loose from its slide and her freckled cheeks were flushed as she'd gamely welcomed the hordes.

Good on you, Maggie, he'd thought. Good on you for accepting the role of substitute hostess with the same grace that you accepted the role of substitute daughter. Compared with her groomed sisters, she still had the look of a country cousin. So much for being made to brush her hair a hundred times a night as a child. He knew so much about her. What was an ex-husband supposed to do with such intimate knowledge?

As the pallbearers took up their positions, Don got ready to make his exit. Churches always made him feel as if he were breathing in the newly disturbed dust of his past mistakes. Even at his own wedding and his sons' christenings, he'd sensed he would fall short of requirements. And he'd not been wrong. The only things he had managed to live up to so far were his own predictions.

He too found it easier to concentrate on the coffin, which was coming towards him now. The bearers wore no trace of effort but then, how heavy could Di be?

As the grim box passed, he imagined her spirit dancing through him. He had missed her decline into ill health, so she was still alive in his mind's eye, bent with laughter, her hands between her legs at the sight of him shuffling through some holiday town or other in the pouring rain, his hooded cagoule tightened around his face, his trousers rolled up to his knees.

Maggie, who hated being outside the joke, used to get so cross with them. 'For God's sake, you two, grow up!' she'd scream, and they'd tease her that she ought to have married good old dependable Stefan instead. Even something as plainly daft as that would go down like a lead balloon with Maggie. She always had to be in the very middle of things, surrounded, protected, an integral part, just as she was now, flanked by her two boys like a celebrity and her bodyguards.

His ex-wife's bloodshot eyes recoiled from

him as she approached, reminding him of a rabbit he'd once glanced with the wheel of his car. Before he knew what he was doing, he put out his arm to touch her but found his hand in his ex-sister-in-law Jane's instead, tugging him from his hiding position and yanking him reluctantly into the family cortège.

'No, I don't think—'

'Oh yes you do,' Jane insisted, pulling him in line. 'Di loved you.'

'But—'

'Come on. You were the brother we never had.'

'Some brother...'

Out in the sunlight, with the coffin on its way to its muddy hole, he fell reluctantly into slow step with the others. Rob shot a worried look his way. The procession carried him along, one heavy foot in front of the other.

'Don...' Maggie croaked, her voice thick and unfamiliar.

'Maggie, I hope you don't mind ... I...'

Jane, her face tight with a pain she was not going to share, put her arm tightly around Don's waist. 'Of course she doesn't.'

'Some warning would have been...' Maggie started.

'Did Rob not...?'

'No.'

'Stop trying to make Don feel guilty,' Jane hissed as a waft of alcohol drifted from her mouth. 'He's here for Di...'

'We all are,' Maggie said. The strong smell

of whisky worried her. It was inappropriate but it was also sad.

'I did ask Rob to give you some advance warning this morning,' Don said.

'This morning? And that would have been OK, would it?'

'For God's sake, Maggie,' Jane muttered, 'let it go.'

It might as well have been Di speaking. *For God's sake, Maggie, you can't let go, can you? Turn over some stones, Maggie, stop being a bloody ostrich, Maggie, do us all a favour, Maggie.*

'Yes...' Maggie murmured, 'yes, I'm sorry. Di would have been pleased to...'

Her eyes stung. She stopped walking, leaving the joyless convoy to carry on without her. Resting her handbag on a mossy tombstone, she busied herself with a search for her sunglasses. Behind them, she would feel protected. Her sons – her and Don's sons – had left the convoy too and were over by the gate with Di's daughters.

Don stopped too.

'You go on. I'm not doing the grave,' she said. 'Di left instructions ... we don't have to if...'

They stood there, blinking into the sun's heavenly rays. Maggie put a finger behind her glasses to wipe away a rogue tear.

'You go on.'

'No, I only meant to ... Jane pulled me into the line, I didn't mean to...'

'It's all right.'

They were close, their shoulders almost touching.

'They're good boys,' Don said, gesturing towards their sons, 'to turn out like this and...'

'Yes, Rob even changed his flight to be here.'

'Unprompted?'

'I can't say that, no...'

'Well, whatever, it's nice to see them looking after Leyla and Carly like that—'

'I asked them to,' Maggie said sharply, looking directly at him for the first time.

'Of course...'

'So, I assume you've spoken to Jamie?'

'Yes, I...'

'And was he OK? Seeing you out of the blue like this after so...?'

'Well, not entirely out of the blue.'

'Oh?'

'We've ... oh Christ, did he not tell you that either?'

Maggie inhaled a whole graveyard of dusty suspicion. 'What?'

'We've ... we've been in touch a little lately.'

She reddened. 'He didn't say...'

'That's teenage boys for you.'

'Jamie is nearly twenty-one, Don.'

He shifted his stance on the gravel path that he wished would open up and swallow him down in one. The realization dawned that Maggie had no idea they had all been together in the pub at lunchtime. It had been Jane's idea, of course, but it had been quite a party. Rob, Jamie, Jess, who'd brought Ben...

105

'We've been texting,' he said.

Maggie let out a measured sigh. The reunion was a small step, not an airport escalator as she had feared. She looked at him longer this time. His beard was greyer. It matched his hair better.

'I got this a week ago,' Don said, opening the flip of his phone. Maggie felt the casing, warm from being in his pocket. On the tiny screen was her grandson Ben, squatting in the mud, digging, the same image she had stored in her own phone. Despite having seen it a hundred times, despite it being *hers*, she smiled.

'Oh, that one! Jamie sent it to me too.'

'He's very blond...'

'Like Jamie was at that age.'

She leaned against the tombstone. She wouldn't have noticed if it had given way and left her lying flat on her back. Don was here and Di was gone. Surreally, the faint sound of Ben's recorded laughter wafted up from her bag.

'That's Ben! Jamie set it as a ring tone...'

'Are you not going to get it?' Don asked.

'Who could it possibly be that isn't right here?'

Behind her glasses, Maggie shut her eyes. Her face was relaxed at last.

'Thank God it's over,' she sighed. 'Maybe we'll all sleep again tonight.'

So she didn't know, Don realized, that a rather rash deal had been brokered in the pub, that Jamie's girlfriend Jess had twisted

Rob's arm to lend his Transit for the afternoon, that Jane had then offered her hire car,
that Jamie and Jess and Ben were moving out
of Maggie's and into a farm cottage as soon
as the funeral was over.

He opened his mouth to tell her, but the
opportunity was lost.

'God, Mags,' said Jane, back from her
sister's grave, her voice still as tense as violin
strings. 'You look like you need a drink. You
should have come to the pub with us at
lunchtime.'

'Mmm?'

'Amanda didn't want us to go, did she,
Don? But I couldn't have got through this
without...'

Maggie pulled herself up and lifted her
glasses. 'You two went to the...?'

'Not just us two. We *all* went. Why didn't
you come?'

'I wasn't asked.'

'You don't need to be asked.'

'I told Jamie to ring you,' Don said.

'Jamie went to the pub too?'

She thought back. Jamie and Rob had left
her home together, a little early, ostensibly to
buy Jamie a tie en route. And yet there he was,
across the sunny churchyard, in an open-
necked shirt. She could hear Di screaming
from her cloud. *Turn over some stones, Maggie,
do us all a favour, Maggie.*

Jane produced a box of Spanish cigarettes.
'Like I said, we all did. It was a last-minute
thing.'

'Who's "we"?'

Jane rolled her eyes. 'Does it matter?'

'Yes.'

'Leyla, Carly, your boys, Jess, Ben ... he's so like Jamie, isn't he?'

'*Ben?*'

Jane lit up. Ben's electronic giggle rose again and this time, Maggie grabbed the phone from her bag. It was a lifebelt, being tossed to her from school.

'Someone obviously needs you after all,' Don said.

Maggie stared incredulously at him for what seemed an age, but much as she wanted to, she could think of absolutely nothing clever at all to say in reply.

Seven

Gatesy couldn't have cleaned the plastic avocado bathroom suite in the entire two years he'd lived there. The dirt from a hundred tractor wheel changes, or something worse, was ingrained in every crack and groove. Jess had been on her knees, scrubbing at the black mould between the cheap white tiles and scraping at the grease on the pale green lino, ever since she had got back from the pub at lunchtime, and the water in her bowl was still turning grey.

She couldn't stop now though. Jamie's brother, Rob, who by rights should have been in Nusa Dua with Gatesy, would soon be here with a van full of things to transform this damp neglected cottage that smelt of last night's farewell curry into a home. *Her* home, something she didn't feel she'd had for two and a half years, not since that last supper when her parents had finally shown their true colours.

'Your father and I...' her mother had said across the previously silent dinner table, '...we cannot pretend that your condition...'

'My *condition*?'

'...does not make it difficult for us to carry

on as if...'

'Come on girls, don't upset the apple cart now...' came her father's standard ineffective interjection.

'...as if everything is the same. We do not find it easy to forgive what you have done to us...'

'What I have done to *you*?'

'...by refusing to marry the father of your child...'

'*Your* grandchild...'

'We aren't ready to be grandparents.'

'No, you're not even ready to be *parents*!' she'd screamed. 'You don't even want *me*!'

'We just don't want you to ruin your life.'

'Me ruin my life? *You're* ruining my life! All you want is a trophy daughter, someone to boast about in church...'

'Well, we certainly don't have that,' her mother had said with her ghastly calm, scraping the uneaten food from all three plates back into a dish. 'You're no trophy any more.'

The brutal memory made Jess stop scrubbing. She rubbed her chapped hands on the small of her back. It was hard to remember, this side of childbirth, exactly who had said what to whom. Being the guardian of a foetus was such a different condition to being the mother of a baby, just as being sixteen and angry was nothing like being nineteen and tired. Her recall was an unreliable witness these days.

Through the open metal-framed window with the frosted glass, she watched Ben sitting motionless on his rocking boat in the garden, his hands gripped around the blue steering wheel just as she had left him ten minutes ago. Would he ever, in the years to come, be throwing clothes into a suitcase and walking out into the night? If he did, would she go after him? Why hadn't *her* parents come after *her*? How could anyone let their child just drift away like that? Why hadn't some solid hidden family anchor kept her safe in the harbour until the storm had passed?

It could have been the lunchtime beer talking, but she felt uncharacteristically weepy. She turned on the bath's cold tap, splashed her face, and turned it off again. Was love like that, capable of being turned on when it was needed and turned off when it wasn't? She tried to imagine a scenario where she would cut all contact with Ben but her vision stretched only as far as a stolen week in Greece with Carl and Amy.

She sniffed three times, as if she'd been sobbing. Why had Jamie's dad had to turn up and get her thinking about her own? She and Jamie had been happy in the same boat. Don used to be the enemy, the selfish defector, the perfect balance to her own paternal deficit, but now Jamie was on the rescue boat. The bad guy of the last few years had turned out to be a softly spoken grey-haired man with a missing tip to his right forefinger which he had chiselled off in his workshop where he made clever kitchens for rich people. Jess was now clinging to the wreckage alone.

111

She sloshed the brush around the bowl, stirring up the grit. The repetitive motion of scrubbing, the rhythm of the bristles, the swoosh of the dirty water as it swirled down the plug made her feel more resilient. She wasn't alone, she had Ben. He had grown in *her* womb, fed from *her* breast, and if he belonged to anyone, he belonged to her. She tipped another bowl of sludge down the green sink. So what if Ben now knew how to say 'Grandpa'?

Jess picked up her phone with its battered pink fascia from the windowsill and tilted it to find a stronger signal. It teased her, flashing on and off, one bar, two, two bars, one. Reception was patchy inside the farm cottage, another minus, along with the bus stop to school being a mile and a half away, the wheels on Ben's pushchair not coping with the track and the fact that Gatesy had left his fucking Jack Russell Stanley behind. ('Why don't you shove the dog in Rob's rucksack and force Gatesy to learn the Indonesian word for rabies?' Carl had suggested.) Her contentment flickered like her phone's signal detection, five bars, two bars, two bars, four.

She rolled away an ache in her shoulder and flicked through her list of contacts. *Home* was still there, above the name of an equally redundant ex-boyfriend. Her thumbnail hovered over the button. It wouldn't be the first time she had played chicken.

Outside in his passing tug boat, her precious son was staring into space. She would go out there and clamber on board with him if she wasn't so close to staring into space herself. When being tired was a permanent condition, Ben's self-contained moments were not to be squandered.

Her skinny arms twinged at the thought of lifting him up. Did other parents wish their children asleep for most of the time? Was it right to look forward to his hours of unconsciousness quite as much as she did? According to Maggie, Jamie had dropped his daytime nap by his first birthday. She dreaded Ben dropping his. But how old had *she* been? How long had *she* been breastfed for? What had *she* been vaccinated against? She glanced again at the phone's screen. Her home number stared defiantly back at her.

Even from the garden she could hear the rattle of Ben's chest. He had coughed his way through the night again and should really be in bed but until Rob arrived with the dismantled cot, there *was* no bed. The bare mattress in Gatesy's bedroom sported too many stains for her to want to go anywhere near it.

Jess tapped on the window and waved but Ben put his hands over his eyes. The excitement of meeting his grandfather had worn him out. Not that he knew what a grandfather was. In the pub, Ben had been calling Don 'the chocolate man'. If all it took for a complete stranger to become a best mate was a Thomas the Tank Engine Easter egg, what could *her* father one day be?

She clamped the mobile to her ear. For as

long as there was no connection, she was able to toy with the idea. What would she say? Whose job was it to make the first move? Were they waiting for her?

Ben came out of his facial hiding and began to rummage in the red PVC handbag he wore around his neck like an appendage. She had no idea why he had chosen this jumble-sale monstrosity to be the keeper of his marvels. It was a mystery as baffling as the marvels themselves. What wonders did he see in the chipped metal tractor, the piece of sea-smooth green glass and the chunky plastic black knight that she didn't?

The sunlight made a direct hit on something shiny and the radiance bounced back at Jess like a flash bulb. Ben flapped a rectangle of chocolatey foil in the air and then held it to his face, breathing in its secrets. The smoothed-out Easter egg wrapper had been bestowed with the highest honour.

'Look, Dad, you're in!' Jamie had said. 'That's a vote of confidence, that is!'

'It's a start,' Don had smiled cautiously, but Jess wasn't sure if she wanted it to be a start. Nor was she sure she wanted Ben to practise saying 'Grandpa' or for Don to bounce him on his lap while he was doing it.

Thankfully, the pre-funeral pub had been a cauldron of distraction, which had been useful for all sorts of reasons.

'You two should get married,' Jamie's brother Rob had kept saying. 'Weddings are more fun than funerals.'

114

'The church wouldn't have us,' Jess had replied quickly.

'Who says it has to be in a church? You could do it on the back of a camel in the Gobi bloody desert if you wanted to.'

But Jess didn't want to. In her recent experience, no relationship was for keeps. Who was to say when the tap would be turned off? There was no point in getting married and no point in contacting her parents. With only one term's worth of her school fees left to pay, both parties would soon be free of obligation. She looked through the window at Ben again and the dead weight of responsibility sank inside her. They would, but she wouldn't. She was trapped now.

Her wet thumb went to press the button to disconnect the call but instead, a ringing tone kicked in. The sudden connection brought up an image of her parents' white cordless phone trilling from the corner unit in their pristine lemon and blue kitchen, of her mother putting down a duster, straightening her apron, irritated to be disturbed from some menial task. The scene felt painfully close.

Deep down, Jess knew there would be no reply, that an instinct for self-preservation had allowed her to make the call only because it was safe, because her mother would, of course, be elsewhere, drying oatmeal china teacups with a damp tea towel in the church hall, 'doing good' for people she barely knew.

'Anne Morley, good afternoon.'

Oh God. Too late.

'Hello? Who's there?'

The signal wavered. Jess's limbs went limp. Hang up or speak? She spoke.

'Mum? It's me, Jess.'

'I can't hear you.'

'Mum, it's Jessica.'

The reception danced backwards and forwards, in and out, like her contentment, her recall, her confidence.

'No, I'm sorry, I can't hear you whoever you are.'

'I'm Jess.'

'Who?'

'JESSICA. Your daughter, remember?'

'No, it's no good, you'll have to call back.'

Trembling, Jess put the phone down hard on the windowsill. She didn't have to do anything if she didn't want to.

A snarl-up had formed on Maggie's drive. The nose of Jamie's driverless pickup, packed with gardening tools, three bikes and a trampoline, was jutting into the road. At its bumper was Rob's Transit van, and behind that, Jane's hire car. The engines of the last two were revving impatiently.

'Tell Jamie we need to leave now, not next week,' Jane shouted from her car window. Nobody had admitted it but the timing of this post-funeral exodus was crucial to its success. Its architect, Jess, had signed them up in the pub on the basis that Maggie's day was going to be a difficult one anyway. 'She won't even notice we've gone. It's got to be done soon, so why not now?' It had all sounded so reasonable four hours ago.

'Where the bloody hell is he?' Rob barked nervously from the van. Strapped in the passenger seat next to him like some half-witted accomplice was a giant purple dinosaur that his nephew Ben sat on to watch TV. 'Are we going or what?'

In the house, Jamie, who could hear the revving and the shouting, could not bring himself to shut the doors. His old bedroom echoed, now that Ben's cot, rug, floor cushion, toy box, books and clothes were in the back of his brother's van. In the guest room, a few wire coat hangers swung in the empty wardrobe, tinkling as if being disturbed by ghosts every time he opened the door to check. In the bathroom there was just one toothbrush left. It felt like daylight robbery.

They were doing this, so Jess kept telling him, to save Maggie the trauma of having to help. This was the best way, kinder than giving her a black letter day to count down towards, cleaner than a long drawn-out, box by box withdrawal. He saw the logic. His new job was waiting for him, there was too much stuff to shift in just his van, Auntie Di was in the ground ... life had to move on.

The familiar yet displaced sound of his dad calling his name came drifting up the stairs.

'Son?' Don shouted from the porch of the house he'd lived in for nine happy years. The memory of the tenth miserable one was what prevented him from trespassing further, in

117

much the same way that it had stopped him doing everything else. 'Are you done? We ought to get going.'

He tried to play down the urgency. Maggie could be back at any minute, but if that was an issue, then what they were doing was wrong. And they had all agreed that this *wasn't* wrong, or at least no more wrong than slipping away from a family funeral on the pretext of work like she had done this afternoon. Poor Maggie. Her sudden departure from Di's funeral had hammered the final nail in her own coffin. God only knew how many Brownie points she had lost by making that decision. Some family members had had a field day over the post-burial sherry.

Don wasn't yet used to casual exchange with his youngest boy again. The difference between the relaxed banter he had going with Rob and his stilted efforts with Jamie was painfully clear.

'We're set when you are,' he called up into the silence.

'Go on without me.'

A sudden paternal response had Don taking off his brown brogues and walking into the familiar hallway where the only thing missing was his coat on the peg. He looked, out of habit, for the bad join in the beige stripe wallpaper that he had hung one wet Bank Holiday weekend. There it was, above the door frame, tormenting him as ever.

Walking in his socks up the stairs, he remembered a thousand fatherly calls to duty.

118

I'm thirsty, I've had a bad dream, I feel sick. For a few years, Maggie and he used to take it in turns to stay with Jamie until he fell asleep.

Upstairs, the lad, still in his funeral suit, was on his knees, teasing out four small squares of flattened carpet where the feet of Ben's cot had been. He didn't look up when his father walked in.

Don took in the bare space. The room had been redecorated, by a professional he guessed, with yellow wallpaper and an alphabet frieze. Gone were the scattered *Beanos*, the dusty Star Wars figures, the tangled heaps of clothing that he would pick up, fold or hang every night as Jamie showed off his latest goalkeeping bruises. A memory of a home-made certificate *'Awarded to Jamie Day for Learning to Dive Today at Big Pool'* Blu-Tacked to the wall above his bed, hit the back of Don's throat and he loosened his black tie.

'What are you doing?'

'These marks from the cot's legs...'

'They'll lift.'

'They make the room look...'

Don got down on his knees too and rubbed his hand over the compacted pile, which kicked up a faint smell of baby talc. For a second, it was twenty years ago, another house, another baby.

'You mustn't worry about Mum,' he said.

'Someone's got to,' Jamie replied, pulling frantically at the wool with his torn gardener's nails. Don noticed them for the first time.

119

My son earns a manual labourer's wage, he thought, shot with disappointment. And it's my fault.

'We need a brush or something.'

Neither of them raised their gaze from the floor. Don remembered how they used to dig holes on beaches together, silently, determinedly, until they could no longer be seen.

'I don't see why.'

'What?'

'I don't see why someone's got to worry.'

Jamie scratched harder.

'That's because you've been gone too long.'

After a tactful silence, Don said, 'Most children do leave home eventually, you know. Parents expect it.'

Jamie blew away an imaginary piece of fluff. But children don't expect parents to, do they? he thought about saying. That damned question, the one he had wanted to ask for nearly five years, was gathering momentum in his throat. *Why did you leave me too?* He swallowed it back down.

'You wouldn't want Ben to live with you for ever, would you?'

Jamie flicked the invisible fluff with his thumb and forefinger. Don thought of the old Subuteo set and the games they used to play on the sitting-room carpet. Once, the plastic ball had gone into the fire.

'You're a parent yourself now. You have a partner and a child and you need your own space. This is the right thing to do.'

Outside, Rob sounded his horn.

Eventually Jamie did look up.

'It's all right for you, isn't it? You've already left.'

When Maggie had put on her red linen jacket earlier that day, it had given her courage. Now it made her feel like a walking target, and the snipers were out in force at Melwood School that afternoon.

She looked and felt a complete wreck. Her hair, a tone lighter than her natural colour to camouflage the grey, had escaped its loose bun, and she had forgotten to swap her rubber-soled driving shoes for the black suede heels that her straight skirt needed. But despite her shambolic dress, Kelly-Ann Drew would not let up.

'You look so smart, Miss,' she said, clinging to Maggie's crumpled sleeve as they crossed the playground. 'I could never look as smart as you.'

'I'm sure you could.'

'No way, Miss.'

Maggie had done enough talking to Kelly-Ann Drew for one day, most of it through a locked lavatory door, and all she wanted to do now was go home, unzip her constricting woollen skirt, take off the tights that cut into her waist and cast off everything that smelt of graves and school toilets. She longed to be sitting on her sofa in her brushed cotton pyjamas that allowed her body to be the shape it really was, reading Ben a bedtime story. The thought of home quickened her step.

'Enough now, Kelly-Ann, OK?'

'You're not cross with me are you, Miss?' Kelly-Ann said, an inch from Maggie's face. Her breath smelt of cheese and onion crisps.

'No, just tired.'

'Why are you tired, Miss?'

'Maybe,' Maggie sighed, 'because you keep asking me all these questions.'

'But people ask *me* questions all the time. It's like "What have you got to say for yourself, Kelly-Ann? When are you going to grow up, Kelly-Ann? Why don't you just eff off, Kelly-Ann?"'

Maggie didn't feel like smiling either but it was the least she could do. She was going home to a comfortable house filled with people who loved each other. Kelly-Ann would be lucky if she saw anyone before midnight.

'I bet you wish I'd eff off, don't you, Miss?'

'Language, Kelly-Ann.'

'I never said the actual word, Miss. Respect and that. But do you, Miss? Do you wish I'd—?'

'No, Kelly-Ann, of course I don't.'

'Mrs Andrews does.'

'No she doesn't.'

'Yes she does. She hates me. You're the only one in the whole school who understands me, Miss.'

'Rubbish,' Maggie lied, but the girl was close to the truth. The line in the staff room was already drawn. There were those who thought pin sucking deserved a hug and those

122

who thought it deserved expulsion.

'Why weren't you at school today, Miss? You aren't getting another job are you? You haven't been given the sack have you, Miss?'

Not yet she hadn't. One couldn't yet be sacked for having a different approach.

'No, I haven't been given the sack. I've been to my sister's funeral.'

Kelly-Ann clamped her hand over her mouth.

'I feel bad now...'

'I'm not going to feel sorry for you, Kelly-Ann, not today...'

'No, Miss. But it was really kind of you to come and get me out, Miss. I wasn't going to come out for anyone else. If you didn't come, I was going to stay in there all night. I didn't know you was at your sister's funeral, Miss.'

'It's OK, Kelly-Ann.'

'I heard Mrs Andrews through the door though, didn't I? She said that this was what came of—'

'Yes, I know what she said, thank you, Kelly-Ann.'

'I'm leaving in six weeks, Miss. I'll have to get a job or something. My mum says I could be a cleaner but...'

'Shall we talk about this another time?'

'Mrs Andrews said you were making it harder for me to leave, didn't she, Miss?'

That wasn't all Sue Andrews had said. She had barely been able to contain her delight that a meeting had been called to discuss the 'growing trend of emotional dependence between velcro assistants and students' and that the head was 'looking to develop a coherent policy aimed at preparing school leavers for the outside world' – which, Sue was keen to point out, probably didn't include giving students private telephone numbers for emergencies. A disciplinary chat was just around the corner for sure. If the head found out that Kelly-Ann had taken to popping round to Maggie's for cups of tea, she'd have a job defending herself.

'Did you get into trouble, Miss? Why did you have to go and see the head, Miss?'

'Nothing you need to worry about, Kelly-Ann.'

Underneath the calm, Maggie had her hands around the girl's throat.

'Did you tell them you'd been to your sister's funeral, Miss?'

'They knew that. It's all fine.'

'There's my bus.'

'Off you go then. I'll see you tomorrow.'

'You promise, Miss?'

'I promise.'

'Thank you, Miss.'

As Kelly-Ann clumped up the bus steps in the heavy black lace-ups that were two sizes too big for her, Maggie rubbed her temples. Home, bath, Ben and bed.

'Miss!' Kelly-Ann shouted from the window. 'What would I do without you, Miss?'

The girl's words ricocheted around the park, bouncing off the milling kids, pinballing between the parked minibuses. By the time they came to rest, the question had picked up its own echo. A lifetime ago, Maggie had asked her dying sister the same thing. You'll cope, Di had murmured, you'd better bloody do. She understood Kelly-Ann more than Kelly-Ann or Sue Andrews or the head or anyone could ever know.

Eight

In another sensitive bedroom clearance, the newly widowed Stefan hooked a bin bag over the back of a metal-framed commode into which he tossed the detritus of his wife's final weeks. He didn't stop to assess. White paper bags full of powders and pills, a piece of sheepskin he had hunted out for her bed-ridden heels and which had once lined their babies' cribs, a lolly stick, a half-finished library book he had been reading to her, a glass bottle and its rubber pipette full of some godawful scented oil that the nurse had sprinkled on the bed sheets in the last few hours to mask the odour of decay. If he ever had the misfortune to smell the same smell again, he hoped he would be dying himself.

In it all went. A freshly laundered night-dress – even as he'd ironed it he'd known she would not wear it again – an unopened glossy magazine brought in by an underestimating neighbour on the penultimate day, a photo-copied sheet from the hospital's physiother-apy department listing gentle exercises for the post-operative, a florist's basket of fading car-nations.

When the black sack was full, he tied its

handles with a sense of achievement and tore another one from the roll. In one cathartic rush went a pile of letters and cards all saying the same thing, a cassette tape of well-meaning but useless spiritual music, a bookmark, a small towel, a pair of velour slippers they had bought together for hospital, the rubber soles of which were still a pristine plaster pink, and a floral wash bag full of things he never wanted to see again.

Stefan jettisoned with abandon, aware of his eccentric timing. Since Di's death, the offers to help him clear out her room had come at him as regularly as the doorbell had rung with condolences, and yet today there had been active discouragement. Not today, Stefan. Leave it until tomorrow. Sit down, Stefan, take a break, Stefan. What did they think? That internment was more difficult than death? That death was more difficult than dying?

Down the open wooden stairs, he could hear the murmuring female voices of his daughters Leyla and Carly, and their two aunts (not the two his girls would have preferred, because both Jane and Maggie had, for their own reasons, chosen some other way to bring the dreadful afternoon to a close). Even from this distance, he could detect the formality.

Di's eldest sister Amanda was a stickler for etiquette and had only lifted the black veil of her hat once, to sip at a sweet sherry, refusing the offer of Pimms with a prudish admonition about it hardly being Wimbledon.

Di would have loved that one, Stefan thought, wiping a film of perspiration from his hair line. To prove to himself that she really had gone, he cleared the surface of her bedside table with one sweep of his arm – pens, a bone-dry glass tumbler, a pack of tissues, half a packet of Polos, the other half of which she had sucked without pleasure to take away a taste she wouldn't name.

The marital bedroom was beginning to re-emerge from its hospital ward guise but like the unconvincing respite one gets after the third of four bouts of vomiting, he suspected there was more to go. He knew, of course, that there was no such thing as a marital bedroom any more, but he wanted to see its mirage just one more time before stepping into the vestibule of widowerhood.

He stripped the bed sheets (the clean set he had put on himself in the surreal minutes after the undertaker had carried away the body) and rolled them roughly into a ball, ramming them into the sack. Two pillows followed, still in their pristine cases, then the summer-weight duvet, folded into a meaning-ful square and pushed in too. He whipped off the mattress protector and dragged the mat-tress from its wooden slats, heaving it into the en suite bathroom where it lay lifeless against the bath that had not been run for a fortnight. Then he leaned over and turned on both taps full blast, letting the water drench the dry acrylic sides and drain wastefully away. There was something about the act of squander that made him feel better.

Back in the bedroom, he flung open the window. As he did, his arm dislodged the lid from a large round dish that had once been a central part of a long-dispersed dinner service. No doubt Bronwen had once served Brussels sprouts from its Empire Ware curves, but for as long as he had known it, it had been the pot into which his wife had tossed her countless necklaces. He lifted the lid off completely and there, coiled like tiny snakes in a porcelain pit, were Di's collection of beads.

Looking closer, he saw that each one had a little sticker attached. At first, he assumed they were price tags left over from some car boot disappointment or other (every now and again, she would have a frantic Saturday morning clearout, piling their excesses into the back of their estate) but the biro marks were not figures but names, carefully written in his wife's hand.

Stefan took a deep breath. The lettering was not the spidery effort she had managed in the final stages of cancer but the confident script of her well self, the script of happy postcards, love notes in his auction-day lunch box, shopping lists written for dinner parties. How early on in her illness had she known?

A double string of grey sea pearls had their younger daughter Leyla's name on them. There was a chain made of three different golds for Carly, an enamel pendant for Judy, a silver hoop on a leather thong for Maggie, and there were other pieces too, labelled with the names of the myriad other women who had constellated Di's female life.

He picked the whole lot up in one handful, letting the necklaces trail through his fingers like pirates' treasure as he turned to open the chest of drawers. The top left drawer was where she had kept what she called her good jewellery. With his spare hand, he unfurled the velvet roll and revealed the rings, brooches and bracelets he had bought her over the years. These too were labelled. Jane, Maggie, Leyla, Carly, Amanda, Judy. His own name was there too, on the dainty antique sapphire and diamond engagement ring he had once tried to slip on to her not-so-dainty finger. She had worn it on a chain around her neck instead, under her wedding gown and on all sorts of days since.

Bewildered suddenly by her absence, Stefan hung to the solid corner of the furniture for a moment and closed his eyes.

'Dad?'

The sound was so sweet.

'Are you all right?'

Leyla was hovering in the doorway. She hadn't been into this bedroom since the day her mother had died in it either.

'I will be.'

'Will you?'

'In time. Come here.'

Leyla hesitated. She'd smelt the smell too.

'Look at these,' he said, holding up her

mother's beads. Their familiarity lured her in and with one tentative step, she crossed the threshold. There was no smell.

'Mum must have...' Stefan said.

Leyla glanced at the wooden-slatted bed frame, unrecognizable now as the deathbed. Fresh air and village noises breezed in through the open window.

'I know.'

'How?'

'Have you looked in the wardrobe yet?'

Stefan put down the velvet roll and opened the pine door. Di's clothes had already gone. In their place was a stack of labelled boxes and bags. His wife had never been this tidy in life.

'Where are all her...?'

'Auntie Maggie took them.'

'When?'

'Mum asked her to...'

'But when did she ... I mean, how did she ... when did she do all this sorting?'

'January?' Leyla said. 'She tried to tell me she was having a clearout for the village jumble sale.'

Her bottom lip gave out before the word 'village'.

'I'll give her jumble sale,' her father said, taking his youngest daughter into his arms, the necklaces tangling in her long auburn hair. 'I'll give her bloody jumble sale...'

At Maggie's, there wasn't so much as a toy train left under a chair.

131

'Go on,' Don urged. 'Jess will be wondering where you've got to.'

'Or should I stay?' Jamie asked again.

'No, you go. I'll sort the rest out.'

'The rest', as they both knew, meant Maggie.

Jamie got as far as the porch before hesitating again but Rob put his arm out of the van window and banged impatiently on the door.

'Do you promise you'll...?'

The word 'promise' hung heavily between them.

'I've told you, I'll wait here until she comes home.'

Home was a strange way for Don to think of a house he hadn't stepped foot inside for nearly five years, but it still meant more to him than his locked and alarmed barn conversion two hours' drive away. He had never said, to the few proper friends he had made in his new incarnation, 'Do you want to come to my *home*?' On the rare occasions he invited anyone back, he'd say 'Do you want to come to my *place*?' It was a significant difference, or it was to him anyway.

As he heard the fleet of vehicles screech from the drive, he relaxed for the first time since he'd arrived. The worst scenario – Maggie arriving to discover her family, like an army of bailiffs, systematically removing the things she valued most – could now fall to the cutting-room floor. So far, not one of his preconceived visions of this visit had proved to be prophetic. He hadn't been cold shouldered, rejected, expelled or stoned – he hadn't even been questioned.

He climbed the metal ladder to the loft. Despite the unventilated heat in the roof space, his head lightened. Whatever else happened today, his ex-wife would not now choke on the conspiratorial exhaust fumes in her own driveway. What was done was done. Finding the old cot, as he'd promised Jamie he would do, was the only remaining challenge.

'How do you know it's still up there?' his son had asked.

'I was married to your mother for fifteen years, wasn't I?'

And Don often thought about fourteen of those. In the darkness, his hand groped instinctively for the light switch, but the bulb had gone. No doubt its replacement could be found in the wicker basket on the shelf in the garage if he had the inclination to sort it out – which, oddly enough, he did.

Electricity restored, he had a good look around. There was the wallpapering table his boys had once used as a home-made lemonade stall, the two vintage wooden tennis rackets in their hinged presses that he and Maggie used to take down to the local park on summer evenings before the kids were born, a box of LPs bought with student grants and first wages, including the David Bowie album *Diamond Dogs* with the cover that used to give Rob nightmares, all in exactly the same places he had put them himself, years ago.

With one foot, he tested a flimsy piece of hardboard that was balanced precariously between two rafters. It flipped up and knocked against something stacked along the attic wall. On inspection, he could make out a rectangle of painted wood inset with three yellow plastic balls on a stainless steel axis. Don flicked one to make it rattle and smiled. Jamie used to be able to spin all three at once with a kick of his tiny bare feet. More by touch than sight, he established that all five components were present and correct, including a small tough polythene bag full of screws and nuts and bolts taped to the flimsy hardboard base. Don had lost count of the number of times he had put these pieces together before – in French gites, Spanish villas, in grandparents' and friends' spare rooms – while Maggie fed a tired baby and entertained a tetchy toddler. Neither of their boys had taken to the nylon walls of an expensive travel cot, which had ended up as a toy pen into which he and Maggie would toss the day's chaos before falling, exhausted, on to the sofa together. Happy days. Maybe if he looked carefully enough, he'd find himself lying between the rafters too.

He began to feed the first plank carefully through the hatch where he could lower it to within three feet of the floor, at which point he'd have to let it go. It landed with a safe thud. The second plank hit the side of the loft ladder with a clunk. The third clattered noisily on to the first.

As Maggie came through the back door, saw the space where Ben's high chair had been and heard the crashing from upstairs, her initial thought was that she was being burgled. Her second, which came almost instantaneously, was that she would have given anything to have been right the first time.

With a bizarre flicker of well-being, Stefan carried the velvet jewellery roll down the open wooden stairs and into the sombre circle of the sitting room. Di's chair by the woodburner was empty but the illusion that she was in the next room had gone. His elder daughter Carly – looking more like her mother than ever now there was no living comparison – smiled at him with relief.

'Dad,' she said, patting the cushion desperately beside her, 'I was just about to come and find you.'

He could see why. He had failed his first solo parenting test already, leaving her alone with these people. Amanda, her black hat on the arm of the chair, was sniffing into a tissue. Peter, legs apart with unbowed back, was on sentry duty behind her. Judy, who had taken her shoes, jacket and scarf off but left her hair band on, was handing around old photographs, more relaxed now that her new partner Clive had taken himself tactfully away.

'This one was taken when we went to London...' Judy turned it over and squinted at the pencilled date on the back. 'Summer

135

1970, it says.'

'It would have been the second week of August,' Amanda said. 'We were always sent away for the second week of August.'

'As in banished?' Carly asked.

'Daddy liked to take Mummy to Europe in August. It was their special time.'

Amanda's theatrical tone struck a false note in a home where Rex's name was not often mentioned. Stefan waited for the challenge but of course none came. Di would have been in there like a shot.

'It was an open secret that Bronwen was prone to depression in August,' Stefan told Carly.

'Really?'

'Oh yes. Rex used to spend a small fortune each year trying to hide his wife away in out-of-season ski resorts, or driving her round and round Belgium and Luxembourg in his Ford Zephyr until September came, didn't he girls?'

'Nonsense!' Amanda tried to laugh.

Judy waved the photo in her sister's face to move the conversation along. 'Diana ripped her skirt climbing on the statue of Eros in Piccadilly Circus, do you remember?'

'No, that was Jane. It was Jane who climbed on Eros.'

'No it wasn't, it was Diana, I remember...'

'Jane...'

'Well, if she was here, we could ask her,' Stefan said. Three faces stared at him in horror. Carly looked at the patterned rug on

136

the stripped wooden floor. 'Jane, I mean...' he added hotly.

'Of course.'

'Although if Di was here, we could ask her too,' he added, feeling a supernatural prod between his ribs.

'Where *is* Jane?' Amanda asked tersely. 'I do think she and Maggie might have...'

'Maggie had some crisis at work...'

'Crisis!' Amanda huffed, again forgetting she was in the wrong camp to express these things.

'It was genuine, she's under fire for being too hands-on with some of the kids apparently.'

'That's so unfair,' Carly said. 'She's so good with them, she makes such a difference.'

'I'm sure there is more to it than that, dear. Maggie gets far too involved.'

'Which is one of the reasons why we love her,' Judy pointed out.

'Of course, but we have to accept it's not always appropriate,' Amanda said.

'Well, it must have been a hard day for her, with Uncle Don turning up.' Carly knew where her loyalties lay.

'Yes, and how *dare* he?' Judy exclaimed. 'I couldn't believe it when I saw him slink in to the back of the church.'

'It wasn't a question of daring,' Stefan said. 'Di put Don on her list of people she would like to be there so I invited him.'

'Are you saying she had a guest list?' Peter checked pompously.

'I am. She organized her funeral right down to the last little detail.'

Amanda made a noise somewhere between a sob and a squeak.

'So where were you lot in the front pew this afternoon, eh?' Stefan asked.

'We were right behind you.'

'Di wanted you up front.'

'We didn't know that,' Peter said.

'You bloody did! I sent you a copy of her wish list.'

Amanda had the grace to blush.

'Perhaps it was overlooked in the shock of her...'

'Not exactly a shock...'

'No...'

'Poor darling,' Judy said ambiguously. 'Her way of coping.'

She put the black and white likeness of one or other of the twins back into the ancient yellow Kodak envelope, and snapped it away in her patent leather handbag.

'Well, we have some wonderful memories,' she said, 'Eros or no Eros.'

'Of course, but you're thinking of the time Diana once tore a cardigan in Hampstead Court maze,' Amanda said like a dog with a bone.

'*Hampton* Court,' Judy corrected.

'That's what I said.'

'You didn't, you said Hampstead...'

Stefan raised his eyes quickly at Carly and moved across the room to sit next to her. 'Look at this,' he said quietly. 'Mum's best bits.' He untied the jewellery roll and opened it out on his lap.

Carly ran her fingers over the gold and silver arcs, the smooth stones and spiky clasps. She picked one out and read its tiny sticky label.

'I bought her this in Ireland,' Stefan said, taking it. 'An emerald, see? We were in Galway. This little shop...'

He handed it over to Amanda.

'Here you are, love. Di wanted you to have it.'

Amanda sat looking at the ring in her palm as if it were a dead baby bird fallen from its nest. She brought the tissue to her nose once more.

'Oh,' was all she said.

Could she not at least smile? Carly thought. She wanted her dad to take it back and tell her she could have it once she made a bit of an effort. If she and Leyla could put on a brave face, then surely Amanda could.

Stefan picked something else from the velvety bed.

'And this ... this Wedgwood cameo brooch we bought together, in Liberty's I think it was, years ago, before you were born...'

He passed it to Judy.

'Mine? Oh, Stefan...'

More tears.

'Another time perhaps?' Peter asked, his sense of correct behaviour already offended by the bedroom clearing that had been going on.

'No, I'd like to do it now if you don't mind, Peter. I think Di would have liked us to do it together,' Stefan said firmly.

'It would be nice if we *were* all together,' Amanda sniffed.

Stefan's hand went back to the roll and his large fingers pinched out the tiny engagement ring, still on its chain.

Carly swallowed. 'Where's Leyla?' she whispered.

Stefan put his hand in hers and squeezed it. The ring dug into their palms.

'Here I am,' came a muffled voice.

Leyla walked carefully down the stairs, her face hidden behind a precariously balanced stack of shoe boxes, files, and a collection of small padded boxes poised on top.

She put them on the table, knocking over a sherry glass and shoving plates with crumbs of half-eaten fruit cake to the edge.

'Help yourselves,' she said. 'It's like Mum's Lucky Dip.'

Amanda's hand went straight to a green leather box file on the bottom of the pile. She lifted the others from it and dusted its surface.

'That's Mummy's,' she said proprietorially and then looking at Leyla and Carly, she added, 'I mean Granny's.'

'I haven't seen that since Mummy died,' Judy squealed.

'She kept all her personal papers in this,' Amanda said, pushing her finger into its brass opener. The lid sprang open. On the top, under the black sprung lever, was a card in an envelope. On the front, in Di's hand, it said 'For Maggie'.

'*Maggie?*' said Amanda in horror. 'Di wanted *Maggie* to have Mummy's papers?'

'It looks like it,' Leyla said.

'But why? Maggie was never as close to Mummy as the rest of us.'

'I think,' said Stefan, 'that could be the whole point.'

Nine

Ben lay on the mottled brown and orange carpet, his head resting on his purple dinosaur, his eyes transfixed by the cartoon images flickering on the ancient TV. His parents, too exhausted to fiddle with the bent aerial any more, sat on the ripped vinyl sofa behind him wishing they were somewhere else. Despite having drunk the bottle of champagne that Don had bought for them to toast their new home, they felt considerably older than the sum of their thirty-nine years.

It was hard to believe that all their worldly goods had arrived. At Maggie's, their clothes had spilled out of drawers, bathroom products had fallen off shelves, books and CDs had taken over every available surface and Ben's toy box had grown like Topsy, but here, with five whole rooms to fill, it appeared they actually owned next to nothing.

Jess, who smelt faintly of pine bathroom cleaner despite the challenge from the curry takeaway foil containers at her feet, was on the cusp between concern and irritation. Jamie had barely spoken a word since saying goodbye to his brother and aunt an hour ago. He'd stood in silence until the Transit van and the hire car had disappeared up and beyond the bumpy track and then he'd gone inside to hunt restlessly from packing box to bin liner for the security blankets of his new life – his alarm clock radio so that he could be up in time for milking, his notes from the tractor-driving course, his hayfever tablets.

He'd set them up in anal formation on the chipboard table next to the grubby mattress that Jess had covered with the faded floral duvet cover he still associated with his own parents' bed. There had once been frilled curtains to match and he remembered the pattern well from the days when he used to sleep between his mother and father during thunderstorms and temperatures.

It wasn't until Jess had finished hanging their clothes in the damp oak-veneer wardrobe that Jamie had made his first verbal contribution to their new life together.

'Happy now?' he'd said, scuffing the beer mat lodged under one of the wardrobe's rolled feet that Gatesy had put there to stop it rocking on the uneven wooden floorboards.

'I will be once you cheer up,' she'd said, but here, staring at the sitting room's woodchip wall, Jess wondered if that were true. This inaugural evening in their own home bore no resemblance to the fantasy whatsoever. Not much in the adult world ever did.

She glared at the pictures either side of the fireplace. Why should she care that Gatesy's cheaply framed Lamborghini Diablo with its vivid sunset and his Shelby Mustang against its American flag were still hanging there? They were no more hideous than anything else in the house.

This was surely not the life she was destined to live. There were several movies she'd seen in which people experienced two different versions of their own existence according to a decision they made, and Jess wished more and more lately that she was in one of them. The door she *should* have walked through led to university and a well-paid career in pharmaceutical research, late motherhood in her forties, marriage to a man with his own successful career. But this was clearly not Hollywood.

'Are you all right?' she said, digging deep. She curled her legs underneath her and leaned over to kiss Jamie's left cheek. The sparse beard he was attempting to grow tickled her lips and she wished he would give up on it. It embarrassed her.

'I said are you all right?'

But Jamie didn't know if he was all right or not, nor whether funerals were sad, if love made you happy, if fathers were useful or if sons just brought you trouble.

'Yeah, I'm fine.'

'Shall we have another drink then? Gatesy's left some beer.'

'I've got to be up in the morning.'

'What, and I haven't?'

'Not at five, you don't.'

On the floor, Ben's head rolled off the purple dinosaur. His eyes were closed and a

144

little trickle of dribble ran from his lips. Jess looked at her watch. It was nine o'clock, two hours after his rigid bedtime. Maggie would be appalled.

'Shall we go to bed then?'

Bed, together, at nine! These were the freedoms she had dreamed of.

'I'm not relaxed enough to sleep.'

'Who said anything about sleep?'

Jamie kept his gaze fixed on the fuzzy pictures in front of him.

'I can tell you what happens,' Jess said sharply, standing up. 'The dog goes on a scooter trip to the park and makes friends with a blue monkey.'

She bent over Ben and put her hands beneath him to haul him up. He hung limply over her shoulder and she could feel the vibration of his permanent wheeze against her chest.

'So is this it then?' she asked, one foot already out of the door. 'Is this the first night in our new home?'

They had sex, as they knew they would, but it was neither the urgent scramble nor the relaxed teasing of their usual repertoire. Jamie, often a two-minute man unless he thought of dead dogs, was reluctant to lose control, and as a result Jess forgot all her usual moves, her foolproof words and rhythms. Even her faked orgasm was uncharacteristically quiet.

They lay there, not quite as satiated as they needed to be, and feigned contentment, too

145

young to know they were simply following an established pattern laid out by a millennium of wedding-night disappointments before them.

Jamie, relieved the day was nearly over, rolled on to his side to set the alarm. As 4.30 a.m. flashed its challenge, a car drew up outside and doors slammed.

'Who the hell is that?' he asked, a little scared, leaping naked out of bed and making a slit in the curtains. Voices were already shouting through the letterbox.

'Yoohoo, sweeties!'

'Get out of bed, you sex maniacs!'

'We've brought gorgeousness!'

Carl's tight white T-shirt gleamed unmistakeably. He was hugging a pot of willow twigs and Amy was waving a bottle.

'Shit,' Jamie said in a quick low voice, slipping back into bed. But Jess was already slipping out.

'Where are you going?'

'To let them in!'

'Leave them!'

She was dragging on her trousers, foregoing the pants that lay next to them on the floor and pulling her top over her loose small breasts. She leant over him.

'Do I smell of sex?'

'Don't go.'

'But they've come all this way.'

There it was again, that bloody word! But, but, but, but, but – it was just another way of saying no.

He pulled on her arm and was shocked by the resistance.

'All this way? We're only a mile and a half out of town.'

'They know we're here. I can't—' she said, wriggling out of his grasp.

'Yes you can.'

But Jess was already pounding down the stairs.

'I'm coming!' he heard her shout, in entirely different circumstances than he would have preferred.

'Are you sure you won't stay?' Maggie asked Stefan on her doorstep as the chill night sneaked past her. 'You'd be more than welcome.'

It sounded too polite given their recent emotional journey, but the atmosphere between them tonight had been formal, despite the way Stefan's mourner's tie hung loosely around his open-necked white shirt, making him look more like a reveller than a widow. She could all but see Di, strappy silver evening shoes in her hand, tiptoeing up the path behind him, giggling 'Sssshhhh! Don't wake the kids!'

'No, I'd better get back. I just wanted to get Bronwen's box to you before…'

Maggie thought he was going to say 'before the end of the day'. She understood his need for closure. It had been the longest twelve hours she had ever known.

'Before what?' she asked when nothing

147

came. His hesitation got her prickling with intuition.

The porch light bore down on him like an inquisitor's torch. He had been about to say 'before the coven got their hands on it', but his other sisters-in-law had sucked his diplomacy dry. He realized he hadn't the energy to take on Maggie's cross-examination as well.

'Well, you know what they can be like,' he ended up saying awkwardly. 'Anything to do with Bronwen and Amanda thinks—'

'Amanda didn't want me to have it?' Maggie pounced.

When he had handed it to her in her sitting room a few minutes ago, the box had just been a box. Suddenly it began to pulsate with significance. It was *Bronwen*'s box of personal papers, *Bronwen*'s, who was all but a stranger to her.

'Whether she did or she didn't is neither here nor there,' Stefan said, shifting to one side to avoid the spotlight.

'But she didn't, did she?' Maggie's speech quickened. 'She wouldn't, of course she wouldn't. It was bad enough when Bronwen handed it over to Di...'

Stefan stepped back, putting his hands up in defeat.

'Maggie love, I've just come away from all this.'

'I'm sorry.'

He nodded to acknowledge her apology.

'Perhaps you should take it home again,' she said, 'if it's going to be an issue...'

'Di wanted you to have it, and that's all there is to it.'

Maggie could hear the green leather box whispering to her. Look inside me, say goodnight to Stefan, open me up, I have things to tell you. There had been no burning curiosity when he'd first handed it to her. It had just kind of sighed contritely, as if to say, *sorry about this, someone's got to have me.* But now that Amanda was in pursuit...

'I wonder why?'

'Oh, there'll be a reason, knowing Di. She's left a card for you, on top. I don't know when she wrote it...'

Stefan's voice wobbled. Maggie grabbed his hand and squeezed it.

'All over now,' she said, hugging him.

He didn't have the strength to disagree. He pulled himself out of the embrace and became almost chipper.

'Right, so ... onwards and upwards ... you must be getting back to Don and the boys.'

Don and the boys. The way it rolled off his tongue sounded right.

'Boy,' she corrected. 'I've just got Rob tonight. Jamie moved out this afternoon, after the funeral. He's starting a new job on a farm, and it comes with its own cottage. It's all happened so quickly, I...'

Stefan threw his head back.

'So he did. I'm not thinking straight.'

'You knew?'

'I had to wait for Jane to come back before I felt happy about leaving the girls. She looked a little better than she did...'

'Jane?'

'White as a sheet under her tan, didn't you think? And she'd been drinking all morning. I was relieved to see her go, to be honest. The distraction of being a removal van for the afternoon...'

'Jane helped Jamie move out?'

'She found today very hard. You would, as a twin, wouldn't you? It must be...'

'Jane helped Jamie move out?' Maggie repeated.

But Stefan had already realized his mistake and was walking towards his car, waving a white handkerchief in the air. Oh, go home then, she thought. Go home. Don should go home. Rob should go home. They should all just go home.

As she watched his car pull away, she cried a little. Di and Jamie and Ben were gone, Don and Rob and Jane were back. She was the only constant, watching the family tide come and go, come and go. The engine noise rumbled off into the distance and she stood there with the door open, letting more and more cold air into the house, until all she could hear was the far-off barking of a dog.

In the kitchen that Don had made ten years ago, the cheese on toast was liquid fat on charcoal. She scraped the ruined supper into the bin and slotted the three clean plates back into the rack above the sink. Her domestic mood was neither artificial nor real and she was neither happy nor sad.

When she walked into her sitting room, carrying a tray of two coffees, a hot chocolate, a packet of biscuits and a bottle of brandy, Don gave Rob's huge feet, which had been resting on the low coffee table, a corrective shove to the floor. There was something so familiar about the action that she took a moment to register how utterly out of context it was. A father who hadn't stepped foot inside his own house for five years correcting the behaviour of a son who had been an adult himself for six.

'Has Uncle Stefan gone?' Rob asked, his eyes still glued to the snooker.

'Yes, I asked him to stay but he needed to get back to the girls. He just wanted to drop off the box before...'

The box! The thought of it shunted everything else over the edge, like a coin in a shove ha'penny machine.

'Before what?'

'Before it became an issue, I guess...'

'Why would it become an issue?'

'I've no idea.'

'What's in it? Why did you have to have it tonight?'

'Closure, I think you call it,' she said.

Maggie put the tray on the table and handed her eldest son the ancient blue and white striped Cornishware mug with 'Robbie' written around its sides. Neither she nor Don thought how silly a six foot four security officer looked drinking from a named cup. They'd seen him drink from it a thousand times before, starting with milk, then graduating to tea with sugar, tea without sugar, milky coffee, black. Equally unremarkable was the way she didn't then offer Don his drink but sat back while he opened the brandy bottle and poured a slosh into both coffees. She was grateful to him for not commenting on the giveaway crunch of crystallized alcohol around the lid which told him just how long the bottle had been at the back of the cupboard.

As the evening's news started, the green leather box sat in the middle of the table, taunting Maggie with its secret. Did it have one, Maggie wondered? Did Di mean her to find something, or had she just handed it on to one sister simply to get at another? *Look in the box*, Di had said on one of those terrible last afternoons. Had she meant this box? If it *did* contain something combustible then why would Di, confrontational to the last, have waited until now to reveal it?

The bulletin droned on about a doctor on misconduct charges, a Downing Street spat, a credit card fraud and a celebrity split. To the rest of the world, the day had been unexceptional.

'Pass us another biscuit, Dad.'

'Get your feet off the furniture and I'll think about it.'

To her relief, neither her ex-husband nor her eldest son paid any attention when Maggie leaned forward and pulled the box on to her lap. Pretending to be still watching the

152

news, she pressed ever so slowly on the release button, her left hand applying a light but firm pressure to the lid. It popped open beneath her palm.

'Let me just see the weather forecast, Rob,' she said casually as he picked up the remote control, but as the rain clouds moved east during the course of the night with another ridge of low pressure coming into the west by morning, her hand slipped under the box's lid and on to its contents. Her fingers worked around the rigid edge of an envelope whose corners were perfect right angles, unbent by time. She slid her forefinger under the flap and pulled out the card, not even bothering to look at its front.

She dropped her eyes. The familiar sight of Di's handwriting, in her trademark turquoise blue ink, stabbed her at the back of her throat. She found herself stroking the words in the way she often touched photographs of Arthur. *'Maggie darling, What a strange letter this is to be writing, knowing that I will have died by the time you read it (I wonder where or what I will be)...'*

'Mum?' Rob asked. 'Can I turn over now?'

'I hope you've stopped crying. I've had a lovely life, and this illness is so completely bloody wretched that to be honest...'

'Mum?'

'Mmm?'

'The weather's finished...'

'...that to be honest, I'd be glad to be dead tomorrow if it meant it would be over and...'

153

'Can I turn over?'

'*...over and done with. I wish I could find a way of letting you all know that. I can see you all grieving already and...*'

'Leave her,' Don told him. 'Watch what you like.'

Maggie looked up. The opening credits to a film rolled over the screen. Father and son shifted in exactly the same way in their seats, settling down a little further. She blinked away a tear and started again.

Maggie darling,

What a strange letter this is to be writing, knowing that I will have died by the time you read it (I wonder where or what I will be). I hope you've stopped crying. I've had a lovely life, and this illness is so completely bloody wretched that to be honest, I'd be glad to be dead tomorrow if it meant it would be over and done with. I wish I could find a way of letting you all know that. I can see you all grieving already and I feel terrible for you, but not for myself. Don't get me wrong. I would snatch at anything that would give me back my old healthy life so I could continue to be a mother to my girls (a grandmother maybe) but that life doesn't exist any more, and so nor really do I.

I have been clearing out cupboards this morning whilst I still can, trying to make the job of sorting things out a little easier for Stefan when the time comes. I'm not sure he knows the time *is* coming yet. We don't speak about it. I have my little chat with the consultant, he has his, and the fact that I am dying is either my secret or ours but I suspect Stefan thinks it is his alone. It is madness really. I know you'll look after him for me after all this is over. He'll need your company – don't be afraid to show him you love him – and he in turn will be able to look after our two precious girls. All will be well, as that rather maudlin funeral poem goes (and no, I don't want it at mine thanks).

I'm sorry I can't say any of this to you now whilst I'm still here on this earth. I have tried, but I open my mouth and something else comes out. I can hear myself being irritable or even hurtful to you and I always feel bad later. You'll understand when you get round to dying yourself, it's all rather surreal, but whatever I have said or will say between now and then, remember that I love you and that you have played an important part in my wonderful life. Don't imagine me weeping. I've done all that. Yes, I feel a little frightened (not unlike how I felt just before my parachute jump), but at the same time relieved, like I've been awake for days and sleep is just around the corner.

Darling Maggie, I am passing on Bronwen's box of papers to you for you to do with whatever you wish. When she gave them to me a few years before she died, she asked me not to look through them until she was gone so I didn't. I had a feeling there was something in there that she half wanted me to find, perhaps something about her unfathomable decision to give you up to Aunt Grace, or a hint that her marriage to Rex was not the blessed union he loved to make out, or one of those other mysteries that lurked just under the surface of our lives. I should have done something about it but by the time she *was* gone, the curiosity had left me. I had another go last year, just after my diagnosis, and I nearly got there. I'm sorry to sound so mysterious but perhaps you'll know what I'm talking about if and when you get there yourself.

When I came across the box this morning, I lifted the lid again but found I had neither the desire nor the energy to do anything more. I'm thinking maybe *your* curiosity is greater. If not, set fire to the lot of it.

I also want to say sorry for one other thing. I am sorry I called you 'the baby who never came home'. I knew even back then, as a not very kind eleven year old, the power of that label, and I have seen how it has stuck with you, but I want you to know that you came home for me many years ago and that in my memory, you have been my kindest and my dearest sister from the very start.

Make the most of what you have, Maggie darling. Don't be afraid to look in the box for the missing pieces of the jigsaw. Search carefully. The answers are there, I know they are. And don't forget I love you.

Goodnight hun, Di x

Maggie let out a sob and both Rob and Don turned from the screen to look at her.

Caught out, Maggie hastily pushed the card – which she now saw had an empty garden bench against a wall of pink roses on the front – into the midst of the papers beneath. Receipts, train tickets, recipes from magazines, a pristine slim leather address book with no entries.

'What's in it?' Rob asked.

'I don't know yet.'

'You're OK though, are you?' Don enquired more skilfully.

'I think so.'

She put the closed box back on the table and stood up.

'How's your hand?' She delivered it as an end-of-conversation question, if not an end-of-evening one.

Don looked at his palm where, an hour ago, a screwdriver had pierced his skin like a stigmata. Unscrewing the brandy had opened the little hyphen of a wound up again.

'It'll be fine,' he said, touching it. It was a mark of goodness. In finding and building the old cot, he'd done what he'd promised Jamie he would do.

Maggie looked at her watch.

'Would you like to take a few clean plasters with you?'

'Er ... I ... yes,' Don said, jumping to his feet, hot with stupidity under his beard. He'd forgotten himself. 'That might be a good idea.'

He picked up his drained mug and left a bloody smear on its porcelain.

'Oh, is it still bleeding?'

He offered up his weeping hand and Maggie held it, inspecting it.

'Some Savlon maybe.'

Rob could see his father was on his way, but he wasn't in the mood to go anywhere himself. His London flat was sub-let. His flight didn't leave until tomorrow teatime, and his mother's sofa was a damn sight comfier than the seats waiting for him in Heathrow's departure lounge.

'I'll have the spare bed now that Jamie—'

'If a guest house was good enough for you last night, it's good enough for you tonight as well,' Maggie said curtly.

'But this is my last night in this country for six months...'

'The bed's not made up and the woman at the bed and breakfast place will be—' Maggie began, but she was interrupted by the opening of the door behind them.

Jamie stood there staring at his family as if he were watching the landing of an alien spacecraft. His mum was holding his dad's hand, his brother, who should have been drinking Indonesian beer with Gatesy in a Bali beach bar, was watching TV with his feet on the table, the brandy bottle was out and a plate of chocolate biscuits balanced on the arm of the sofa.

'What in God's name are you doing back already?' Maggie cried.

It was like hearing a nun blaspheme.

'Forgotten your teddy bear?' Rob asked through a mouthful of digestive.

'Don't mind us,' Don said. 'We were just off.'

'I thought I'd come and see if you were ... I'm sorry about this afternoon.'

He looked it. Maggie sighed.

'Oh, don't worry. I can quite see how it might have seemed like a good idea at the time.'

'You can?'

'Of course. Now if none of you mind, I'm off to bed. You know where everything is if you need it.'

She glanced at the box on the table and then at her sons and their father, standing awkwardly in what was once their home. Tomorrow, they would all be gone again, one of them to the other side of the world. It seemed a shame to break up the party. She gave Rob a hug and told him to look after himself.

'Don't do anything silly,' she said.

'Nor you,' he replied, holding on to her embrace a little longer than usual.

159

Ten

Against all the odds, Maggie managed to leave Di's legacy untouched for the next five days. On the sixth, she poured herself an early drink, took the box by its recessed metal handles and tipped the whole lot upside down, causing a document avalanche.

Postcards, bills and birthday cards slid across the table, releasing paper dust from the last century into the expectant air. Maggie leapt on a safe-looking A4 piece of low-grade blue card decorated with crushed tissue-paper flowers. On the back it said *'Get Well Soon from all your pupils in Class 4C'*.

Maggie had similar greetings from her own pupils, so this one meant nothing to her. Bronwen's teaching career, which had spanned at least two decades, had touched her own life not a jot. She had no fond memories of her mother in the classroom, no picture of school books on the kitchen table, no recollection of report writing, parents' evenings, sighs of relief when the holidays came round. No doubt Amanda could provide the detail should she want it.

She made a jealous nick in the side of the card with her fingernails and tossed it to one

161

side, but the neatly written list of children's names – Philip, Stephen, Maxine – lured her back. How old were they today? Did they feature in 1968 – the year the 'truth' came out? Maggie had such a vivid picture of the trends of that time – in particular a popular pink rose pattern on a white dinner plate – that she measured all neighbouring years against it.

She smelt the card, hoping to catch something of what had made it special. Get well soon from what? Flu? A broken leg? Maggie tried to place herself in the story too. A ten-year-old girl telling her boarding school friends she was adopted? A nine-year-old wondering why she had nothing in common with her mother? Nothing fitted, as usual. The fact was, she didn't have enough pieces of the jigsaw to complete the picture. She had the four corner pieces in Rex, Bronwen, Arthur and Grace, she had the side pieces in Amanda, Judy, Diana and Jane, and she had her own middle piece, and yet still something was missing.

One image of her childhood dominated, of Arthur bending over her, buttoning up her velvet-collared coat and reminding her to give 'Auntie Bronnie' a kiss. Naturally, Maggie would then do anything she could to wriggle out of the obligation. To assuage her grown-up guilt, she would force herself to imagine Rob or Jamie rejecting her in the same way, but for them to do that, she had to imagine herself rejecting them first and that was beyond her. Parental ostracism wasn't a question of why, it was a question of *how*.

Maggie tore the card in two and slapped it on the table in an act of liberation. Half the contents of this box were memories belonging to other people, and there was no reason on earth why she should be their reluctant curator. She picked up a postcard sent by Amanda from Venice in May 1981 and ripped that up too, followed by a handwritten recipe for tiffin, an order of service for Judy's first marriage and a curled black and white photograph of her four sisters holding baby rabbits. I never knew you had rabbits, she said to the remnant showing Di's squinting young face, you never told me that.

'God!' she said out loud as the phone made her jump.

'Maggie, it's Don...'

As if she didn't know his voice.

'I'm sorry to trouble you.'

'Oh, you're not ... I mean, I'm sure you're sorry, you're just not troubling me...'

'Good, I was just wondering...'

'So was I...'

'You were?'

'No, you first.'

'Did I leave a screwdriver there last week by any chance?'

'Oh.'

Maggie realized she'd been expecting him to say something else.

'In Jamie's room?' Don clarified.

'You mean the little bedroom? Would you

163

like me to look for it a minute?'

'I could look for it myself if you don't mind me popping round.'

'Isn't that a rather long way to come for a screwdriver?'

'It might be worth it.'

'I understand.'

'I've already lost it once...'

'And good screwdrivers are hard to come by.'

'Exactly. So if there's a chance I can find it again...' he said cautiously, not sure how far to push the metaphor.

Maggie wasn't sure he was pushing it at all, so they left off with a casual 'see you later'. Although there was nothing casual about the way Maggie put the wine back in the fridge, defrosted a ciabatta, found a jar of olives, ran upstairs, dumped her work clothes in the laundry, showered, dressed again in a pair of black linen trousers and a red crinkle cotton shirt which came off in favour of a white skirt and navy T-shirt, which then came off in favour of a denim skirt and a white T-shirt, which she then tried with a pink blouse which became the white T-shirt again. Eventually, she changed the denim skirt for the black linen trousers and went back downstairs to make it look as if she had been there all the time – just in case.

In an entirely different mood now, Maggie selected something else from the avalanche – a slim red leather diary with 'Birthdays' embossed in gold on its front. She checked for her own birthday first. There, pleasingly, on September the third, was her name, in Bronwen's distinctive teacherly script. She found Diana and Jane's in May, Amanda's in March, Judy's in October and Rex's in January. As she flicked through, she saw Carly and Leyla's names, Stefan's, Amanda's husband Peter, and noticed that Rob shared his April birthday with someone called Lottie. To an untrained eye, Bronwen passed for the queen of all mums.

Maggie turned to August the eighth to see if Jamie was there, which he was. Three dates down, on August the eleventh – the day in 1968 that the 'truth' had come out – Bronwen had simply written the letter 'C'.

'C' for what? Catastrophe? Calamity? Collusion? Not expecting to come to any understanding, Maggie reached indiscriminately for something else. It was a typed letter, separated over time from its envelope, from an organization called The Joseph French Foundation. The strap line read *Is your child different?* and at the top of the sheet on the right-hand side was a pencil drawing of a young boy's smiling face.

With one ear out for a car on the drive, Maggie turned the sheet over to see a faded ink signature – not computer generated as she'd expected.

Thank you for your enquiry, it said. *We are a new independent charity, set up in 1976 by Joseph's parents to help couples, like them, who have had a child diagnosed with severe dis-*

165

abilities. John and Mary French's experience of anger, confusion, helplessness and exhaustion, is typical of thousands of other parents in Britain today. This charity has been born out of their needs...

It was the sort of letter Maggie saw lying around in the Melwood School staff room all the time, so she put it down. After a few disappointments, she came across a matching envelope, this time with the pencilled picture of the young boy's face in the bottom left-hand corner. She'd been wrongly assuming that John and Mary French were parents of a child Bronwen had once taught, but Bronwen had never had anything to do with special needs – that was *her* domain.

Inside the envelope was a compliment slip, showing a donation in 1987 of five hundred pounds. Five hundred pounds! 1987 was the year Jamie had been born, and Rex had made a great deal of opening a bank account in his name in which he and Bronwen had placed twenty-five pounds. She glanced at the clock. Did she have time for this?

Dear Mrs Barton,
  Once again, thank you for your generous donation. The work your money represents is not only for the Joseph French Foundation but for you, because you, or someone you know, has a child with a disability, rare disorder, chronic syndrome, behavioural problem or chemical imbalance. Your donation will make a

significant difference to the lives these diagnoses touch.

With best wishes, Mary French.

Outside, a car pulled up. Maggie stacked half the papers hurriedly back into the box and closed the lid; the other half she patted into something resembling a pile. And with just a brief check in the mirror, she went to answer the door.

In the musty farm cottage that was still irrefutably Gatesy's, Carl's pot of willow twigs sat mockingly in the empty grate. He'd placed them there with a camp flourish as if they were the perfect finishing touch, but all Jess could think as she looked at them now was that they reminded her of a fossilized prehistoric bush, put there to make Ben's purple dinosaur feel at home.

Having her own place had fewer ups than downs, as it turned out. Carl and Amy had taken to using her sitting room as their local, but Jess had never wanted to run her own bar. She would pay an inflated price for a drink every time if it meant she could leave the washing-up to someone else.

As she stood up, her foot caught Amy's latest bottle of supermarket cava and it rolled on the tiled hearth that was the colour of mushroom soup, leaving a trickle of sticky liquid in its wake. Three drained cans of Gatesy's left-behind beer were the mantelpiece's only adornments, one of them an ashtray for Carl's Marlboro Lights. Jess wouldn't mind if the pervasive odour of stale smoke and curry had been the legacy of a good night in, but her friends had moved on to another party.

'Come with us,' Amy had trilled, fiddling coyly with the body jewellery in her navel. 'Jamie will babysit.'

But Jamie had disappeared into the night again. When Jess had gone upstairs to wheedle her way back into his affections, she'd found an empty bed. The music had been turned up so loud she hadn't even heard him go, but she could put money on where he had gone.

She turned off the thump of summer festival rock and wandered drunkenly into the hallway, the chemical taste of cheap fizz still in her mouth. In the new quiet, a strange noise seeped down the stairs, getting through to her only when the hollow wheeze ended in a lupine yelp. Suddenly, fear was whirling round her like a Spielberg ghost. She stood stock still until the whine, like a distant siren, came at her again. Then she took the stairs two at a time, the sinister barks rising and falling with her own feet.

'Oh shit, oh God, oh Ben, oh shit oh God oh Ben.'

In the doorway, she slammed her hand on to the light switch.

'Mummy's here,' she said, lifting her son's head off the wet mattress. 'Mummy's here.'

Ben was heavy and damp, his body writhing

with the effort to breathe. He greeted her with several short yips, his lips and the neck of his Thomas the Tank Engine pyjamas sticky with a foamy saliva like the cava on the hearth tiles downstairs.

Jess's mind was racing. Who could help?

'Sit up, like a good boy, sit up.'

Where was she, in this darkness? What road were they on, which turning? If she ran to the farmhouse, which lane should she take?

Holding him upright made no difference. He didn't speak, but only stared into the next cough.

'Ben? Mummy's here. Ben?'

She carried him into the bathroom that she had spent three days scrubbing, and dampened the corner of a towel to wipe his mouth.

'Ben, come back to me! Ben? Look at Mummy, Ben.'

But his hooded eyes were somewhere else.

'I didn't mean it when I told Daddy I wanted my old life back ... I'm young, Ben, too young...'

The high-pitched whooping began again. She couldn't do this on her own – she was a teenage mum, a single parent, a useless statistic. Jamie, where was Jamie? Maggie would know what to do! If Ben died, would—

She swiped her mobile from the windowsill, its signal flickering as she fumbled with its buttons. All Outgoing Calls flashed up, the last number dialled already in the process of being redialled. Was that the one she wanted? With one hand stretched over Ben's retching

169

body, she tried to halt the call but the buttons refused to respond.

'Answer it, Jamie, answer it.'

No, it wasn't Jamie she needed, it was the emergency services, the NHS helpline ... oh God *please*, what did real mothers do?

Ben's colour changed from red to purple then red again. With his all but dead weight over her shoulder, she opened the bathroom window and tried to position his face to the cold night breeze.

'Breathe, baby, Mummy's here. Breathe for Mummy.'

The ringing tone stopped and a male voice, calm and solid, spoke to her.

'My son can't breathe!' she cried. 'I can't stop him coughing, he's gagging on his own—'

Ben vomited down her back and she felt her shirt wet and warm against her skin.

'It's a bad line, I can't hear you. Who is this?'

'Jess ... Jessica Morley. My son, he's choking! I need an ambulance.'

Her baby fell exhausted back on to her chest. She shook him, scared by his lifelessness, and he began to cry.

'Jessica, where are you?'

'I don't know,' she screamed. 'Long House Farm cottage.'

'Where is that?'

'A mile and a half from a bus stop that goes to the college.'

The line crackled.

'The name of the road, Jessica.'

'Past the Highwayman pub. Please, I need an ambulance...'

'Are you in Bridgeford?'

'He's choking ... he can't breathe. It's the cottage next to Long House Farm, Bridgeford...'

'Towards Gateborne or Newmill?'

'I don't know!'

The signal faltered.

'I can't hear you, Jessica. Did you say Newmill?'

'Yes, maybe,' Jess shouted. She shook her son again, just to feel his movement. Ben's head lolled horribly. 'He's not responding...'

'I'll find you on the OS map. Talk to your mother...'

With the night wind blowing in through the bathroom window came a gust of recognition. 'Daddy?' she cried into the phone. 'Is that Daddy?'

Ben's mortal yelp began again.

'Jessica darling? What's going on?'

'Mum?'

It was like regaining radio contact with Earth.

'It's Ben, he's not responding...'

'You're not at Jamie's mother's?'

'We moved out, I was going to—'

'Don't worry about that now. Listen, Jessica, your father has found Long House Farm on the map, so I'm going to put the phone down and call an ambulance and then I will call you right back.'

171

The signal began its dance again.

'Mum? Are you there? You've gone, I can't hear you...'

'I will call you right back...'

'Don't go!'

The line went dead. Jess could no longer stand up. She fell against the bathroom door and slid down its flaking painted panel.

'Mummy's coming,' she whispered into Ben's wet hair, 'Mummy's coming to get us...'

A hot flush rushed across Maggie's cheeks as she heaved her end of the desk up the last stair on to the landing. Using his shoulder, Don levelled it and shunted it along the floor to Jamie's old bedroom.

'I didn't mean you to spend your evening...' she said, wiping her upper lip with the back of her hand.

'No problem. I spend my entire week shifting furniture, my kitchens are a darn sight heavier than this...'

'I could have got someone else to help me.'

'This makes much more sense.'

'Only on a bottle of wine.'

The room had undergone a metamorphosis already. Maggie had painted over the alphabet frieze with a wide terracotta stripe, the curtains had been replaced by a wooden blind and the cot that Don had resurrected on his last visit was in a relegated position under the window, full of threadbare towels he recognized from their first home together. A nursery it was not.

'You weren't wrong when you said you'd been having a bit of a clear out.'

'As I said in the pub, I'm in the mood to move on.'

Together, they shoved the desk into place over the carpet marks that Jamie had been so worried about. Don lifted the computer that was still in its box on to it, and Maggie pushed the wooden chair on castors neatly into its new space.

'One study,' she said.

To Don, having missed a few steps in the evolutionary process, it was still Jamie's bedroom. 'That's what the estate agents say people want these days.'

'I know, that's why I've done it.'

'You're serious then?' It was a bit rich of him, but he wasn't sure how he felt about not being consulted. 'It's not a knee-jerk reaction to Jamie moving out?'

'So what if it is?'

The conversation felt too dangerous and he made an effort to move it on.

'So, what are you going to study in your study then? You could always start with a trip to the Family Records Centre.'

'No thanks.'

'You'd be in good company. When the 1841 census went online for the first time, the site crashed – they had something like two million hits within the first three hours...'

'But I don't need to know if my great-great-grandmother had an illegitimate child, or married a bigamist or went to work in a mill

173

at the age of twelve...'

'No, but wouldn't it be marvellous if you found—'

He stopped, realizing he had moved from the frying pan to the fire.

'Yes?'

'Well, whatever it is you're looking for...'

Maggie screwed up her nose.

'Diplomacy really doesn't suit you, Don! Go on, say it! It'll be something along the lines of me looking too hard, or how it's about time I accepted things as they are, or what a bloody relief it would be for everyone else...'

Don laughed.

'You still think I'm the same woman you married, don't you?'

'Would that be such a bad thing?'

'Don't ask me difficult questions!'

Don wished he could have shown his pleasure at her answer in some easy physical way. Instead, he said, 'I'm hungry, what have you got to eat?'

But down in the kitchen, they discovered they were not alone. Jamie was helping himself to the last beer in the fridge. It came as a shock to Maggie to find herself annoyed by his presence.

'What are *you* doing here again?'

Jamie was so taken aback to see his father then appear that he tipped the bottle too quickly into his mouth and it went down the wrong way. When he finished coughing, he confronted them.

'Oh, that's *your* car outside, Dad?'

'Whose did you think it was?' Maggie answered crossly.

'I thought Dad had bought Rob's Transit van.'

'I have.'

'But not to drive?'

'It's for work.'

'And this is pleasure?'

'Of course.'

'Oh, sorry,' Jamie said pointedly. 'Am I interrupting something?'

'Not at all. Your father came to find a screwdriver...'

'And did you find it?'

'Not yet, no.'

'Dad's going to measure up for a new kitchen,' Maggie said quickly. It was not a total lie. They had talked about it briefly in the pub, in the early stages of the evening when conversation had been awkward and thin.

'At ten thirty at night?'

'We've been out for a drink,' Don said, 'to discuss it.'

'So this *is* work?'

'Well, if I'm going to put this place on the market it really needs...' Maggie said, busying herself filling the kettle. The water gushed noisily from the tap.

'What did you just say?' Jamie asked.

'Every room could do with a lick of...'

'Did you say we're putting the house on the market?'

'*We*, Jamie?'

'All right then, *you*. Are you?'

'I'm thinking about it.'

'But don't!'

'I beg your pardon?'

'Don't. I mean, you won't be able to afford anything comparable...'

'It could do with a new kitchen regardless,' Don said tactfully.

Jamie cut himself the end of the ciabatta.

'Oh, posh bread now is it?'

He hacked the corner off the cheese. Maggie could tell by his movements that he was upset but something was stopping her from being her usual comforting self.

'Don't tell me,' she said, flicking the kettle switch on. 'Carl and Amy have turned up to see Jess again?'

'They seem to think we're licensed premises...' her son mumbled through his sandwich.

'What, turning up at bedtime, helping themselves to beer from the fridge, that sort of thing?' Don joked.

'Oh, I'll go then, shall I?'

'Don't be daft, Dad's only teasing you.'

'I wouldn't bother,' Jamie said crossly to his father. 'Your audience is all the way over in Bali. Rob'll never hear you.'

Eleven

A lonely Jamie dragged himself into the sitting room of what he was going to have to stop calling home, although judging by this evening, it seemed the cognitive process was already being helped on its way.

He shouldn't have been surprised at the speed of his metamorphosis from resident to visitor. He'd seen the same thing happen to Rob after he'd first left home – that unspoken right to raid the fridge or make toast subtly withdrawn.

'Of course you can, love, you don't need to ask,' his mother said to Rob these days. But surely the very fact that she said it meant that he *did*.

Not for the first time tonight, Jamie wondered what his brother was doing now. His lazy imagination had Rob and Gatesy in Hawaiian shirts propping up a beach bar under a roof of giant palm leaves, but he supposed they could just as easily be trying to get some sleep on an overcrowded bus. One thing was certain though – neither of them would be thinking of him. Nor would Jess, and nor, it appeared now, was his mum.

Maggie had gone to bed a while ago. He'd

tried to signal with his eyes – *no, don't go, don't leave me with Dad, I don't know what to say to him* – but his mother had dodged his gaze and left them shifting awkwardly from foot to foot, swapping polite opinions about cricket, discussing the virtues of Transit vans for transporting kitchen units, and talking about farming. How are the early starts? Good to be out in the fresh air! Absolutely!

Outside the window, the gravel path was crunching with Don's assured footsteps. Jamie listened for the engine to start up and the car to drive away before he collapsed. Damn it! If he'd been feeling more confident, he could have used the opportunity to pose a few burning questions. *Have another beer, Dad. Nice car, Dad. By the way, how did you manage to walk away from me too, Dad?*

What was he still doing here? The expected behaviour would be for him to go 'home' now, to his girlfriend and baby son, but the prospect of finding Carl and Amy giggling through their alcopops made him take his shoes off instead.

He thumped the side of the sofa and an open box of chocolates slid on to the dented cushion. They were his mum's favourite but he hadn't seen them in the house since the divorce. She used to let him have the big flat round one in the middle in the light green foil, much to Rob's fury, but that one was already gone.

'Sod it,' he said quietly. He shouldn't have come. He should have stayed in the pub. He'd made a fool of himself again.

He didn't want to be a mummy's boy, he'd moved out precisely to avoid that accusation, but somehow he and his mum were inextricably linked in a way that she and Rob were not. How had she come to be his responsibility, a force that drew him home, kept him close? It wasn't a relationship against his will – he loved her as much as she loved him – he just wished she loved someone else as much too so the load could be shared.

Or did he? Something had changed. Why, when she'd looked less than pleased to see him earlier, had he felt so utterly crushed? Was it *jealousy* he'd felt when he'd seen his dad standing there too?

Jamie lay back on the sofa, feeling superfluous. *Forgotten your teddy, have you?* Rob had teased him last week. Oh ha ha. 'Don't mind us,' Don had said, 'we were just off.'

Us. That was it. Don and Rob were, and always had been, an *'us'*. They used to go off together like that when Jamie had been growing up. Cycle rides that Jamie was too young to go on, runs that Jamie hadn't the stamina for, a mountain climb in North Wales that Jamie didn't have the right boots for. He used to stay home and help his mum make cookies or plant sunflower seeds in little plastic pots. That was his *'us'*, the *'us'* that smelt of flour and sugar and the inside of Arthur's shed. But hold on, his voice of reason overruled, what about Big Pool? Did Dad ever take Rob to camp with the cows or learn to dive into the icy water from the branches of an old oak? Well, did he?

Fair dos. Jamie spotted an almost full brandy bottle on the table and the warmth slid down his throat and into his churning stomach like medicine. He should be heading back to the farm cottage, back 'home' to get some sleep before another early start. Should but wouldn't. Big Pool he'd concede, but there was definitely no 'us' waiting for him at Gatesy's. It hurt him that spending time with a couple as irritating as Carl and Amy was apparently more appealing than lying in bed with him. Just *what* would it take to make Jess happy?

Not a bad question to ask, that. If his battery hadn't been flat, he might well have done. Too right he might. He tossed the dead phone on to the table and sat down. A chocolate trapped under his thigh had melted on to the velour cushion and with a filthy fingernail, he scraped it off. Ben had wrecked the sofa anyway so one more mark wouldn't be noticed.

The house was quieter than it had ever been. He'd been on his own in this room on this sofa a hundred times before, but the quiet then used to be the sound of his mother awake. Tonight, it was the sound of her fast asleep.

What the hell was it all about? The sand was shifting under his feet so fast that nowhere felt like the place it was meant to be. He took another swig from the brandy and put the bottle back on the table next to a green leather box he hadn't seen before. It held his gaze, looking significant. He *knew* the inventory of this house and this box was not on it.

Had it played a part in the evening just gone? Was that why his father was back so soon? He imagined his parents sifting through its contents together. See here, our divorce papers. And these, our wills. This, our marriage certificate – we'll rip it up, shall we? The deeds, the mortgage, and oh look, the children's birth certificates. You take Rob's and I'll have Jamie's.

He leaned forward and opened the lid. There was far too much to make sense of in his increasingly drunken state. The best thing to do was to shut his eyes and pull something out. A Meaning Of Life Lucky Dip. His fingers pinched a scallop-edged envelope with a tissue-paper lining addressed to Mrs R. Barton.

September 1957

My dearest Bron,

I received a letter from Rex an hour ago and I am numb with sorrow at your sad news. How I wish, as your oldest friend, I could think of something to say to bolster you but I cannot.

Bron? Bronwen. Granny. What sad news? Rex's death? No, she had died first and anyway this was 1957.

181

You must be emotionally and physically exhausted from the event of the birth itself, let alone what has happened since. I have read Rex's words over and over again looking for the truth, but it is well hidden. I don't expect him to tell me, but please don't feel you need to hide it from me.

We are used to being outspoken with each other. You forgave me for telling you my misgivings about your choice of husband all those years ago as I forgave you when you said much the same about mine. And here we are, still married to them, most probably regretting it a little.

What neither of us regret of course are our children, *all of them*. Our babies have made it all worthwhile. They are each and every one special in their own ways. I know you too well not to be certain that you feel this way too, which is how I know you must be hurting very much.

I have telephoned the railway station and I can catch a train tomorrow morning which will get me to the hospital at two o'clock. Rex asked me not to come but I am ignoring that. I will arrive announcing my intention to help with the girls as you recuperate but my real motivation is to be there for you. We will do our talking when Rex is at work. Do give my love to your darling daughters who you must continue to keep close to you.

My special love,
Lottie

Jamie took another mouthful of brandy. A postnatal spat between his grandmother and some long-forgotten friend of hers was of little interest. Bronwen had had her fair share of depression, from what he'd picked up obliquely over the years.

Maybe Jess is postnatal, he thought dimly. Maybe we should go on holiday, just the three of us, camp in a tent by a river, a fire, moonlight, away from the possessive clutches of Carl and Amy. What did that letter say? *You forgave me for telling you my misgivings about your choice of husband* ... Did Amy tell Jess *her* misgivings? Did Jess listen?

He pulled out another envelope, thinner, more businesslike, with tighter, smaller writing.

August 17th

My dearest wife,
    I am writing to ask you to please come home. The girls are becoming restless in your absence and I am running out of excuses. Diana in particular is asking too many awkward questions. I have told her that Lottie is ill and needed you but if she persists, I will tell her the truth, that it is you who is ill, and it is I who need you.
    Your loving husband,
    Rex

So his grandmother Bronwen had walked

out on her marriage for a while? Good on her! Rex was a bastard by all accounts. Certainly, he sounded like one here. Everyone said Rob was like Rex. Was Rob a bastard? What sort of a father would he make? Jamie felt a rare superiority. He was more like Arthur and everyone knew Arthur had been a good father. More brandy. Another dip, another letter.

Bron darling,

Oh, not her again. Jamie wanted something more. A truth or a revelation, something to do with *him*.

Our awful estrangement is over and I cannot tell you how happy it makes me.

I know I should say sorry now for all the things I said about Rex, but instead, I shall say sorry for the fact that in saying those things, I hurt you.

I will not shy from asking, from time to time, if the pain is still with you. Someone must, and I cannot think who else but me will.

I am so looking forward to next week.

My fondest love as always,
Lottie

Jamie tossed it on the table in disappointment. Lottie, Bron, Rex. What did these people have to do with him? He put another chocolate disc into his mouth, where his brandy-flavoured tongue toyed with the mint centre. The next letter was in a child's handwriting, on lined paper ripped from a notebook.

August 12th 1968

Dear Bronwen and Rex,
This is a letter to announce my decision to stop calling you Mummy and Daddy and to call you Bronwen and Rex from now on. Please do not try to stop me.
Love from Diana.

No, too much, that one. Jamie pushed it frantically back into the box and pulled other papers on top of it but it was too late, the memory of his dead aunt was back with him, digging him too hard in the ribs. 'Tell me I'm your favourite aunt! Tell me!' 'OK, I submit!' He had to hand it to her – she had always been the one who said what she felt, when she felt like it, but what use was that now?
He looked at his watch. It was nearly midnight but he was over the drink-drive limit now. Jess would have to spend a night in the cottage on her own – at least it would give her something legitimate to belittle him about for the next few years. He would sleep on the chocolatey sofa among the foil wrappers. A few hours' kip in familiar surroundings would make tomorrow's challenge loom less large. It was market day. Would he be expected to drive the tractor on a road? And he didn't

want his mother to sell the house either. Where would she go? Where would *he* go? Two of his cats were buried in the garden. One more dip into the box and then he'd sleep. His hand went to a pale green envelope decorated with a darker green tree.

June 1976

Dear Aunt Bronwen,

Thank you for your letter. I am glad you sent it because I could tell you had thought hard about what you had written but I don't really know what to say in return, other than there is no need to worry about me as much as you do.

I don't really know what you mean when you say you wish I would cry. I keep being told that things will get easier and I want to reply that they aren't hard anyway. Something is in the way of me feeling sad. If I have lost anything, I lost it a long time ago, maybe when I was born.

Mum's death was a shock as you say but Daddy and I are getting over it. If Daddy had been the one to die I would not know how to cope, but I have realized in the last three months that I did not have the sort of relationship with Grace that most people seem to assume I had, otherwise I think I should be feeling more afraid. The fact is, I am used to feeling motherless.

This was more like it! A letter from his

mother, aged eighteen, to *her* mother, when she was Jess's age. The voice was strong and bitter, confrontational even – did it ever occur to the two women in his life that they had so much in common? How could he use this to improve relations between the two of them? The words floated across the page in front of him.

I am going to go back to school for one more term to re-sit my A levels in January. I probably should have sat them last month anyway and taken a chance but I didn't want to leave Daddy on his own.

Have you heard we are supposed to be having a heatwave this summer? It is so hot here I can believe it. I expect you know that Diana has written to me from Uni asking if I want to go to France with her next month. Perhaps you suggested it. I haven't asked Daddy yet but I think he will tell me to go.

I am sorry for not being able to say the things I think you want me to say. I can't call you what I know you want me to call you but one thing I would like to do is to drop the 'Aunt' and start calling you just Bronwen. Would you mind?

I send my love to everyone and of course to you.

Love from Maggie

Jamie fell back into the sofa cushions, one sentence of the letter still going round in his

187

head. *I am sorry for not being able to say the things I think you want me to say. I am sorry for not being able to say the things I think you want me to say.*

Sleep would be a sensible idea, but the contents of the box were now scattered over the coffee table and a remnant of expected behaviour told him he should put it all back. He picked up a handful of papers and plonked them on the pile. The lid wouldn't shut. He shuffled and tried again, really tired now, eyes already closing. There were too many secrets in this house – probably in this very box. He could just place the letter from his mother on the top and leave it at that. But his fingers wouldn't let go. He wanted to keep it in his back pocket as a talisman to encourage him every time he needed to say 'I am sorry for not being able to say the things I think you want me to say'.

He put the letter between his teeth as he swung his legs up on to the sofa, then, lying on his back, he put it to rest on his chest. In his mind's eye, he was showing it to Jess. She was lying down too, on her tummy on the bed in the farm cottage, studying her chemistry notes. He was walking into the bedroom and taking out the folded letter from his pocket and now she was reading it, really reading it, in the way she read the results of experiments. She was looking up at him and nodding. She would start seeing Maggie properly then – a woman who deserved to be loved with the same ferocity with which she loved others. After all, they were both women missing the guidance of a supportive mother, determined to offer something better for their own children, keen to hang on to the structure of a family. Kindred spirits, Jess might say they were.

In his dream, Jess and his mum were together, in an embrace. Ben was there too, sitting on the ground between their feet. The women were smiling at something ahead of them. *Take a picture*, Jess was saying. *Store it on your phone! Send it to your dad! Go on, he'd love it!* Jamie pointed the lens – come on, they were laughing, hurry up! – but his phone was ringing, a call was coming through. What should he do – answer the phone or take the pic? 'Jamie!' his mother was saying, 'Jamie!'

'Jamie, wake up!'

He really did wake up.

His mother was standing next to the sofa in her white towelling robe. He knew there was something wrong by the colour of her lips.

'It's Jess,' Maggie said, handing the telephone to him. 'Ben's been taken to hospital.'

Twelve

It had been hoped that the recent refurbishment of the staff room at Melwood Special School would create a much needed retreat from the madness that lay beyond. Painted in shades from what the interior designer had called her 'sanctuary' range – biscuit beige with a cool blue strip running horizontally at dado rail height – it was meant to invoke 'an ambience of serenity and calm'. Brief failed then, thought Maggie as she walked in to the morning conference late for the third time that week. The walls might as well have been redecorated by a paranoid schizophrenic.

Her colleagues were too busy launching their opinions like missiles into a riot to notice her arrival. Their words exploded in space before reaching any target and all Maggie could hear of the discussion was a cacophony of squeaky outrage and languid sarcasm. It was variation on the same old argument, full of the implicit hierarchy that teachers and learning assistants pretended not to recognize. What had triggered it Maggie hardly cared. It was just a relief not to have to explain herself.

With the runaway chaos at home, her 'work'

head had finally unscrewed itself. Left in a classroom earlier in the week, it was now in the lost-property cupboard with the mouldy lunch boxes and smelly trainers, and there she was inclined to let it remain. She couldn't entirely blame the shock of Ben's illness. There was the bizarre truce she seemed to have signed with Don, and then there was Bronwen's box, which was sometimes more distracting than the rest of it put together.

'Hospital again?' Vicky Haines, the art teacher, whispered. Vicky was one of the few members of staff Maggie saw out of school. Maggie nodded.

'How's he doing?'

'Ben's in good hands – it's Jamie I'm worried about now.'

Her son had looked like the living dead in the hospital cafeteria that morning. You need to go and breathe some fresh air, the tea lady had advised him, sloshing hot liquid not unlike the colour of the staff room walls into thick-rimmed cups. You don't want to start believing this is your home, mind, don't matter what's going on in here, you've got a life out there too remember. We see it all down here we do, and you, my love, are definitely a candidate for some fresh air.

'She's right,' Maggie had reiterated once they had sat down, but Jamie had pushed away three-quarters of his beans on toast and told her to go to work.

'I can take the morning off. You go back with Jess. Have a bath and a sleep.'

191

'Back where? Her parents won't have me in their house.'

'What are you, the devil incarnate?'

'All but.'

'Go home then. The two of you go home and...'

'None of our stuff is there...'

'I meant the farm cottage, Jamie.'

'Jess says she's never going to set foot inside the place again.'

'She'll come round. Go on love, do what the woman told you and get some fresh air.'

But Jamie was too busy breathing for Ben to be thinking about his own lungs. With the latest diagnosis he couldn't bring himself to leave the boy's side. Whooping cough he'd been able to deal with, pneumonia he could not, and for once Maggie accepted there was nothing she could do to make it better. She took a deep breath of her own and forced herself to join the meeting.

'If anyone thinks I am going to sit there with my arms around a fifteen-year-old boy all day,' Sue Andrews was saying, rocking forward on her chair, her right calf resting on her left knee exposing a few unflattering inches of pale skin between her trouser hem and her ankle, 'like some sort of tree-hugger...'

'But that's what his mother has suggested,' the head repeated calmly.

'Since when did parents have anything to do with it?'

Misanthropic laughter rippled around the circle.

'What's his problem exactly?'

The question was asked with the interest of someone who knew it was going to make absolutely no difference to him.

'He's addicted to being held.'

'How can you be addicted to being *held*, for God's sake?'

'You can be abnormally dependent on anything,' the head reminded them. 'You only need to take a look around this staff room to realize that.'

Maggie slunk on to an upholstered office chair at the edge of the group.

'A new pupil?' she asked.

'Year Eleven. Family moved down from Scotland. One of seven. Single parent.'

'Does he have a name?'

'Rory Irvine.'

'I think you'll find that's Ryan Irvin actually,' came a gruff admonitory voice from the sofa. The men at Melwood specialized in reproof. They'd let the women do all the talking while they sat on the sidelines listening for the first slip of the tongue, whereupon one of them would grunt 'silly cow' and genuinely believe it to be the wittiest comment of the morning. It was all part of their conspiracy to belittle the female authority.

'One for you, Maggie,' Sue suggested disparagingly. 'Apparently, he needs to feel *restrained*. If you let him go, anything could happen.'

'We have to restrain him all day?'

'That's hugging to you, surely.'

'We'll have to start him off with a velcro assistant,' the head said. 'Sue, you're the only free—'

'No thanks.'

'You'll have to drag Kelly-Ann Drew off Maggie then.'

'Wonderful. Although if she thinks she can start turning up at *my* house for a cup of tea she's got another—'

'Yes, thank you Sue, I think we've been through all this before. Maggie, perhaps you'd...?'

'What sort of restraint?'

'That isn't clear. Hand holding might do it. I don't see how we can keep him in a permanent embrace...'

'But that's what his mother does, is it?'

'So she says. I, er, I wouldn't let him know your address...'

'I've never given out my address. Kelly-Ann *found* it...'

'Yes, yes...'

'What does it matter what his mother does?' Sue huffed. 'You're *not* his mother.'

Maggie frowned at the head to see where the support lay. Nowhere, apparently. The meeting to 'discuss the growing trend of emotional dependence between certain velcro assistants and students' that Sue had been so victorious about had yet to happen. That was the problem with the leadership at this place. It kept changing its mind.

'Well, if that's what it takes to get him settled,' she said wearily.

'Terrific!' Sue shouted, putting her empty coffee mug down hard on one of the new beech-effect tables. 'The logical extension to that argument is that we give our problem drinkers vodka shots at break. Or how about we introduce cannabis to the canteen menu so no one has to roll a joint in the toilets?'

A cheer rose from the fringes of the room.

'So, what do you suggest then?'

'No, no, do it your own way,' Sue replied, getting up and busying herself with a pile of books. 'It'll be fun to watch.'

Watching another person sleep had never been so mesmerizing, not even, Anne Morley thought, in her brief postnatal bliss of nineteen years ago. Sixteen of those nineteen years had passed smoothly – too smoothly, she now realized. Maybe if Jessica's path to womanhood had thrown the odd pothole every now and again, then Anne's maternal shock absorbers might have been better maintained, but when she'd finally needed them, they'd seized up through lack of use and the shock had not been absorbed at all.

Never mind, no harm done, she told herself. She truly believed she was a very different woman to the one who used to pretend not to understand this room with its trashy steel furniture and its nauseous lime green and silver walls. Three years ago, at the start of what her husband referred to as 'the trouble', the garishness of her daughter's bedroom had mocked her. Jessica's choices had been so at odds with her own that Anne had only drawn one message from them – their cherished daughter was in the process of rejecting them.

The satisfaction of being right was all Anne had to hang on to, and how easily that satisfaction had turned to self-righteousness. But hours of contemplation had since passed within these four hallucinogenic walls, many of them more soul searching than anything that had ever happened in a church pew. Her husband believed a few more hours wouldn't have gone amiss, but Anne chose this morning to believe her prayers had been answered.

Their mercy dash in the pitch black to rescue Jess three evenings ago had been a divine intervention, she was sure. It was God's work that had made Jess's fingers redial their number that night. His forgiveness had led them through the darkness to their lost child, and His love had brought Jess home again, to her own bed, where she belonged. Anne was trying her hardest not to look as happy as she felt. Her daughter, she had to keep reminding herself, was still in the middle of her own parenting nightmare. Her grandson (*there* was a phrase she hadn't expected to be using last week!) was back in the place of his birth, being pumped with antibiotics to fight off secondary pneumonia as a result of advanced pertussis. He had a face mask over his little snub nose and infant lips and a needle pushed into his tiny arm like an extra in a hospital drama. And yet for Anne,

196

the overwhelming relief of having her own baby back was making it hard to find something more than an obligatory concern for the boy. *Ben.* She *must* start referring to him as Ben.

As she sat in the uncomfortable chair smoothing the electric-blue fluffy cushion cover on her lap, she wondered if she might, one day, love him too. Well, if she didn't, she would fake it. She was well acquainted with the feeling of the cold metal at her back and the ridges of the seat that made unflattering imprints into her already dimpled thighs. She had sat in the same chair for hours and hours over the last few years, feasting on her own anger and jealousy until she had been so full of both, the Lord had become a stranger to her.

Her faith might have returned but she still rued the day that Jamie Day had been born. She tried hard not to actively hate him, but he was a damaged child from a broken home who had no right to damage *her* child and break *her* home, and her Christian forgiveness simply didn't stretch that far.

Her anger had so nearly spilled over in the family room at the hospital that ghastly first night as they had all sat staring at each other, waiting for news. Jamie's mother, with the privilege and advantage of the last two years written right across her face, had been the hardest to look at, so Anne had directed all her conversation towards Jamie's father. 'Do you live in the area?' she'd asked pointedly, as

197

if she didn't know.

'No, I was here by chance this evening.'

'How much do you see of the child?'

'Not as much as I would like.'

'It's not easy, is it, being an absent grand-parent...'

'There's no need to be absent,' Jamie's mother had had the gall to say. 'I've always told Jess you are welcome any time...'

Well, there was no need for invitation now, was there? Anne stared hard at the figure on the bottom bunk to make sure there really was a living breathing daughter beneath the psychedelic purple and orange duvet cover this morning. She longed to reach over and stroke the long mousey brown hair but two things stopped her. One was a reluctance to wake Jessica up. The other was habit.

Anne Morley was not a toucher. Her way of showing someone how much she loved them had always been to display her pride – the wall in the downstairs cloakroom, for example, was still plastered in Jessica's certificates of achievement. For a long time, it had all worked so well. Every time her clever girl had come home with a commendation, up it had gone in a hammer-and-nail moment of celebration. And then one day, Jessica had come home with a bit more than a piece of paper and Anne's pride had been replaced by a shame acute enough to propel her across streets. The love hadn't gone away of course, but the method of expression had disappeared almost overnight.

She patted the cushion with satisfaction. It was her turn to host the weekly house prayer group this Thursday and it excited her to think she might at last be able to give her long-overdue testimony. The theme would be Pride. Pride was every bit as dangerous as the Bible said it was. It was pride that had once led her to believe she had an angel for a daughter, pride that had prevented her from catching Jessica on her fall from grace, pride that had stopped her hammering on Maggie Day's front door and begging through the letterbox for her girl to come home.

Jess stirred under the vivid swirls. Anne checked her watch. Her prodigal daughter had been asleep for the full two hours she'd asked for. 'You promise to wake me up at twelve?' she'd begged. 'I need to get back to the hospital.' But the baby's father was at the hospital, so there was no need for her to be disturbed. She could stay in bed all day if she wanted to.

Anne eased herself quietly from the chair, took one more glance at the gift God had returned to her and then tiptoed out. On the landing, she bumped into her husband Derek.

'Oh good, you've got it,' she whispered. 'Was there any opposition?'

'Didn't see a soul,' he whispered back, propping the cot head against the wall. 'I got everything on your list bar the big purple dinosaur.'

'But Jessica asked specifically for that. It's

the baby's favourite.'

'To be honest, love, I didn't think it was the sort of thing you'd care to have in the house.'

'How big is big?'

'Big.'

'How purple?'

'Very.'

'Go and get it,' Anne said.

'Are you sure?'

'Well,' she muttered, putting up her hands in defeat, 'she comes with baggage now, doesn't she?'

With her arms folded and her scabby face fixed in a bully's scowl, Kelly-Ann Drew blocked Maggie's path.

'Why are you holding his hand, Miss?'

Maggie wasn't holding Ryan Irvin's hand, she was clutching his wrist. The two of them had come to the arrangement by silent trial and error, since her new charge had so far refused to speak.

'This is Ryan. He's going to be joining your class. Ryan, this is Kelly-Ann. She's not usually quite so rude.'

Maggie smiled hopefully but the girl did not smile back. The crusted top of one of her self-inflicted wounds had been picked off and a thin smear of blood disappeared into her hairline. Maggie handed her an antiseptic wipe that she carried in her bag for the purpose.

'I don't care about that,' Kelly-Ann spat. 'I want to know why you are holding his hand.

Is he blind or something?'

'We can both see perfectly well, thank you.'

'Have a look at this then.' Kelly-Ann open-ed her mouth and stuck out her newly pierced tongue. 'Gold stud. Like it?'

'Charming.'

'I bet if he had it done...' Kelly-Ann thrust her head towards Ryan. 'I bet you'd like it on *him*.'

Maggie felt the muscles tighten in Ryan's wrist and caught a glimpse of his curling fist. She didn't know his habits well enough to interpret the movement so she made an attempt to walk on.

'Where are you going?' the girl asked, walk-ing backwards in front of them.

'We're on a tour of the school, aren't we, Ryan? We've been to the gym and the hall, now we're going to the canteen.'

'I want to come.'

'You've got English.'

'Yeah, well, if he's' – Kelly-Ann jabbed a finger in Ryan's face – 'in my class, he's got English too.'

'He has a name and I would like you to use it.'

'All right, *Brian*?'

'The bell's gone. Mrs Andrews will be wait-ing for you.'

'I've got Mrs Andrews? That's shit. Why do I always have to have—'

'Language...'

'Mrs Andrews is enough to make me fuck-ing swear...'

'That's enough.'

'No. Not until you put him down,' Kelly-Ann demanded.

Ryan's fist clenched so tight his knuckles turned white.

'I'm not a fucking dog,' he growled. They were the first words Maggie had heard him speak and they frightened her. The restraint she was offering was suddenly more muzzle than blanket.

'Hey hey hey, that's enough. Kelly-Ann, English, now. Ryan, come on, canteen.'

She yanked his wrist and he pulled his arm into the air but put up no further resistance as she dragged him away.

Kelly-Ann unfolded her arms and slid her hands up her regulation school fleece and into the waistband of her trousers. Her fingers touched the curved top of her mum's new boyfriend's folding pocket knife. Its blade was still stored safely in its die-cast metal body. For now.

Jamie lined up the toy trains on the tray over Ben's hospital bed and placed a finger on each one in turn.

'That's Thomas,' he murmured, 'and that's Percy the small engine, and Henry is green...'

Ben's nose twitched in response, causing the two little prongs that fed oxygen up each of his small nostrils to dislodge.

'I'm just going to check your nasal specs, mate,' Jamie said, moving them gently back into place. His son took no notice – apparatus up his nose had become the norm. Nor did he protest any more when the nurse held the nebulizer over his mouth or when his pulse was taken, his intravenous drips tweaked or a thermometer shoved under his tongue.

Jamie was used to it all too. At first sight, the activity had made him fear for Ben's immediate survival, at second, it had made him fret over his son's entire childhood. Was Ben destined to linger at the vulnerable end of the playground hierarchy with the kids who didn't run around for fear of losing their glasses or needing their inhaler? But now he'd had time to take a third look, these prongs were as much a feature of his baby's face as the ridiculously long eyelashes or the tiny strawberry mark on his left temple. They were, for the moment, a part of him.

'Percy wishes he was as big as Thomas,' Jamie continued, pushing the little engine round in circles on the tray, 'because sometimes it's tough always being the smallest, but of course if he was as big as Thomas, he wouldn't be able to do this, would he?'

He made an arch with his thumb and forefinger and drove the train through it, hooting. Ben's eyes flickered and then – and it seemed like a miracle to his father – he laughed. Percy joined the celebration, looping the loop in the air over the bed in synch with the aerobics of Jamie's heart. Neither of them noticed the nurse with the hair braids approach until she took the metal clipboard from the foot of the bed.

'Is your silly daddy playing with your toys again?'

Jamie let the train drop on to the pristine flatness of the bedclothes. The reach of Ben's little legs had no impact at all on the bottom half of the mattress.

'No need to stop,' she said, 'I'm only going to check oxygen saturations.'

Two days ago, the phrase had forced Jamie to imagine lungs so drenched with air that they were about to disintegrate like a rotten sponge. It conjured nightmares of Ben on an artificial respirator, his puny chest rising and falling only because a machine was telling it to. But today, Jamie nodded his acquiescence. Pulse, respiration, colour, temperature. These observations were as routine as nappy change, bib, breakfast, face wipe.

'Amber,' Ben said.

'That would be me!' the nurse smiled brightly at her patient, and then to Jamie, 'He's looking better, isn't he? Which is more than I can say for you.'

Jamie put his hand to his chin where the first signs of stubble were beginning to appear. His bed-shaped hair stuck up in peaks and he hadn't taken his grey T-shirt off for four days.

'I should have a shower...' he apologized.

'But?'

'I don't want to leave him.'

'He'll be fine. Trust us.'

'It's not that,' Jamie said. 'I just don't want to leave him.'

Amber clicked her biro and put it back into her breast pocket.

'I wouldn't be surprised if he was back home by the weekend.'

'Isn't that a bit soon?'

'We'll keep him until he comes of age then, shall we?'

Jamie looked back at his son, away from the banter, but Amber came to perch on the bed.

'You're not still beating yourself up about this inoculation thing, are you?'

She picked up Percy and flew him back to Ben's tray. Jamie remembered now. She was the one who had been on duty in the dark hours after Ben's admittance, the one who'd made him tea in the parents' kitchen and sat with him on the leatherette seats, listening to his muttered confession. He raised his eyebrows quickly at her.

'Look,' she said, 'you made a decision you thought was best for Ben at the time. That's the most any parent can do.'

'It wasn't *my* decision. It was his mum who refused to...'

'You don't want to start thinking like that.'

'No...'

'It doesn't matter who suggested what. You went along with it. If you'd felt strongly...'

'You don't know her.'

'I don't know you either, but I do know that both of you love your son and neither of you would do anything that you thought might harm him.'

'But it was the wrong decision.'

205

'Might not have been. Might have been the right one. Who's to tell? It's a lottery, this business is.'

'We're young, Jess and me, we don't have the experience to—'

'No one does until it happens. And anyway, you're not as young as all that. Some of the parents we get in here are children themselves.'

'Younger than us?'

'I mean *children…*'

Jamie shut up.

'You three want a holiday. When you get out of here, you should go away for a few days. Where would you go? The coast?'

'Camping. Far from the madding crowd and all that.'

'Go on, go and have that shower. Ben's not going anywhere, are you, Ben?'

Jamie eased himself from his sentry chair and took his roll bag from the neighbouring bed that he had been sleeping on in shifts for the last ninety-six hours. The only item in it he recognized was a towel. The new toothbrush, the new underwear, the new T-shirt and the new Nick Hornby novel – all untouched – were courtesy of his mum who had kitted him out from the high street rather than go to Gatesy's cottage. His phone fell off the top, indicating two new messages. One was a text from Jess with no kisses. The other was a voicemail from Mr House, his new – or possibly former – boss.

'Glad to hear the little lad is on the mend. The

missus tells me you've been shifting stuff out of the cottage so I'll take it you're not planning on staying then. Tell you what, I'll either see you at work tomorrow morning or not at all. I don't want to be harsh but I got a farm to run. Catch you later.'

'You make your bed and you lie on it,' he said to Amber, throwing the phone back down on the pillow.

'Not in this place you don't,' she said lightly. 'In this place, I make the bed and everyone else lies on it. No wonder you lot never want to go home.'

Thirteen

Anne Morley put her palms into the tight neck of Ben's Thomas the Tank Engine pyjama top and gave it a businesslike stretch. She was on the morning shift, resenting the fact that outside the sun was shining and her conservatory would have been just perfect for breakfast. However, her mouth remained in a rictus smile for anyone who might be judging her competence.

'Draw the curtains, Derek,' she hissed, 'give the boy some privacy.'

'No curtains,' Ben cried.

'Now, now, we want to tell Mummy what a good boy you've been this morning, don't we?' Anne said, pulling the cotton ribbing in and out as if it were a chest expander, releasing a little of the tension that built up inside her when she was left to deal with her strange grandson.

The child looked at her without connection as she pulled the hole over his head. Only a sprout of blond hair made its way through. The material caught on his bottom lip and dragged it down to reveal tiny milk teeth and pink gums. It was just a relief that his nasal tubes had been removed.

'Mummy's got an important day so Grandma wants you to be a big boy and—'

He started to cry.

'What's that for?'

'Grandma!' Ben wailed.

Anne tugged on his dressing gown and tied it quickly. She'd forgotten the golden rule. Maggie was Grandma, on the grounds that she had got there first.

'Well, today you've got Granny,' she squeaked, 'and Granny wants you to be a big boy because...'

She meant her voice to sound bright and cheerful, not trill and sinister. She was no good with children, not even, as things had turned out, her own. Her touch was too practical, her tone too efficient. But now, as she had told her prayer group on Thursday, she had been offered a second chance. The Lord had seen fit to send her daughter Jessica home. It wasn't too late to put things right, to see her through university, marriage and a respectable career, to steer her into a life like the one they had planned for her.

'No big boy,' Ben sobbed. His voice reverberated throughout the entire ward. She glanced across at another grandmother who had her head in a magazine while her granddaughter played on a hand-held computer. The scene of negligence comforted her. 'Do you know what's happening today?' she chirped in the voice of a children's television presenter from the 1960s. 'Mummy's going to take an exam. She should have taken it last year, but she was too busy looking after you, wasn't she?'

'I want Grandma,' he wailed.

'Mummy used to be a very good girl at school. She worked very hard and both Granny and...' Anne stopped. What did the child call Derek? 'And Granny and Grandad were very proud of her, and they would very much like it if she could...'

'Come on, little chap,' Derek said helplessly from his side of the bed.

'I want Daddy.'

'Oh, Daddy now is it?' Anne tried to smile, as if it were a game.

'Where's my daddy?' the child sobbed.

'Don't you want Grandad?' Derek tried, tickling him under the chin.

'Chocolate man,' Ben cried. 'Chocolate man!'

'You're not having any chocolate at this time of the morning,' Anne told him sternly, wiping his wet face with a flannel that lay next to the bed. 'My, my, there's been some spoiling going on somewhere.'

She looked at the ward clock. It was eight thirty.

'He means Don,' Amber told them, arriving with a small plastic beaker of red syrup. These people looked so inept she felt sorry for them, but not as sorry as she felt for the little boy. She'd never seen so many people vying for supremacy round one bed before.

Ben thrust his arms out to her, desperate to be released from the unfamiliar clutch.

'Don brought you some chocolate yesterday, didn't he, Ben?'

'Put it on the list,' Anne whispered to her husband once Amber had moved away. 'Chocolate, get some chocolate.'

'I thought you said...?'

'I don't care what I said. We need chocolate. How else are we expected to get through this?'

Across the classroom, Maggie's trouble radar picked up a surreptitious movement. Kelly-Ann was fumbling around under her regulation school fleece as if she had a small furry animal up there. For a moment, Maggie, whose own hand was still firmly wrapped around Ryan's left wrist, entertained the naïve hope that this could be a possibility. The woman from the Wildlife Trust had been a couple of dormice down after her special assembly to thank Year Nine for the nesting boxes they had made in design technology and a Chinese whisper had spread through the staff during the course of the morning's lessons to keep an eye out. That hope drained away when Maggie saw the telltale flash of silver.

'Put it away,' she mouthed across the blue Formica table.

Shaking her head, Kelly-Ann provocatively lifted her top to reveal the blade's red handle as Maggie's throat squeezed with fear.

Sue Andrews looked up from the maths worksheet they were all supposed to be working on.

'Problem?'

'Not at the moment.'

Ryan adjusted his position and Maggie loosened her grip, noting that he seemed relaxed with the relative freedom.

'Miss?' Kelly-Ann leaned away from Sue towards Maggie. 'I'm stuck, Miss.'

'Leave Mrs Day alone,' Sue said, dragging Kelly's blank sheet towards her. 'You're going to be staying in at lunchtime at this rate.'

'I can't do it.'

'Look, if Asif has ten sweets which he is selling at three pence each and Jill wants to buy half his stock...'

'Half his sock? What does she want to buy half his sock for?'

Marcus the runner cheered and hammered on the desk with his fists.

'She wouldn't want to buy Connor's socks. They stink!'

'What about half his cock?'

'Settle down!' the maths teacher shouted in his repetitive way. Kelly-Ann pushed backwards on her chair, making a scraping noise. Her hands were still beneath her fleece.

'Where do you think you're going?'

'To sit with Mrs Day.'

'You're with Mrs Andrews today.'

'Not any more I'm not.'

'That's enough, Kelly-Ann. Go and stand by the door.'

'Why? Why can't I just sit by Mrs Day?'

'Mrs Day is helping Ryan today.'

'Ryan can have Mrs Andrews.'

'Kelly-Ann, door, now. You can do your work during lunch break.'

'No.'

Maggie tried a particular smile they used as their own private code to encourage her but Kelly-Ann shut her eyes and bit her lip. Under the blue polyester, she exerted a little pressure on the knife's blade and nicked the top off her thumb. It produced enough blood to daub a long wide stripe down the unsullied maths sheet.

Maggie stood up, letting go of Ryan completely. So suddenly and so unexpectedly that she couldn't think what to do, he was on the table, ripping off his clothes. Naked from the waist up, his muscle-bound torso was such a threatening surprise that even the maths teacher scraped back his chair and stepped away.

The boy next to Ryan scrambled over his neighbour, a small girl who cried at any sudden noise dived under her desk as Ryan screwed his white cotton shirt into a ball and threw it into the air. Some of the class roared in confused excitement, others shrank back into their seats.

Forgetting every procedure she had ever been taught, Maggie lurched for his ankle, but the adrenalin coursing through the boy's veins had transformed him and she was no longer any match. He grabbed a chair and held it above his head, showing a thatch of armpit hair.

Kelly-Ann pressed her thumb and flicked a

213

few droplets of blood up at him. He threw his head forward.

'She's fucking *mine!*' he thundered from his platform.

'No she's not, she's mine!'

Kelly-Ann whipped the knife out and brandished it in the air in front of him.

'Go on then, fucking kill me!' he screamed.

'Evacuate the class!' the teacher ordered as Ryan bounced the chair off a bookshelf. Bodies scattered, squealing and screeching. Kelly-Ann launched a ball of spit into the air as Melwood's newest student jumped off the table, yanked a computer from its leads and held it aloft like a trophy.

If ever there was a look that said 'Got you!', it was the look Sue Andrews gave Maggie as she filed the rest of the class away from the battleground. And if ever there was a moment at which Maggie decided she was in the wrong job, it was the moment just after that, when the window glass shattered and Kelly-Ann put the blade to her wrists.

In his farm overalls and dung-encrusted boots, Jamie waited for Jess outside the gates of the private school he'd once attended himself. He found a perverse enjoyment in standing there in so much filth, enjoying the wary looks he got from parents, knowing he was more like their offspring than they'd ever dream. *They had me down for Oxford*, he imagined telling them, *look me up in the school magazines, you'll find me under the poetry prizes.*

214

Instead, he amused himself by listening for their frantic plays for position. Who had the gap year edge – Freya and her Venezuelan orphanage or Adam saving turtles in Costa Rica?

Their silly competitiveness made him feel superior. In the back of his rusting van was a breathable nylon family dome tent and three sleeping bags with hollow-fibre filling, all acquired on eBay. Personal growth was nothing to do with the number of air miles you clocked up. Gatesy and Rob and Freya and Adam could keep their beach party tales. But as time ticked closer to noon, insecurity started to flutter in his guts. He began to entertain the possibility that Jess might not be pleased to see him. If she'd wanted him to know it was her final chemistry exam today, then she would have told him. Instead, she'd left him to find out from her mother half an hour ago.

'Hello Mrs Morley, sorry to trouble you. I've got some good news. The doctor says Ben can come home tonight.'

Her ensuing silence had rocked his foundations.

'It would be a lot easier if he stayed in until tomorrow as planned,' she'd eventually replied.

'I'm sorry?'

'Jessica is going out tonight to celebrate the end of her exams.'

The phone clicked and in that moment, Jamie understood once and for all how the rift between Jess and her mother must have come about. Nothing, but nothing must interfere with Anne Morley's plans, not even the welfare of her own grandson.

Was the fault genetic? Had he and Ben interfered with Jess's plans? The thought made him shrink. Perhaps he should go? But he was at the school gates, he reminded himself, to congratulate her, not to claim her. It was the sort of gesture any boyfriend, let alone any father of her child, would make. And why wouldn't he, with such good news to report? But there was a hole in his argument through which the last grain of his confidence fell. He and Jess were living apart, he was feeling less and less like a boyfriend as every day without her passed, and in truth, he *was* here to claim her, if only as the mother to his son.

It was time to celebrate. God knows, he'd been working himself up towards this moment as much as she had. Ben's illness, this damned exam, his new job – their path to happiness had led them into a dark forest, but now it was at least moonlit, and they could start feeling their way towards a proper family life. Jess and Ben could both come home!

'Where's home, Jamie?' she'd provoked the other day when he'd asked her yet again to please come back.

'Gatesy's cottage.'

'Gatesy's! Not *ours!* That's my whole point!'

'Give it a chance.'

'I don't need this now,' she'd snapped, slamming the door of her parents' house in his face.

She'd all but shut him out of the rest of her life too. Every day, he'd made a bid for some time together, and every day she'd had an excuse. I'm revising, I'm really tired, we're about to eat. Not once had he been invited in. He could no longer even pretend to believe the reasons. Jess was in the process of leaving him.

'Jess!'

He saw her before she saw him. Her skip through the sports hall fire door turned his insides. To his further delight, she started to wave and broke into a run. He badly wanted her in his bed again, not for the obvious reasons but to believe she was his.

As he stepped forward, he caught a rival movement out of the corner of his eye. Like a fellow sprinter about to rob him of first place came a flash of denim and white. There was no need to confirm who it was. Jess became lost in the middle of arms that weren't his, her words were drowned in a chorus of other people's congratulations. As if in slow motion, a cork popped and a spray of sparkling wine bejewelled the hair he'd been going to touch.

'Congratulations, sweetie!' Carl sang, kissing her on both cheeks.

'It's all over!' squealed Amy. 'You're free!'

As Jess went to take a swig from the bottle, she caught sight of Jamie.

'Oh hi. God, you're filthy...'

'I came straight from the farm.'

217

'It's so embarrassing!'

Carl and Amy were both wearing tiaras.

'So, how did it go?'

'Fine.'

She stood awkwardly in front of him, wiping the wine droplets from her face.

'I've got the best news,' he said, trying to rally some conviction. 'Ben can come home tonight if we're ready for him.'

'But we're not,' she snapped, unnervingly like her mother.

'Why is there always a "but" with you?'

'We're *not* ready...'

'Yes we are. You wouldn't recognize the cottage. Mum's worked really hard on it, Dad's going to give us his old sofa and buy us a new bed, we can pick Ben's cot up from—'

'Oh, give the girl a break!' Amy complained.

'A break? Our son has been seriously ill in hospital and he is well enough to come home – what does she need a break from?'

'How about you?' Carl suggested.

'Jess, we could go for a drink, get some lunch,' Jamie said, stepping between Jess and her bodyguards.

'With you like that?'

'I've got a change of clothes in the van.'

'Aren't you working?'

'I'm milking at four.'

'I...'

Amy took the bottle of sparkling wine and tipped it towards her lips. Carl took his tiara off and perched it on Jess's head.

'Come on, Jessie babe! You've done it!'

Amy rested her head on Jess's shoulder and smirked at Jamie as if he were pointing a lens at her. 'Don't take her away from us,' she wheedled.

'What about Ben?'

'Look, the hospital said he was allowed home tomorrow. That's what I've been working on.'

'So they've changed their minds. We can pick him up after milking and...'

Jess's eyes hardened.

'This is my one night of freedom, Jamie,' she said stonily. 'No revision, no sick baby to look after...'

'No boyfriend to get in your way?' The moisture pricking his eyes was nothing to do with the spray that laced Jess's hair.

'You can come if you want.'

'I want *you* to come with me.'

'Today is planned. I don't want to mess with the arrangements. This way everyone knows what they're doing.'

'Everyone except me.'

Jess took off the tiara and tried, half-heartedly, to put it in Jamie's hair. He ducked, and the cheap silver plastic arc fell on the floor.

'Spoilsport.'

'I've bought us a tent...'

Carl snorted in derision.

'A *tent*?'

'Family time, Jess—'

Jess winced.

'Forget family time, this is *party* time!' Carl looped a sky-blue pashmina over Jess's head and pulled her towards him. She trotted helplessly away from Jamie as if caught in a current.

'Come home with me!' he called desperately after her. 'We'll get Ben and go camping...'

'I don't do camping!' she laughed, tripping over her own feet, still harnessed by the scarf.

'If you go, I'll—'

'No you won't!' Amy mocked. 'You say you will but you won't. You're all mouth, you are!'

'You go and milk your cows!' Carl shouted. 'Save some cream for me!'

Over her shoulder, Jess tossed him a crumb of hope.

'We'll get Ben tomorrow, yeah?'

And then she merged so effectively into the rest of the post-exam euphoria that only someone who knew could have picked her out as the mother of a child waiting to be collected from a hospital ward.

Fury coursed round Jamie's veins as he walked, red with disbelief, back to his van.

'Jamie Day,' a voice boomed from behind.

He swung round on the rubber soles of his mud-caked boots to face his former English teacher. The last time they had been in such close proximity, a university application had been on the desk between them.

'Mr Midway,' he replied politely.

'Farming these days, are you?'

'Looks like it.'

'What a bloody waste.'

And shaking his head, the teacher stepped off the pavement and moved on in disgust.

'I should roll your shirt sleeves down now,' Maggie suggested as she switched off her engine in the staff car park. Her voice had a hardness behind its usual powdered calm.

For the entire journey back from hospital, Kelly-Ann had been examining the bandages on her wrists as if they were silver bracelets, twisting her palms this way and that. Her expression was reminiscent of a pupil walking down the stage steps at speech day holding the prize for achievement.

'I'm letting the air get to them.'

'If you're worried about that, you shouldn't have insisted on them being bandaged up in the first place.'

'The nurse told me to keep the wounds clean.'

'They're not wounds, they're scratches.'

Her patience had been worn so thin, Kelly-Ann could see straight through it.

'Roll your sleeves down and let's hear no more about it.'

'No. I like looking at them. They look cool.'

'You'll be questioned about them, you know.'

Kelly-Ann's eyes flashed at the idea of being a celebrity for the afternoon.

'Not as much as you,' she smirked. 'You're the one who let go of Ryan.'

Maggie got out of the car and slammed the door. She had spent the last hour and a half sitting in the disinfected bowels of a hospital that she had come to know too well lately.

First Di, then Ben, now this. She had grown restless on her vinyl seat, watching people with largely self-inflicted cuts and bruises come and go, while a few floors up someone's sister or son lay dying.

'Back to your lessons,' she told the girl so sharply Sue Andrews wouldn't have recognized her.

'Aren't you coming with me?'

'I've got to go and see the head.'

'But who's going to write for me?'

'You can write for yourself.'

'I'm injured, Miss!'

'I'm going to be in trouble for sticking up for you,' Maggie told her, wanting appreciation or apology.

Kelly-Ann shrugged.

'Don't you care?'

'I never asked you to. You did it because you wanted to.'

The girl pushed her shirt sleeves even further up her elbows and sauntered across the gravel in search of her new-found fame.

'What about a thank you?' Maggie called after her.

'A what?'

Just then, the door from the art room opened and children swarmed round Kelly-Ann like autograph hunters. So, Maggie thought as she watched her charge disappear into the throng, Mrs Day has finally served her purpose.

The next time Maggie saw her was an hour

later, this time from behind the safety of her steering wheel. Piled on the passenger seat were the entire contents of her metal locker – box files, paper folders, books, tissues, antiseptic wipes, sanitary pads, Savlon, plasters, a stash of mini chocolate bars, scissors, a pencil case, a camera. She had gathered them up with very little regret.

Through the sealed quiet of the windscreen, she watched Kelly-Ann peel back the bandages to show the criss-cross surface marks underneath. She kept watching as Marcus put his arm around her and walked her proudly towards the hut. They were part of a world that already had nothing to do with her.

'I'd rather you go home and think about it,' the head had said fifteen minutes ago. 'I can sign you off on sick leave for a week or two.'

'But I'm not sick,' Maggie had told her. 'Sick of being misunderstood maybe, sick of trying too hard...'

'It's no good for her in the long run, you know. She's got to leave here in a few weeks, and she won't have you to lean on out there, will she?'

'It's best I go now.'

'The children will miss you.'

'They won't even know I'm gone.'

They'd hugged – it was that kind of school – and that had been it really. A funny old way to end four years of one's life.

'Come back and see us sometime,' the head had said feebly, but as Maggie turned her key in the ignition and drove out of the iron gates, she knew she wouldn't.

She didn't feel like going home. She wanted to go and see someone – anyone – and tell them what she'd done, but who? Her friends were teaching, her family had dispersed. Driving through town she toyed with the idea of buying herself something, a habit she had fallen into since Don left, a guilty treat when what she really wanted was company. But what? Clothing was no fun these days. She looked middle-aged in everything, and yet at the same time her body seemed to be changing back to its girlhood stockiness – straight from the neck to the ankles. The only difference was the outward curve of her tummy in profile. Some days, if she stood naked in front of a full length mirror (which she did more often than was sensible), her bloat could pass for a mid-term pregnancy.

She circled a roundabout for the second time, thinking how if she wasn't careful, she could circumnavigate life for ever. It wasn't only a waist she no longer had. Today, she had no job to worry about, no Kelly-Ann, no husband, no dependent children, no dying sister.

A scene from years ago suddenly burst into her head. Diana was helping her tie a cheesecloth shirt in a knot above her jeans.

'You're cutting me in half!'

'You see, you *do* have a waist!'

Maggie put a finger into the restricting band of her skirt and remembered how, when she used to lie in bed on her side, Don would run his hands down and up the dip in her outline. Had her tummy slipped and collected in a bag of soft flesh then like it did now? Her car seemed to be taking her in the direction of Jamie's cottage. She could pretend she had come to clean the windows or shampoo the carpet or any of the other spring-cleaning promises she was ticking off the list.

As she bumped down the lane, a tractor appeared from a field entrance. She flashed her lights, hoping it would be Jamie in the cab, but it was his employer Mr House who jumped down to shut the gate behind him. He walked towards her with the look of a man who had something to say.

'You Jamie's mother?'

'Yes, I was just...'

'He's not here. I was expecting him back for milking b'now.'

'Oh, where is he?'

She regretted the question immediately. Nineteen years ago, she had left baby Jamie in his carrycot in the car while she dashed into a shop for some milk, only to emerge to the sound of his red-faced bawling and a furious woman standing by her locked car. The only thing she'd been able to think of to say in response to the torrent of rebuke had been 'How long has he been crying for?'

'How the hell should I know?' the farmer laughed. 'I've been as good as I can to 'im but...'

'We've been very grateful to you.'

'I'll be having to let 'im go now. He's no

225

good to me. I shall be lookin' for someone else from tomorrow.'

'I understand,' she said, putting the car into reverse. She didn't want him to be telling her this. He should be telling Jamie.

'No need for 'im to move out before the weekend. You want to tell 'im, or should I?'

'You, if you don't mind.'

Mr House touched his hat and walked back to his tractor. Her car screamed its way backwards up the track. On the open road, she checked her phone. It showed no missed calls or messages. Jamie's unemployment is not my problem, she told herself, not my problem, not my problem. My problem is what to do about *me*.

Fourteen

Stefan didn't know whether to be grateful for the flurry of mail that came through the letterbox that morning or not. The six hand-written envelopes staring at him from the dusty wooden floor could have represented anything from a racing certainty to a complete surprise – he had no clue where to place them in the scheme of things. All he knew was that he had been dreading today, when Di would have been fifty-two.

As he bent to pick them up, he had a bet – four would be from Di's sisters, Amanda, Judy, Jane and Maggie, the other two from his daughters. He hoped the flowers he'd sent them all had arrived before they'd left for the office or the coffee morning, the shops or the lecture theatre, or whatever else they had planned to keep their sorrow at bay. He ought to have planned something for himself too, but Di had been too good a social secretary for him to have learned by necessity. There was an auction he could go to, a dead man's art collection to value, a dining table and chairs in the lock-up he should try and shift. It was about time he renewed his trade contacts, checked on prices and stimulated his old appetite for antiques. Not today though.

He flicked through the cards quickly to confirm his guess, faltering as he realized he'd been expecting them to be addressed to Di, like the charity circular that had arrived a week ago, her name teasing him in the envelope's window behind a square of transparent paper which he had smoothed with his thumb to bring her closer. His recall still brought her back thin and frightened, and he didn't yet believe the well-meaning comments from people who told him that one day he'd remember her curves and laughter again.

He was right. One card had a Spanish stamp, another was in Judy's odd italics, and Leyla and Carly had both written SWALK across the flaps as family tradition dictated, their rounded letters still young enough to evoke their childhood selves.

Stefan carried the little stack down the tiled steps into the basement kitchen and placed them neatly on the table, not yet ready to read them, for what would they say? *Thinking of you. With fond memories of a wonderful sister. Love you Dad.* Kind but hopeless gestures.

He made himself a cup of tea and tried to concentrate on the newspaper. As he turned the front page, Di's birthday date on the top right of page two and the top left of page three ran like a double taunt. Every story he read had a resonance. A twelve-year-old boy had been crowned British champion of Sudoku, Di's hospital obsession. The death of

Layla, a gorilla named after Eric Clapton's celebrated song, had a whole city in mourning. That was Layla with an 'a', and therefore a point to Di. He imagined her licking her forefinger and painting the air. Three hundred and seventy-four nil. He'd been the one to register the birth, written 'Leyla' with an 'e', condemning their eldest daughter to a lifetime of spelling correction thereafter. If Di had been here, he might finally concede that now, seeing as it was her birthday and all.

'Cheers, my love,' he said, lifting his bone china mug in a solitary toast with his absent mate. It was going to be a long day.

It was going to be a long day for Jess too. To halt its progress, she tried to make her shower go on for ever and ever. The temperature was turned up so high, the bathroom was like a sauna. She could almost see the decadence of the night before being drawn from her guilty body and rising in the steam around her.

Guilt was a strange thing, she decided as she squeezed a wiggle of body scrub on to her palm. It made one feel unclean from the inside out, and she knew she wasn't going to be able to wash this one away no matter how long she stood under the gushing water for. It might help if she knew what she was feeling guilty *about*. Her best guess was that she was ashamed of the way she had treated Jamie yesterday afternoon, but really, when it came down to it, was she? She knew she ought to be, so maybe that was where the offence lay.

She put her hand on the control dial to turn off the water and then took it off again to lift her face to the torrent a few seconds longer. When it stopped, that would be it. Finito. The end of this shower would mark the end of what had been an oasis of other small luxuries lately, like lie-ins and haircuts and her own private taxi service. If truth be known, she wasn't ready – and especially not with a hangover – to go back to 6.30 a.m. starts and the constant presence of a demanding toddler.

She didn't want her leisurely cup of tea to end either, nor the uninterrupted half hour it took her to get ready, nor the peaceful trip across town in the back of her parents' clean comfortable car, even though it felt like a journey to the scaffold.

'Watch the exhaust!' Anne Morley screeched as they turned off the main road into the bumpy lane leading to the farm. 'Derek, watch the exhaust!'

Gatesy's cottage looked even more like an illustration than it had the first time now that the geraniums that lined the path to the freshly painted front door were out.

'It looks better in the daylight,' her father said hopefully.

Jess got reluctantly out of the car, her conscience dormant as she looked across the deserted farmyard and walked slowly up the path to the front door. Someone had mown the lawn, which made it look bigger, inviting enough to fall asleep on in the sunshine. Tubs of bright blue lobelia covered the broken paving stones around the porch. It looked like the sort of place she'd like to live in, but appearances were so deceptive.

She knocked, aware that her decision not to use her key and let herself in spoke volumes. When no one answered, she avoided a glance towards her parents in the car and walked across the farmyard to the house.

'He's not here, my love,' the farmer's wife told her, wiping floury hands on an apron. 'We haven't set eyes on him since yesterday morning.'

'Do you mean gone?'

'Without so much as a by your leave.'

'He wouldn't...'

'Oh, he would. We've seen it all before. A lad with money in his pocket goes out and has a skinful, ends up sleeping on someone's floor and can't get himself up for milking...'

'That's not Jamie, something must have—'

'He's not alone, love, we get through dozens, we do. These young men, they don't have the right attitude these days. In our day, a job was a job and you were lucky to have one ... I'm not saying he's all bad, he's worked harder on getting that cottage back up together for you and the little one than he has on the farm. We've had our money's worth from him just from that.'

Jess tried hard to feel the disappointment that Mrs House wanted her to feel, but the sensation of escape and relief was too strong.

'Well, that's something...'

'The baby's on the mend, is he?'

'He's much better, thank you.'

'You'll be wanting a ring on your finger now, I expect...'

It was a quick end to the conversation and after a polite goodbye, Jess turned back across the yard, shrugging at the expectant faces of her mother and father behind the windscreen.

'He must be already there,' she said unemotionally, plonking herself on the back seat.

'I told you not to have that shower. I wanted to be there before him.'

'It's not a competition, Mum.'

On the way to the hospital, as she waited for Jamie to reply to an unfriendly text, her mother launched into an even longer speech than the one Mrs House had delivered. It still amounted to nothing more than 'I told you so.'

Jess felt no need either to argue or agree. At least she knew the heaviness she couldn't seem to shake was nothing to do with Jamie after all. All she felt when she thought of her ex-boyfriend now was a mild irritation.

Her father parked the car in the visitors' car park, buying a day's stay even though they were only going to be there for less than an hour. The three of them trudged through the reception doors, along the wide main corridor, into the lift to the third floor, along another corridor and up to the double doors with the intercom system, exuding all the enthusiasm of a wet Monday morning.

'Hi, it's Jessica Morley,' Jess announced into

the grid.

The security doors opened and Ben's favourite nurse Amber bustled towards them in her flat black lace-ups, the beads in her hair clacking together like her own personal percussion band. There was an unsurprised smile dancing across her expression that Jess didn't understand.

'What's he forgotten now? I could tell he was going to leave *something* behind, the speed he was packing all Ben's stuff up...'

'Jamie is here, is he?'

The question wiped the smile right off Amber's face.

'No-oo, he took Ben at six o'clock last night,' she said, her eyes carefully patrolling the small group's response. 'Doctor gave Ben the all clear yesterday lunchtime. But you knew that, didn't you? I was here when Jamie made the phone call from the ward and spoke to your mother to tell her the good news.'

Beside her daughter, Anne Morley reddened.

'That's right, isn't it?'

'Yes, I...'

'Oh good,' Amber said, pleased to have been able to make a point. 'I must have been off duty by the time you came to pick him up...'

Jess's cheeks grew red too now. Behind her, she could feel her mother boiling with the shame of being caught out.

'You didn't come, did you?'

'Well, no, there was...'

'But you did know Ben was discharged yesterday, didn't you?'

'Yes,' Jess said quickly. 'Yes, of course.'

'But you didn't come with Jamie to collect him,' Amber confirmed.

'No.'

'OK, as long as I've got that clear. So what's he forgotten then?'

'We're just here to ... well ... he left a train here ... his favourite train ... I...'

'I'll tell you what,' Amber said with the voice of a nurse who had seen it all before, 'we'll put it in the lost-property book and give you a ring if it turns up.'

Back in the car park, where the ticket in the windscreen had another twenty-three hours and forty-five minutes to run, Jess realized through her humiliation why she had been feeling guilty. The one thing she now wanted more than anything else, she hadn't for the last few days been wanting at all.

'I need Ben,' she said, bursting into tears.

When Stefan answered the door to both Maggie and Amanda, his immediate reaction was dismay, assuming they'd arrived at his cottage together by accident, two competing Angels of Comfort.

'What a lovely surprise,' he lied, resigning himself to a morning of tiresome diplomacy. But to his astonishment, it turned out the two of them had come on a planned mission to carry him through the day. Or at least, that was one agenda. The other one didn't emerge until lunchtime.

'What would you like to do?' they asked him, and he was honest enough to say he couldn't care less, so they drove five miles down the road and placed themselves in the fail-safe care of the National Trust.

An historic garden was as good a place as any to remember Di. She would have loved the bluebells, they agreed, they were better than ever this year, and you had to admit how life affirming spring always was. The camellias, magnolia and narcissi of April had given way to May's gaudy riot and there was a tangible relief that the warmer weather had finally arrived. Stefan found the sight of so many elderly people with time on their hands sauntering along the paths in their shirt sleeves oddly reassuring. Pleasant old age really did come to some. But even so, he took his own jacket off and put one finger through the loop in its collar, carrying it over his shoulder in a way that made him look less like one of them than if he'd draped it in the crook of his elbow.

They wandered into a Victorian red-brick summerhouse, which prompted a conversation about a piggery in the Bartons' paddock years ago, an old stone building which all five girls had been allowed to paint one summer. A whole tin of lilac gloss had been tipped over – by Diana, both sisters remembered – coating a section of flagstone path.

'It's probably lilac to this day!'

'We should sneak in and take a look next

time we're passing.'

'We'd have to knock. There's no back gate any more. The land backs right on to a housing estate.'

They passed by a rock garden where spring water babbled into a tiny stream, over a rather twee bridge that reminded Amanda of the time she and Di had seen *The King and I* in London, starring Yul Brynner. Maggie held her sister's hand as they crept through a long dark tunnel of giant bamboo while Stefan followed behind, unmoved by the plants but pleased to be out of the house.

In the sun again, Amanda stopped under a tree to pick up one of its fallen white blossoms. On closer inspection, the flower was creased and browning at the edges so she discarded it with a disappointed grunt.

'It's called a handkerchief tree,' Maggie said. 'See how its petals hang like little squares of cotton?'

'I've always called it a dove tree,' Stefan said, 'on account of the way the leaves flutter when the breeze catches them.'

'Handkerchief.'

'Dove.'

'Handkerchief.'

'I think Maggie's right,' Amanda ruled. 'Handkerchiefs, definitely.'

'Steady on, you two,' Stefan teased as they wandered through a gazebo dripping with old wisteria, 'you'll be seeing eye-to-eye next!'

'Oh, sisters never see eye-to-eye,' Amanda said. 'They don't need to.'

'Don't they?' Maggie asked.

'It's not like friends, is it? You don't have to worry about offending a sister, they're there for the long haul, aren't they?'

For a split second Maggie thought, at last, that she understood, but at that same moment, maybe the sun went behind a cloud or an easterly breeze began to blow, because she suddenly needed her cardigan.

'I don't know about you two, but I could do with a drink,' Stefan suggested quickly. 'They do a nice little straw-pressed cider in their tea-rooms here.'

'Just an apple juice for me,' Amanda said.

The restaurant, a restored barn with beamed ceilings and wooden floors overlooking an inner yard full of old farm machinery, was already well into its lunchtime rush by the time Stefan, Amanda and Maggie got there. Women in ankle-length floral dresses and white frilly aprons carried trays of pork and apple casserole, apple shortbread and apple ice cream to patient-looking customers, hoping, Maggie suspected, to give the impression that the almost unacceptable delay was down to the fact that they had been out to the orchards themselves to pick the ingredients.

She wished Stefan would hurry back to the table, but from where she was sitting, the queue for drinks looked to have about as much sense of urgency as most of the diners. Huddled couples in sensible outfits chewed slowly and swapped notes about their choices, making weak attempts to use the building's famous post-war restoration as a springboard for conversation. She and Amanda were running out of small talk themselves, which meant there was always a danger of succumbing to the big.

'Do you think all these people are retired?' she asked.

Amanda's eyes widened in disapproval as if Maggie were a child making an inappropriate comment about the size of someone's nose.

'Keep your voice down!'

'They're not listening. I just want to know what they *do* all day if they don't work?'

'We do all the things that you workers always moan you don't have time for.'

'Like what though?'

'Hobbies, travel, I don't know! I'm not going to be made to feel guilty just because Peter has had the good fortune to reap a decent army pension. Retirement isn't a sin.'

'I'm only interested,' Maggie said excitedly, 'because I'm about to join the ranks. I've handed my notice in at work.'

Telling people her news was like tossing a pebble into a pond. The ripples that passed across their glassy eyes thrilled her. *She* had chosen the disruption this time. *She* was in control.

Amanda frowned again. 'What on earth for?'

'Me,' Maggie smiled.

'Can you *afford*...?'

'Not really, but things at school came to a

238

head and...'

All morning, she had been working up to telling Amanda about the classroom fight, about Kelly-Ann Drew's unsuccessful wrist slitting, about her moment of epiphany in the head's office when she was told her job was on the line. My job is already *over* the line, Maggie had said. I resign!

But this time, the ripple effect failed.

'The big mistake of course is to retire without having a *project*...'

'Right...'

Maggie suddenly wanted to laugh. This was classic Amanda and Di would have loved it!

'That's why Peter and I took on a larger garden, of course. It's not just the actual physical work. You wouldn't believe the number of hours he spends researching leaf blowers on the internet.'

Maggie thought she would, actually.

'The danger lies,' Amanda continued, 'and I should really be saying this to Stefan as well because both Peter and I are worried about his lack of interest in the business...'

'Just in time,' Maggie said with relief to her brother-in-law as he arrived balancing three glasses on a wooden tray.

'Say what?' Stefan asked, sitting down. Amanda didn't even stop to blush.

'I was just telling Maggie what a mistake it is to stop work and fail to replace it with another interest. That way lies boredom and dare I say it, depression. I've seen it happen...'

'I'm going to an auction tomorrow, if that's

what you mean.'

'No, no ... I just wanted Maggie to understand the pitfalls of having too much time on her hands.'

'Oh, I can't wait,' Maggie said, wincing at a sip of sharp cider.

'It's not always healthy,' Stefan said, sinking half his glass in one go. 'You can start dwelling on all sorts of things.'

'You see? I hope you're listening to us.'

'No, really, I can't wait,' Maggie repeated, thinking of Bronwen's box still sitting on the coffee table.

'To do what?' Amanda asked. 'You really will need a project. I mean, you don't even have Jamie's little boy to worry about any more, do you? And you of all people should not dwell...'

Despite the chilled cider, Maggie felt her insides go hot. She hadn't been intending to use the box as ammunition but as Amanda said, sisters didn't have to see eye-to-eye.

'Don't worry. I've already got one,' she said.

'Taking up macramé, are you?' Stefan teased, wishing the alcohol would start working.

'No.'

'Candle making? A language ... Russian, is it?'

'No. I'm going to find out why Bronwen and Rex gave me up for adoption.'

Stefan felt the table shudder. The apple juice in Amanda's glass shook. Maggie took another mouthful of cider.

'But you know why,' Amanda said tartly. 'Mummy was in her forties and ill, money was tight, and Aunt Grace and Uncle Arthur...'

'There's more to it than that.'

Amanda stared implacably at her for a second. 'You'd like there to be.'

'I've already begun actually,' Maggie said shakily.

'Oh?' Stefan asked.

'Yes, did you know, for example, that she made an annual donation to a charity called the Joseph French Foundation for nearly forty years?'

'Do you mean the cat's mother?' Amanda said, anger sibilating through her vowels.

'I mean Bronwen.'

'You mean Mummy.'

'I don't know if you remember, Amanda, but I always called her Bronwen.'

'The Joseph French Foundation?' Stefan asked, pouncing on the opportunity for neutral ground.

'Five hundred pounds a year every August to a charity set up to help the families of handicapped children.'

'Well, well. Lucky Joseph French.'

'Yes, but why?'

'She was a very generous woman,' Amanda said. 'Why does there have to be a why?'

'Why *doesn't* there?'

'Fair question,' said Stefan, thinking of Di.

'Did you know, for example, that she ... Bronwen ... once walked out on Rex, leaving him to look after you four?' Maggie said, looking unflinchingly at Amanda.

'I don't believe that for one minute.'

'She did. She went to stay with someone called Lottie.'

'Ah, Lottie,' Stefan said.

'I think she was Bronwen's old school friend. They were very close, I know that much. The letters suggest—'

'Oh, *her*!' Amanda spat out disparagingly. 'Daddy used to say she was a terrible trouble-maker. She used to bribe us with sweets to stay out of the kitchen so she could tell Mummy about her latest lover.'

'I'd like to talk to her.'

'Daddy refused to speak to her in the end. She became very much a persona non grata.'

'I don't think Lottie liked Rex very much either, judging what she says about him in the—'

'Do you really think you should be reading other people's—'

'Oh come on!'

'It's just not something I would feel happy doing.'

'Neither of you remember the rest of Lottie's name, do you?'

'No, I don't.'

'Judy might,' Stefan suggested.

'Forget it,' Amanda said quickly, picking up the menu and pretending to read it. 'She died years ago. I remember Daddy being delight-ed.'

Stefan's eloquent eyebrow went up, but it passed unnoticed. Maggie clicked her tongue in regret.

'Oh, that's a blow.'

'Are you two hungry?' Stefan asked hopefully. His glass was empty and he needed another. The village pub was beckoning. 'We could get a bite to eat here or...'

Amanda tossed the menu down and it skittered across the table.

'I don't think so.'

'Amanda, don't be like that,' Maggie said.

'I just think it is wrong to pry into someone else's personal business, that's all,' she hissed, loudly enough for an elderly couple to glance up from their soup.

'Bronwen was my mother too,' Maggie said, refusing to lower her voice.

'She still has a right to some privacy!'

'And I have a right to know—'

'Oh, for God's sake! Know *what*?'

'Well, if I knew that...'

Amanda tightened her thin lips.

'I just think Di left me the box for a reason,' Maggie added.

'Talking of whom,' Amanda snapped, standing up, 'shouldn't we be on our way? I'd like to visit the grave before I leave.'

The three of them walked through the restaurant in silence, but as Stefan held open the heavy door for the sisters, he murmured something so quietly to Maggie that she had to check with him later to make sure she had heard correctly.

'Lottie's not dead,' he whispered. 'Di had tea with her last Christmas.'

Fifteen

Lottie Buchan-Jones couldn't help wondering if sometimes these days, she didn't merely remember the past but somehow actually visited it. She wasn't yet senile enough not to realize that entertaining the idea of time travel verged on the delusional, but toying with the possibility was surely better oil for her ninety-year-old brain than gaping at mindless television for hours on end, which is what most of Fir Lodge's residents did.

It worked like this. Something – a visitor's fragrance, the taste of fudge, the sight of rain on the window – would trigger a distant memory. At first, it would be just a memory, foggy and incomplete, but sometimes, if she then stared into space somewhere to the top right of her vision and really excavated for detail – What was that perfume called? When did I wear it? Who gave it to me? What was the texture of the glass, the design of its stopper? – the present would invariably recede and the glorious past would come rolling in.

'How are you today, Mrs Buchan-Jones?' a member of staff would enquire too loudly if they caught her like that, with her head cocked, her limpid eyes focused, unblinking.

'Tidal,' Lottie would reply mischievously. 'Tidal today.'

And she would be left in peace then to scratch archaeologically away at the recollection until she could smell those sweet peas, feel the sun on her bare shoulders, hear the full river rushing through the valley, taste the retsina or watch that last school play. Lottie only ever travelled somewhere within her own lifetime but she didn't mind about that. The twentieth century had been a marvellous stamping ground.

Today, she was gazing somewhere beyond the wall-mounted frosted shell light and thinking about her boarding school, in particular the way the tepid bath water used to splash against the iron-orange stain that lurked at the bottom of the deep unforgiving tub and the feel of the rough blue-edged towels that scraped you dry.

'Come on girls! Get that lather going! Cleanliness is next to godliness!' Miss Slade barks as she patrols the rows of naked bathing girls, casting stolen glances that are greedy enough to make Lottie clamp her thin arms around her knees to hide her newly rounded breasts...

Really! She snapped open her ninety-year-old eyes and clapped her hands. So that's what the Saturday evening bathing ritual had been about – nothing to do with clean hair for church the next day at all!

'Voyeurism!' she leaned across and said triumphantly to her crony Douglas Rogers, a familiar spirit and the only other Fir Lodge resident who understood the comic potential of mental infirmity.

'A man can look, can't he?' Douglas batted back, unfazed as always by their nonsensical exchanges.

'Oh, a *man* can look all he likes, darling.'

The trigger for Lottie's startling insight into bath time at St Hilda's School for Girls had been the arrival of Fir Lodge's morning post. It was the way the diurnal hope and disappointment of the postie's bag could make or break one's position in the rest home hierarchy that had brought school flooding back for Lottie. Letters, somehow, made you popular. The more letters you got, the more likely you were to end up as head girl, or in charge of the remote control at any rate.

Today it was Fat Pat's turn to play postman. Douglas had named all the other day care staff in the same vein – Lean Jean, Moaning Mona and Cool Hand Luke who, as the only male carer, got to give Douglas his thrice-weekly bath. 'So I can vouch for just how cold his hands are,' he'd told Lottie confidentially.

It made no difference, Lottie thought as Pat bustled round the room in her mauve pinny and matching slippers, whether the kingdom was an overheated lounge or an oak-panelled canteen – recipients of the postbag ruled while the unloved tried their best not to look as if they cared. Well, Lottie hadn't cared then and she didn't care now. More often than not, today's communications from the outside world were nothing more than death notices

246

anyway. Since the postbag would almost certainly not be coming her way, she closed her eyes again and returned to her thoughts.

Douglas missed Lottie when she time travelled. He had developed various techniques to keep her in the present as his sidekick, all of them based on making her laugh, which, much to his delight, he found very easy to do.

Having finished and folded his newspaper, he watched Pat weave her way through the velour chairs singing 'Po-ost! Po-ost!' as if she were auditioning for an amateur musical. 'It being a Monday,' he started his subversive commentary, 'we have the inevitable white envelope for Mrs Murray from her daughter in Evesham with the ugly husband and irritable bowel ... there goes Mrs Murray's hand, she's making a bid for it, and yes, as we thought, straight into the handbag! But we have trouble on the left here with Mr Knight. Wake up, Mr Knight, your criminal son with the new wife you refuse to acknowledge has sent you a postcard from Spain. He wants you to know they had paella again for lunch yesterday ... no, Mr Knight is not going to wake up today...'

But if it was for Lottie's benefit it was wasted because she was too busy back in 1931.

She is making her iron-framed bed in the sixth-form dormitory she and Bronwen share. Their 'cubie' is no bigger than the en-suite bathroom attached to her current bedroom and it has a curtain made from wine-coloured velvet for a door, except the colour has faded to stripes of watery pink.

'Oh, now this *is* a surprise!' Douglas was saying as Pat waddled towards their corner. 'Could it possibly be a rare letter from Mr Hedges' negligent son in New York City or ... no, no, it seems to be heading the way of Mrs Charlotte Buchan-Jones...'

But Lottie still wasn't listening.

The velvet door curtain has come down on Bronwen's head and the hooks are scattered across the dark herringbone lino, hiding themselves in the rag rug. The two of them are on their hands and knees, searching...

'Mrs Buchan-Jo-ones! Po-ost!'

With a nudge from Douglas, Lottie snapped open her eyes to see Pat's chubby hand stretching towards her. At once, St Hilda's ebbed and Fir Lodge washed back in, bringing with it a surprise piece of driftwood in the form of a lemon-coloured envelope addressed in a hand Lottie did not recognize.

Dear Mrs Buchan-Jones,

I do hope you don't mind me writing to you out of the blue like this, but I am also hoping that I may not be a complete stranger to you. I am Maggie, the youngest of Bronwen and Rex Barton's daughters (the one brought up by Rex's sister Grace and her husband Arthur).

As you know, my sister Diana sadly died this spring. She left me a box of Bronwen's personal papers and in it are some

248

letters from you. I wondered if you would be interested to see them again? Either way, I would love to meet you and talk to you about my mother sometime. There are so many things I don't know about her.

I hope this letter finds you well. My apologies for troubling you if you would rather not be in touch.

Best wishes,
Maggie Day

'So many things,' Lottie told Douglas knowingly, slotting the card into the pages of her large-print library book.

'So many indeed,' he agreed, and decided this time to leave her be as she tilted her head and tried to find what she was looking for beyond the frosted wall light once more.

Lottie must have been in the mood for institutions that day because before long, she found herself smelling the antiseptic, cabbagey whiff of another nursing home sometime in the late 1950s.

It should be a happy place, populated as it is by newly bestowed mothers and their host of cherubic babies, but walking along the cream-painted corridor listening to the echo of her own heels on the tiled floor, Lottie is aware of feeling wretched.

She must buoy herself up before reaching her friend's bedside or she will be of no use at all. Come on, Lottie, she urges herself as she hurries past a room with sinks too large to pass as a washroom, dredge up some reason to be positive for pity's sake!

Well, how about this? Between them, she and Bronwen have so far managed to produce six healthy children. Six! That isn't bad going for a couple of schoolgirls who used to vow they'd never even get married. And yet this is the first time either of them have ever been in a maternity hospital. Her own boys, Oliver and Charles, who are already back at boarding school, were born at Mrs Tyler's just outside Chelsea – a splendid arrangement, like home delivery without the mess. Poor Bronwen of course, being married to a tight-fisted man like Rex, has just had to put up with the mess, and she was planning to put up with it all over again until her blood pressure went sky high and she was shipped against her wishes to this unfriendly prison. But why – now that the baby is born and her blood pressure has dropped – is she still here?

Lottie walks on, feeling none the cheerier. Perhaps it is the after effect of the train journey that seemed to go on and on and on. Travel is always tedious when you are keen to get somewhere, particularly if that somewhere also contains a someone, but really, the three-hour trip from London had been insufferable. Despite the sweltering August day, her unwanted fellow passenger had been dressed in one of the worst examples of the ubiquitous Fair Isle sleeveless sweater Lottie

250

had ever seen. His face had got shinier and shinier as the stations rolled by.

'This line is scheduled for electrification, you know.'

'They've got a cheek, charging the prices they do when you can still buy a terraced house with an outside toilet for £850.'

'I've written to the British Transport Commission to tell them that eighteen shillings to get to Bournemouth is daylight robbery.'

Boring little man. She had dearly wished to lean forward and tell him to shut up but she had eventually blocked his monotonous interjections by concentrating on her friend's dreadful letter.

It wasn't so much the decision itself that had kept her awake all night, but the way Bronwen was so matter-of-fact about it. Emotionally bankrupt – that is the phrase that comes to her as she clips along the corridor, but when she dodges a porter pushing an empty wheelchair, it comes to her. The letter is in Bron's handwriting but it is Rex's voice. He must have made her write it! A flicker of hope for her plan to talk Bronwen out of it passes across her face.

A stern sister with a uniform starched to the point of cardboard is coming towards her, sizing up Lottie's sleeveless summer dress and flouncy underskirt with a disapproval Lottie puts down to jealousy.

'Yes?' the nurse inquires brusquely, staring through her horn-rimmed glasses with accusing eyes.

'I'm here to see Mrs Barton,' Lottie says loftily.

The sister's attitude softens – rather falsely, Lottie thinks – at the mention of Bronwen's name. She smiles with such a rehearsed sympathy that Lottie wants to push past her, snatch Bronwen and her baby and whisk them far away.

'We'll be putting Mrs Barton in the side room off Ward Three this afternoon,' the sister says, 'but for the moment, I'm afraid you'll still find her in Ward Two.'

Lottie appreciates the need for apology as soon as she walks into the room. Five of the six inhospitable iron beds are occupied by women still waiting for labour to begin, their huge swollen bellies embarrassingly visible under the thin white sheets. In contrast, the shape Bronwen's tummy makes under her own inadequate covers reminds Lottie of a giant hot-water bottle.

'How insensitive can you get?' Lottie hisses, pulling up a hard wooden chair.

'It doesn't matter,' Bronwen replies almost serenely, 'since I am entirely desensitized. I can't feel a thing.'

'Then you shouldn't be making such big decisions,' Lottie says, grabbing her friend's hand. 'You should wait until you are in your right mind.'

'I don't think I shall ever be in my right mind again.'

'Well, can I at least see her?' Lottie asks. 'I *so* want to see her.'

'Mmmm?' Bronwen responds absent-mindedly as a short fat nurse arrives at her bedside carrying a silent bundle.

'The little man needs feeding I'm afraid, Mrs Barton. So if your visitor wouldn't mind waiting outside...'

'Little man?' the ninety-year-old Lottie said suddenly to Douglas, who put down his newspaper crossword at once.

'Six feet exactly in my stockinged feet,' he said without missing a beat. 'Used to be six feet one.' He was always pleased to have her back.

'Oh, for heaven's sake,' she cried, 'I've been in the wrong blessed birth!'

That was the problem with time travel. If two separate situations were in any way similar, they tended to merge into one and Lottie could never be entirely sure which one she had landed up in. She had the same problem with her two weddings. The mistake she'd made there was to have married such identikit men – tall, blond, effete, selfish. The other day, her recall had *Laurence* changing Oliver's nappy on the tombstone at Charles's christening, when of course, the boys' father was Eric – and that was the just the tip of it!

'At least I know exactly where I am with you,' she leaned over to tell Douglas, who said that was only because these days, he never went anywhere.

Douglas was being awfully kind, but then again he never could resist a good story. After lunch (spring lamb and new potatoes, factory-produced meringue and peach slices), he invited her into his ground-floor room, which, despite the fact that he was in a wheelchair, always got the other residents at Fir Lodge raising their eyebrows. It was the only place they could have a private conversation, and this conversation was turning out to be very private. It started openly enough, but Douglas wasn't an ex-Fleet Street editor for nothing.

'What do you remember of this Maggie woman then?' he began.

'The word "woman" is not going to get me anywhere, Douglas. She was a *child*, a nervous little girl who hid behind her cousins too unsure of her position to—'

'Sisters,' Douglas corrected.

'I'm glad to see you're keeping up.'

'Doing my best.'

Lottie flashed him a dose of affection and tipped her head back in Douglas's winged chair. Her eyes closed and for a moment or two it was the summer of 1968.

The air is full of tiny golden pieces of hay, swirling into the garden from the field beyond. But it won't be a field for long, and Bronwen's beastly husband Rex is furious. He has been trying to start the lawnmower all afternoon, pulling angrily on the starter cord and interrupting the few moments of peace his wife is trying to enjoy with her oldest friend. Lottie can't help making matters worse. He is such an easy man to irritate, and he deserves it, the way he treats Bronwen.

'So just tell me again, Rex,' she says, drawing on the cigarette in her holder and taking a sip of the afternoon gin and tonic she asked for instead of the tea that was offered, just to get on his nerves. 'How many homes are being built next door, did you say?'

'Sixty.'

'How nice for the girls,' Lottie says. 'They'll have neighbours at last.'

Bronwen laughs for the first time that day into her home-made lemonade. Lottie winks across the wrought-iron table. And then the telephone rings from inside. Rex comes striding across the lawn and tells his wife it is Arthur Wetherham, calling to say the twins are being sent home on the next train.

'What on earth for?' Bronwen asks.

'For calling Maggie their *sister*,' Rex tells her as if it were somehow her fault.

'And that is how it all came out,' Lottie told Douglas, opening her eyes again. 'A game of tea parties, the three girls playing at being sisters, but of course, they weren't pretending and...'

'Yes, yes, we've done all that. The tall woman you couldn't bear smashed that plate and—'

'Grace,' Lottie shuddered. 'She was almost Shakespearian in her plotting, was Grace. I always picture her standing behind pillars or just beyond an open door, listening in.'

'But we're not interested in Grace, are we? We're interested in *Maggie*.'

'I'm getting there...'

'Now, earlier, you mentioned that she was exactly like her mother...'

'Only to look at. There was a stockiness about Maggie that the other girls didn't have. Amanda and Judy and the twins, they all had Rex's elongated stature, but Maggie had her mother's younger build exactly. Bron lost it over the years of course. It was as if all that guilt put her on the rack and stretched her...'

'Oh, heavens above,' Douglas pleaded. 'Don't think about Bronwen. Think about Maggie.'

Lottie shook her head. 'But what can I say? I never really knew her.'

'You said you were at her birth, didn't you?'

'Oh,' Lottie exclaimed, closing her eyes, 'why, so I was!'

It takes her no time at all to travel back to a deserted hospital corridor in 1958. Lottie is marching purposefully past the metal and vinyl chair intended to block her entry with the 'Visiting Time Strictly 3–4pm' sign propped on it, and is beginning to scour the wards for her friend. She knows Bronwen needs her – she's been feeling it in her waters ever since she left London. The further she goes, the louder the bovine moaning grows. Her footsteps quicken, and when she reaches its source, her stomach lurches into her throat. A sister, two nurses and a medical student are

256

crowding around a bed. Just as she is about to push them aside to rescue Bron in her hour of need, she hears a reedy voice behind her.

'Lottie! Thank God!'

Bronwen is calling to her from the side room opposite. She is shifting uncomfortably on a narrow bed, trying to position herself into a squat, her voice quiet with pain.

'Can you get someone? I've been calling but...'

Lottie runs across the tiled floor to the high delivery couch where Bronwen is soaked in perspiration, her white knuckles gripping the hostile sides of the bed.

'Darling, are you...?'

'Get someone!'

But the only available staff are the four in the noisy room, where the air is now thick with profanities coming from the woman who is not Bronwen on the bed.

'Please, could one of you come and help my friend?'

No one looks round.

'Mrs Barton in Room Four is about to have her baby,' Lottie says loudly.

'Nonsense!' the starched sister snaps. 'I examined her an hour ago.'

'She has her babies very quickly. I really think—'

'Lottie!' Bronwen screams from her bed.

She gets there just in time to lift the damp sheet and feel the baby's slippery head.

'Push!' is all she can think of to say. The floor seems such a long way down. She holds the crown of hair in her trembling hands and, to the sound of running black leather and crisp uniforms swooshing around her, she catches the little body as it shoots out of its mother into a world that will not be immediately kind to her.

In the overheated ground floor bedroom of Fir Lodge, Douglas Rogers clapped his hands.

''Owzat! Thank goodness you were there!'

'Oh, that wasn't everyone's opinion,' Lottie said darkly. 'Not at all. Poor Bronwen went on to contract puerperal fever.'

Douglas's brow furrowed. He knew all about 'childbed fever', his own mother having been taken by it in 1917, a month before his father was blown to pieces in Northern France.

'The fever that turned maternity hospitals into morgues...'

'Yes, and me into a scapegoat. They said that I had brought the infection in with me and passed it on to the mother as I delivered her child. Even Bronwen believed them.'

'Not for long, surely?'

'Long enough for Grace to get what she wanted.'

'Your Shakespearian plotter?'

'Think of it! Bronwen pumped full of drugs lying in an isolation cubicle, unable to feed her baby, sinking into a postnatal depression that had been bubbling under the surface for a year...'

Lottie took a handkerchief from the cuff of her ancient blue merino wool cardigan and pressed it against her eyes. 'She wasn't allowed to keep that one either, you know. That bloody husband and his scheming sister ... two babies snatched from her like that...'

She sniffed, quickly wiping her nose.

'What *are* we doing?' Douglas cried suddenly. 'What *is* the point of resurrecting sadness?'

'I beg your pardon?' Lottie looked at him in complete surprise.

'Surely the whole point about old age is that, finally, we can put on those rose-tinted spectacles...'

'Oh! Is that how you see it? I thought the whole point was that we no longer had to pretend.'

'I won't have you upset!' Douglas brought his mottled hands down on the armrests of his wheelchair. 'If this letter is going to cause you...'

'Not at all,' she assured him. 'It is a *relief*.' Her liquid eyes glassed over and she tilted her head.

'Oh no you don't,' he said. 'You stay right here with me. I'm seeing this one out to the end.'

'The end hasn't happened yet,' Lottie told him from behind her closed eyes. 'Nor indeed have I told you the beginning. That was the whole problem. We all spent far too long pretending that there was nothing more to Bronwen's monumental mess than the middle.'

Sixteen

Big Pool, now that Jamie finally came to show it to his own son, wasn't actually that big at all. It was more of a large pond really, and unless the roots of the old oak tree had sunk into the banks by five feet or more, then the drop from its overhanging branches into the water below can't have been the daredevil plunge that Jamie had impressed himself with all these years. But Ben, hyperactive with recovery in the tussocky buttercup-rich meadow beside him, seemed suitably in awe and that was all that mattered.

'Big Pool!' Jamie announced with a fanfare that was more for his own benefit than his son's.

'Big Poo!'

A grainy image of the toddler standing solemnly outside the tent in his wellies, pyjamas and fleece in the summer morning sunshine was already captured in perpetuity on Jamie's phone. Who to send it on to was no longer a problem – he was going to have it all for himself. He was having no difficulty ignoring the message icons that flashed constantly from the screen either. His text last night to all the important numbers – *'I've picked up Ben, he is safe and well and we are going away for a few days'* – was good enough. It wasn't abduction. He was his *father* and he had the moral upper hand here, Jess knew it.

'When I was ten, I climbed that tree, I did. I crawled along that branch there until I was right over the water, and then my dad shouted "One-two-three JUMP!" and I leapt off and felt the air rushing past my face...'

'Two-three jump!'

'My legs were running in mid-air and I shouted "Geronimo!" and hit the surface of the water with such a splash—'

''plash!' Ben mimicked, throwing his hands up.

'—and it stung my legs like a billion wasps, man, and I came up gasping for air and had to swim to the edge where my dad was cheering and clapping...'

Jamie put his hands under Ben's arms and swung him up to kiss his face. The relief of his boy's regained health trumped even the euphoria of resurfacing from Big Pool's muddy depths. He'd discovered something else worth celebrating here too. Despite what Rob or Jess or old Mrs Bertoli thought, his own boyhood had passed.

His adult confidence was, this morning, as sturdy as the old oak in front of him. Yesterday, outside the school gates as Jess had rejected him in favour of a couple of plastic tiaras, his heart had fallen into his stomach and his stomach into his boots. He had almost been able to hear Rob and Gatesy's

261

laughter from the shores of Nusa Dua. But then, like a tap on the shoulder from his other self, his former English teacher had called him a bloody idiot and finally, his disappointment had hit something solid. Indignation burned in his eyes as the muck from his farmyard boots fell in organic shards on to the urban pavement.

'Mr Midway?'

'Mr Day...'

'I'm not a bloody idiot. I'm a father and that should be good enough for anyone.'

The decision to go to the hospital alone to collect his son and disappear had been an easy one after that, despite the shrill female voices in his head. *You're going camping the night your two-year-old son comes home from hospital having recovered from pneumonia? I don't think so!*

But Ben had been warm and content and safe for every single second of the last eighteen hours; he'd had plenty of fluids, enough to eat, a good sleep, a healthy temperature – a tick in the box for everything Amber had told him to look for. The boy's cheeks were a joyous colour this morning, neither the flush of fever nor the cheerless pall of a hospital ward. And so Jamie didn't care what flak he would have to face.

His son pulled a snail off a stone and watched its horns grow and shrink back. With a quick glance up at his father for permission, he opened the flap of the jumble sale handbag hanging around his neck and put the

262

snail inside, with the chocolate Easter egg wrapper, the chipped metal tractor, the piece of sea-smooth green glass, the chunky plastic black knight and the crumpled photograph of him and Maggie on a swing.

'We'll let him out a little bit later on for some fresh air, shall we?' Jamie said.

'Later.'

'He can't live in there for ever, can he?'

'No.'

No more than they could they live in their tent for ever either.

'Shame,' he said.

'Same,' his little boy agreed.

For the last two years, they had carried out their relationship in a goldfish bowl, with the women who fed them keeping an eye, tapping on the glass, getting them to swim this way or that. This morning, no one knew where they were nor what they were doing. They might cook some breakfast, dig for worms, visit the cows, eat some biscuits and read books in their secret blue dome. What they were going to do after that, Jamie didn't know, but what he *did* know was that his defining role was neither farmer, English student, gardener, nor even Maggie Day's youngest son – he was Ben's dad and he would fight for the privilege and win.

He carried his son on his slight shoulders over the bridge and across the field back to the tent which he had pitched yesterday evening just inside the gate, close enough to his van to have turned its wheels at the first hint of concern. But the two of them could not have been cosier in their Thermolite sleeping bags, the third bag – the one that Jess could have joined them in if she'd wanted to – unzipped and over them like a blanket. She didn't know what she was missing, and it had occurred to Jamie in the middle of the night that he no longer wanted her to find out either.

Only on the last bite of his sausage did Ben feel the first fat drop of rain. ''Plash!' he laughed, putting his hand to the sudden patch of wet on his fine blond hair. Another one fell, hitting him on the thigh, and Jamie watched his own trousers darken in three places. It was the sort of summer rain that came from nowhere and soaked you in seconds. Burning charcoal in the disposable barbecue started to hiss and let off puffs of white ash, and thunder rumbled ominously in the not too distant distance. 'In the tent, Ben!' he cried, making a game of zipping the doors and climbing back into their bags.

The storm growled louder as it approached and then, with one almighty overhead crack that sent Ben leaping into his father's arms, the heavens opened. The rain hammered against the taut blue nylon, the thunder roared, flashes of static electricity flickered on the canvas walls.

Ben put his hands over his ears. Jamie sang 'Rain, rain, go away! Come again another day!' but still it poured. Jamie sang louder. Ben shouted 'Go away!' at the top of his voice, Jamie sang some more, but outside, the sky roared and poured and forked.

The phone rang.

'Go away!' screamed Ben in delight.

'Jamie? Where are you?'

Jess's anger was no match for the bedlam above.

'We're fine,' he said loosely.

'But where are you?'

'Does it matter?'

'Can I speak to Ben?'

Jamie handed the phone to his son, who snatched it and shouted 'Go away!'

'Ben, it's Mummy,' Jess said.

'Go away Mummy!'

'Give the phone to Daddy.'

'Yes?' Jamie asked, tickling his son's tummy.

'Bring Ben home.'

'Go away Mummy, go away Mummy!'

'And where would home be, Jess?'

'Here, with me.'

'Really? Because I would say it could just as easily be here, with me.'

'Bring him back, Jamie. You've got no right.'

'I'm his father, Jess. I have every right.'

And with that, he turned his phone off and lay back to listen to the rhythm of the falling rain.

'The law is the law,' Anne Morley said as she slammed the iron down on the board and pressed her eighth church hall tea towel in five minutes. 'What does he think he's playing at, taking the child off like that and refusing to say where they are? It's criminal! It's kidnap! It's entirely irresponsible!' She was still crawling with the shame of being caught out at the hospital, and shame, as her family well knew, made her as tough as old boots.

But her outrage was proving a useful hiding place for another inadequacy of hers too. Unlocking the door back into her peaceful tidy house an hour ago, she had thanked God for answering her secret prayer. He had granted her a reprieve of a few hours more in a house without noise or clutter or demands on her love. The awful fact was, she hadn't been looking forward to bringing her grandson back as much as she should have been.

'I'm sorry to say it again,' she repeated.

No you're not, thought Jess.

'But just who *does* he think he is?'

'He's the child's father,' Derek Morley said equably, aware of his daughter's slumped form at the table, 'and there's no court order...'

'There will be after this. No court in the land will give him equal rights after this.'

'Who said anything about courts?' Jess asked, opening her mouth for the first time since the tirade began.

'As I said, the law is the law.'

'Why does he always have to be the baddie with you? Jamie is not *bad*.'

Anne couldn't tell her daughter that the father of her child would always be bad in her eyes. She was a Christian, she should forgive.

'You don't take a baby away from its mother

266

the day it comes out of—'

'*He*,' Jess said miserably, dunking a second cookie into her milky coffee that had been made by Anne just the way she liked it. 'The day *he* comes. He's called Ben, Mum.'

'I know he's called Ben, dear, I'm just making a point.'

'And he's not a baby, you missed that bit.'

'Give Jamie another ring,' Derek suggested to Jess. 'Tell him you're worried.'

'But I'm not.'

'Of course you are, love, you're just in shock.'

'I'm not. I trust Jamie, he's very good with him, better than I am.'

'He might well be. But the fact is, you want Ben back here with you.'

Jess picked at a loose thread on the hem of her T-shirt.

'You don't take a child away from its – from *his* – mother the day that child comes out of hospital, regardless of *who* you are,' Anne continued ranting from behind her ironing board.

'You do if the mother refuses to come with you to pick him up.'

Jess began to peel at the clear varnish on her fingernails. Now she knew that Ben was safe, the guilt had returned. She wanted to go back to bed, to put the duvet over her head and to sleep, sleep, sleep.

Her mother was too busy dialling a number to hear her admission. 'I'll call Stuart Royden, he'll know what to do.'

'I don't want you to do *anything*!' Jess cried. 'Ben told me to go away. He's happy with his dad, let's just leave it.'

'He'll have been put up to that, for certain sure!'

'He didn't mean it,' Derek reassured her.

Maybe not, but *she* did. Please, Jess felt like begging her mother, please leave it. I'm tired. I want to go back to bed and wake up when I want, and have a bath if I feel like it, and think about it when I'm not hungover. I want more nights like last night. I want to be free. But the truth made her into a monster and her parents thought she was an angel. If only she could sleep...

'Stuart's a better than average community policeman, he was terribly good when Jenny Maxwell's son got done for drink driving.'

'No, Mum, really, leave it.'

Derek leaned forward to put his hand over his daughter's. 'What do you mean, "if the mother refuses to come with you to pick him up"?'

'Well, how *could* she refuse?' Anne butted in, holding the phone to her ear. 'She wasn't *told*. I put my hands up to that. That was *my* mistake. I should have phoned you after Jame—'

'*Jamie*, Mum...'

'After Jamie phoned me...'

'The thing is, I *was* told—'

'Ah, Stuart,' said her mother, putting her hand up to *sssh* her daughter. 'It's Anne Morley here.'

268

'Jamie met me at the school gates,' Jess told her father. 'He wanted the two of us to go and get Ben last night...'

'Stuart,' said Anne into the mouthpiece, 'we have a family crisis...'

'But Carl and Amy had planned a celebration in town and I hadn't had a night out for so long...'

Derek Morley got up wearily and took the phone from his wife. 'Hello, Stuart. I'm so sorry, I think Anne might just have jumped the gun...'

His wife, red hot with humiliation, picked up a folded, pressed tea towel and shook it out on to the board. The iron came down on it with a slam and Anne started pushing it backwards and forwards over the neat rectangle of linen.

'Well?' Derek said to his daughter, whose head was resting on her arms on the table. 'Are you going to call Jamie again or not?'

'Not,' said Jess, sounding a muffled thirteen years old again, and pushed back the chair to run upstairs where the sanctuary of her duvet awaited her.

It took Jamie just fifteen minutes to decamp – the exact time it took for Ringo Starr to read a taped story from the classic collection of *Thomas and Friends* to Ben in the van. The downpour had made the roof of the tent concave with the weight of water and they had a laugh pushing it back out with their heads. After that, they'd unzipped the nylon

269

door to assess the damage and seen the foil tray of their disposable barbecue bobbing away from them in the distance.

'Big Pool,' Ben had said.

'It is a bit, isn't it, mate?'

When Jamie waded to retrieve it, barefoot and with trousers rolled up to the knees, all he could think of as he sloshed through the cold cowpat soup were the *E. coli* warnings from his two-day agriculture and farm mechanization course.

'I know, we'll go and see chocolate man, shall we?' he suggested as he put the soggy tent into the back of his van as far away from the dry sleeping bags and sharp edges of his gardening tools as he could. The desire to be with Don was strong but not impulsive. He'd had it ever since Rob had left the country, and after standing by the oak tree at the water's edge and remembering Geronimo it had turned into a physical ache. It wasn't *just* that there were things he needed to ask.

'Chocolate man,' Ben agreed.

'Good stuff.'

'Good 'tuff.'

Don's barn was not hard to find. There was only one village called Outleigh in Hampshire on the road to Southampton, and helpfully Don had fixed a large sign – 'Don Day Bespoke Kitchens' – at the top of the unmade lane down which he lived. It was as good as balloons tied to the gate of the party house.

They found him in his workshop, bearing down on an electric sander, his nose, mouth and beard covered with a disposable dust mask like the one Mr House had given Jamie for handling mouldy straw. Ben didn't like either the noise or the mask and he burrowed his face between his father's legs and whimpered. The golden particles of wood in Don's grey hair took years off him but his brow was furrowed, although not with concentration as Jamie assumed. Don's phone next to him on the workbench was full of futile attempts at contact with his younger son.

'God alive!' he shouted when he finally looked up and saw them both through the sawdust cloud. 'Where the bloody hell have you been?'

'Big Pool,' Jamie grinned.

And Don could have sworn that the dust cloud parted just then and that every single tiny piece of woody debris he had created floated straight to the concrete floor.

When the knock on Jess's bedroom door finally came a full two hours after she had flounced off, it was a tentative sort of knock – nothing like the assertive rat-a-tat-tat Anne Morley usually employed. At the sound of her father's voice, Jess shoved the pile of university prospectuses under her bed and fought a blush. It wasn't just that he hardly ever came into her bedroom. She didn't want him to discover she had been enjoying herself when she should have been pining for her not-quite-missing son, and nor did she want him to see the irony. Two and a half years ago, her

271

secret reading material had been the instruction leaflet to a pregnancy testing kit.

Derek appeared apologetically, carrying the drop side of Ben's pine cot.

'Sorry to disturb you.'

It was little courtesies like this that made the choice so straightforward for Jess. If she'd spent this much time in her bedroom at Maggie's, the door would have been beaten down hours ago. He leaned the cot side against the wall and disappeared to fetch the base. Jess, suddenly realizing the gravity of the situation, scrabbled to her feet.

'I'm afraid your mother thinks I should build this,' he said, dragging in two more bits.

'It's going in *here*?'

'Apparently.'

'But there's no room.'

'We'll have to make some.'

'Why can't it go in the spare room?'

'*It?*' her father said.

'The cot, I mean.'

They both stood there ashamed of different things.

'Maybe if we take this out,' he said, putting his hand on the cold steel rim of Jess's café chair.

'No! I sit on that to—' She'd been about to say 'paint my nails'.

'We could move the chest...'

Derek caught sight of the pair of jeans on the carpet like a shed skin, the wet towel hanging from the end of the bed, the crumpled duvet on the bottom bunk. She was surely

272

back, but he could see no space for a baby.

'Is he old enough to sleep in a bed? Perhaps he could have the bottom bunk?'

Jess looked at him in horror.

'I'm nineteen years old, Dad.'

Derek let the cot pieces rest against his golfer's shins. 'And your point is?'

'I can't sleep on a top bunk.'

'Then we have a problem,' he said quietly, 'don't we?'

'Chocolate man' had delivered big time as far as Ben was concerned. The toddler sat on the lawn outside the kitchen eating Maltesers straight from the packet and watching the tent flap itself dry on the washing line. But a little distance away, sitting at a table on the terrace drinking beer with Jamie, Don had yet to come up with the goods owed. Whether it was an explanation, an apology, or some new declaration of commitment Jamie was after, he wasn't getting it.

'Your face when you jumped!' Don laughed. 'I'll never forget it.'

'It's *your* face I remember. Relieved, like I'd finally measured up.'

'Where do you get this stuff from?'

'I don't look for it, if that's what you think.'

The admission sat self-consciously between them. Jamie wanted to ask Don when he'd stopped being happy and whether it had anything to do with him but the conversation stuck like phlegm in his throat. Instead he called out a silence filler to Ben.

'That's enough chocolate now, mate, yeah?'

Don got up and walked to the washing line to feel the tent. 'I had to literally force you up there though!'

'It was a long way up! I was small for my age!'

'I told you I'd catch you if you fell, didn't I?'

An image of Jamie snagging his swimming trunks on the bark, Don's arms outstretched like a walking safety net, came to them both.

'I was still scared.'

'You were always scared. Everything was always too high or too noisy or too fast for you...'

'Only because you compared me to Rob all the time.'

'I didn't.'

'You thought it was normal for a child to have no fear.'

'No, I just knew I had to push you to be brave.'

Jamie took the deep breath he'd been practising. 'Yeah, well ... you left me to it in the end though, didn't you?'

Don came to stand directly in front of him. 'The truth is, Jamie, I was there the whole time. On one occasion, I even trod that icy muddy water for what seemed like hours whilst you deliberated up there on your nice dry branch, trying to find the courage to—'

'I don't mean at Big Pool.'

His father ran a hand through his sawdusty hair.

'Nor do I, son.'

On the lawn, Ben was getting his snail out of the red shiny bag.

'So how did you do that, then?' Jamie asked.

'Do what?'

'How did you walk away?'

'I got my marching orders, didn't I?'

'I didn't give you them.'

'I didn't have any choice.'

'You could have chosen *me*.'

'It doesn't work like that.'

'It does if you want it to.'

'No. Ask any father in my position. Ask *yourself*.'

'What?'

'Fathers don't count.'

Something in Jamie snapped then, like one of the twiggy footholds of the oak tree that would sometimes fail under his trainers. 'Well, *I'm* going to count,' he shouted, finding a safe place again. 'No one is going to give *me* my marching orders.'

'Bully for you, Jamie.'

They sat in a slowly boiling silence for a while until Don broke it. 'I did try, you know. I did ask your mother to forgive me.'

'Then you didn't try hard enough.'

Jamie put his beer down on the wrought-iron table and walked over to Ben. After a while, Don followed. The three of them passed the snail between them like William Golding's conch.

'Would it help if I said I'm sorry?' Don asked after a bit.

'Yes.'

'Then I'm sorry, I really am.'

Anne Morley's fridge-freezer was full of fish fingers and pots of strawberry-flavoured fromage frais – compensation, she was hoping, for the empty shelves elsewhere in her grandmother department.

'Is there anything else he likes?' she was asking Jess who was lying on her bunk staring at the springs of the bunk above, where she had been all day. Ben's cot was still resting in pieces against the walls of the lime green and silver bedroom.

'I've sent Dad to get the purple dinosaur...' Anne said, twisting her wedding band round and round her finger.

Jess bit the inside of her cheeks.

'Perhaps the two of you can sleep in the spare room tonight ... and we'll think about where to put him long term tomorrow?'

As Anne bent down to pick up a magazine and tidy a pair of Converse trainers together, a salty droplet fell out of Jess's eye and ran into her hair. Her mother saw it from the foot of the bed and stood there, twisting and twisting her ring.

'What's wrong, Jessica?'

'I can't tell you.'

Anne's fleshy bottom and thighs sank through the ridges of the uncomfortable metal café chair and she suddenly felt more at home.

'Yes you can.'

276

'I can't.'

'Could you perhaps try?'

At the same time that in a barn garden somewhere near Southampton Jamie was taking his deep breath, Jess took hers.

'I don't want to live with him any more...'

Thank you, Lord, Anne said silently. She would never have to grow to love Jamie Day after all.

'Then you don't have to. We'll see to it that—'

The relief of actually saying it out loud made Jess start to sob. 'But it's not normal. I should want to...'

'Why should you? You were very young. You were put in a position that—'

'What's wrong with me?' Jess's words surfaced in fits and starts and a bubble of watery mucus popped from the end of her nose.

'Nothing,' Anne said, dearly wishing she knew how to cuddle. She put out a hand and rested it on Jess's arm. 'Nothing's wrong.'

'I just want to be able to go to university on my own, without the responsibility of having to think of someone else...'

'Of course. I want that for you too ... and there are crèches...'

'He won't understand,' she wept convulsively, 'he'll never forgive me—'

'He will. He's a grown man. He won't be the first to have his heart broken ... we can sort it out...'

'I'm not talking about Jamie, Mum.'

Anne stopped playing with her wedding

ring. The penny dropped, not the metallic sound of something spinning out of control but the plop of a coin into a slot.

'You're talking about Ben,' she said calmly.

And at last, here was something she understood.

Seventeen

As soon as the porridge bowls, egg cups and toast racks had been cleared, Lottie brushed aside a few crumbs and pulled a greetings card out of the handbag she always took to breakfast. She opened the cellophane and flattened the card against the pale green tablecloth too quickly for Douglas to see what was on the front, but his best guesses included a silver cross, a vase of lilies or a shaft of sunlight through trees.

'Anyone I should also be sending my sympathies to this morning?' he enquired, peering over the tea cups for a clue.

'Douglas,' Lottie said, pulling the steel lid off her black fountain pen, 'you have not had a secretary for thirty years, and I am not interested in applying for the vacancy.'

'Not a condolence then?'

'Not today,' she said brightly.

He watched her write, not noticing how her hand shook every time she paused for thought, but thinking instead how lucky he was to have landed up with her. Neither of his wives had ever made him feel quite so grateful.

She was better at surprise than they had been, too. Before sealing the envelope, she –

the most sure-footed woman he'd ever met –
asked him if he would mind checking over
what she had just written. To be useful at
ninety-six was a privilege indeed.

'My handwriting is not up to much these
days so I have kept it short, but sometimes
short can seem rude, so if you think I ought
to add a little news of my own or...'

'Give it here,' he said fondly. 'Let an old
hack decide.'

'Dear Maggie,' he muttered,

How nice to hear from you. I was terribly
sad to hear of Diana's death, not just for
her and her family but because I thought
(wrongly as it turned out) that I had lost
my last link with your mother. Old age
makes one very selfish I'm afraid. Do
come and visit if you would like to. Morn-
ings tend to be better than afternoons as
far as my powers of concentration are
concerned. And of course I remember
you. I delivered you, you know.

With best wishes,
Lottie Buchan-Jones

'Honest,' Douglas said, handing it back,
'but friendly. And you're right about the
afternoons.'

She got up from their breakfast table in the
bay window – Len Hedges and Mary Forbes
had already eaten and gone – and started to
make her careful way towards the hall. Before
she had reached the dining-room door,

Douglas's wheelchair was alongside her. She preferred it when their faces were at the same level because he was too intelligent a man not to hate being looked down upon, but this was only achievable when she sat too, which she wasn't always prepared to do.

A canvas sack hung by the main door into which all mail was dropped, but mostly Lottie liked to put on her tailored coat and walk down the drive to the little red postbox in the wall. If Douglas was coming too, and it looked like it was going to be one of those days when their togetherness went without saying, it would all take too long. A member of staff would have to enter a four-digit number into the keypad to open the wider side door, someone would have to accompany him down the ramp, he'd need a blanket for his legs and so on. She pretended she was too tired to make the effort.

So,' she told him as she heard the letter fall into the sack, 'the secret I have been keeping for fifty years is not going with me to my grave after all.'

'Much healthier all round,' he said. He was too deep-rooted a newsman to react to such blatant bait.

Lottie, in need of more reassurance than she would ever let on, tried to hook him again. 'I thought I might have told it last Christmas you know, when one of the twins, Diana, came to see me so out of the blue like that.'

Not a flicker. She cast her line a third time. 'I was all ready for her to ask me. I dropped

281

some very big hints.'

Douglas was finding the tentative quality to her chatter quite charming.

'It was rather an anti-climax when she didn't pick up on them. I'd sorted through all those letters and cards, do you remember?'

'Last Christmas? My dear Lottie, I don't even remember last night!'

'So you *claim.*'

'Are you doubting my senility?'

'You doubt mine!'

'I do not! I am more than happy to accept there are times when you are as doolally as the rest of us.'

Lottie didn't need to ask *which* times. 'Is it doolally to talk to the dead, do you think?'

'Out loud, certainly.'

'And silently, in the privacy of your own room?'

'Normal behaviour.'

Lottie's lip twitch subsided.

'Let me guess,' he said. 'You have been seeking your old friend Bronwen's advice. You want to know if she minds you revealing her little secret.'

'It wasn't little...'

'But you still talk to her?'

'Often.'

'So what does she make of you and me then?'

'Oh, you're all right.'

'I am, am I?'

Douglas took two wrapped chocolates from the dish on the hall table, dropped them into

282

the pocket of his tweed jacket and gave her a playful wink.

'I offered, you know,' Lottie carried on, 'to tell Diana the truth.'

Ah! The twin who died. Douglas nodded in acknowledgement. He was pleased with himself for still having the mental agility to leap where Lottie leapt.

'I told her there was nothing I didn't know about her mother but she just smiled at me and said she was sure that was true.'

'That rather sounds to me like someone who didn't want to know.'

'I think now she was probably only coming to say goodbye, dear girl.'

They made their way slowly down the carpeted corridor to the day room where the Thursday talk – about badgers this week – was just about to take place. Why the residents of Fir Lodge might want to learn about badgers, no one either knew nor asked.

'Are *you* not curious?' she enquired with a coy tilt of her head.

'They've never interested me much. Filthy creatures, spreading TB and—'

'No, about my secret! I really have kept it for fifty years, you know.'

'Well, there's curious and then there's nosey.'

Lottie clicked her tongue and walked deliberately in front of his wheels.

'Although...' Douglas added, catching an uninviting sight of a large piece of card propped against the door that said *Foraging,*

Hibernation and Sanitation, '...I am tempted to advise you to break your silence in a controlled environment first.'

Lottie peered into the day room. A short man in a shapeless T-shirt with a badger's face on it was holding slides up to the light.

'What could you mean?'

'If the secret has been worth keeping that long, you really ought to get the excitement of its telling out of your system. That's what I always used to advise my new reporters before their first piece to camera. Tell the cameraman first, I used to say. That way, your delivery will be sensitive rather than sensational.'

'Are you saying,' Lottie asked with a smile tugging at the corner of her mouth, 'that you would like to hear it first?'

'What, and miss the badger film? Are you mad?'

In his ground-floor bedroom with the view over the paved terrace where, any day now, it would be warm enough to sit out, Douglas agreed to be the perfect audience.

'No complaints about me drifting off,' Lottie warned. 'There might be something I need to revisit. And no journalistic questioning. It will put me off my stride.'

'And no weeping,' Douglas said, 'because that puts me off mine.'

She settled herself in his winged armchair and concentrated for a moment on the pewter globe on the shelves to the right of the

284

window.

'One of my press awards,' he told her, following her gaze, 'won in 1965 for my coverage of Liverpool's FA Cup Final win.'

'In 1965,' she said, 'no, no, it all began much earlier than that.'

'The little man needs feeding, I'm afraid, Mrs Barton. So if your visitor wouldn't mind waiting outside...'

It isn't just the broad West Country accent of the squat, tubby maternity nurse that makes Lottie want to burst out laughing. It is the idea that Bronwen, famed for feeding her four other babies whenever and wherever they were hungry, might need some privacy in front of her oldest friend. Why, Lottie has seen her reclaim one of them from a vicar's arms during a baptism and undo the buttons of her blouse right by the font before now. Rex had barely known where to put himself!

It is a real shock when Bronwen doesn't wink back. That is when Lottie also notices the lack of flowers and New Baby cards on the bedside table. And then, when the nurse hands the quiet little bundle over, she takes so much trouble to pull the cream cot blanket over the baby's head like a hood that Lottie can't help herself. She opens her own card, which she has chosen especially for the size of its embossed blue *Congratulations!*, and plonks it by the solitary glass of water.

'Do you really want me to wait outside, Bron? I'm longing to see him.'

'No, stay,' her friend says, but she looks at the nurse in a cryptic manner, as if they have prearranged a silent code between them about who can and who can't see this small but special newcomer.

The nurse draws the bed curtains around them and Bronwen carefully opens out the blanket to reveal her three-week-old son.

'Hello, you!' Lottie exclaims, leaning forward and stroking the flat back of his little head and marvelling at the perfection of his miniature low-set ears. 'How dare that naughty nurse try and send me out!'

'She's just trying to be kind,' Bronwen says quickly. 'People can be funny and she's been very protective.'

Lottie isn't listening. She never could take her eyes off a newborn.

'Oh, this is no good, I can't see you properly here, can I? Big fat Mummy's in the way!'

Lottie hurries round the end of the bed to sit on Bronwen's other side. The baby's face is perfectly round but his colouring is delicate. He is a good size but he still looks fragile.

She pulls more of the blanket away to see his tiny toes but they are tinged with blue.

'Is he cold?'

'They don't believe in swaddling,' Bronwen says. 'I wish they would.'

She clasps his foot motherly in her hot hand and holds it tight. At the same time, Lottie takes the baby's palm and traces a finger down its crease.

'That's how they diagnosed him,' Bronwen tells her. 'Just that, and a little fold on the inner corner of his eyes.'

His short limbs squirm and his face crinkles as he begins to wake up and smell his mother's milk.

'Oh Bron, he's so sweet! Hurry up and give him a name!'

Bronwen adjusts herself ready to feed. She pinches her swollen nipple between her thumb and finger and toys with it around the baby's mouth to try and interest him, but his face lies against her large workhorse of a breast as if he is far too comfortable to move. Lottie unwraps the tissue paper of the present she has bought and makes the powder-blue knitted teddy bear dance on the baby's long white brushed-cotton dress. His miniature lips begin to tug almost imperceptibly, so leisurely and detached, so unlike the engrossed sink-plunging technique her own boys perfected, that Lottie has a sense of his character already.

'He's not going to do anything he doesn't want to do just because a short fat nurse tells him to!'

She watches as his eyes, which slant upwards and outwards as she had imagined they would, start to close. He really is truly beautiful.

'We haven't quite got the hang of this yet,' Bronwen says apologetically as the milk flows down her nightdress instead of into his mouth. 'The sucking doesn't seem to come naturally and he splutters rather, then he falls asleep before he's had enough and...'

'Bron, this is your *fifth* baby – what are you talking about?'

'It's different, Lottie.'

Lottie takes hold of the baby's translucent foot and tickles it. His brand new lips begin to suckle again in tiny movements.

'*Every* baby is different. Every baby is unique.'

'Did you rehearse that?' Bronwen asks without looking up.

The comment is so harsh, Lottie is momentarily lost for words. By the time she finds one – a hoarse and lonely 'no' – it is too late. Tears as well as milk are streaming from Bronwen now.

'Because I wouldn't blame you if you had,' her friend says quietly. 'Nobody seems to know what to say, least of all Rex.'

'Not now!' Douglas suddenly shouted.

A knock on his bedroom door to tell them the badger man was about to start his talk brought Lottie skidding back to the present. She had been talking with her eyes shut and the shock of opening them again made them water. She took a tissue from the sleeve of her cardigan and wiped her eyes.

'So *had* you rehearsed it?' Douglas asked once the care assistant had said 'Suit yourselves' and they had replied that they would, thank you.

'You said you wouldn't ask questions,'

Lottie said.

'Ah, but you said you wouldn't cry.'

He took the two wrapped chocolates he'd pinched from the hall table out of his tweed jacket pocket and passed her one. Lottie unwrapped it and popped it into her mouth. The sweet caramel melted her resolve.

'It's possible I might have rehearsed it a little,' Lottie said, smoothing the wine-coloured velour of the armrest with her fingers so that it lightened and then darkened. 'You couldn't have blamed me. I had to go into that hospital armed with every positive thought I could muster. Someone had to.'

'Oh, so you *knew*?'

'Knew what?'

'You knew *before* you saw the baby that he had problems?'

'Of course. I had Rex's letter, didn't I?'

She reached into her handbag and pulled out several age-old envelopes, held together with an elastic band.

'This one,' she said after some deliberation. 'Read it. It still has the power to shock me.'

Douglas took it from her eagerly and quickly found his glasses. He liked a story that had a reliable source.

September 2nd 1956

Dear Lottie,

I took the liberty this morning of opening your letter to Bronwen, a decision

289

which I trust you will accept as a sensible one when I tell you why.

You ask why you have received no news of the baby and wonder if all is well. I am sorry to say that it is not. Bronwen gave birth to a boy a fortnight ago, an event which would have been the cause of much joy had it not been for his not immediately apparent disability.

We decided not to announce his birth in the traditional way since neither of us feel it is a cause for celebration. The child suffers from what the medical experts refer to as 'mongolian idiocy', a mentally defective condition often found in children born to older mothers, and we have already been told that his life will not have much value.

Bronwen and I are still in a state of shock as to how this can have happened. It is a genetic disorder and yet we have four healthy girls to prove otherwise. Before you think it, I have asked about the possibility of there being a weakness in the male line but I have been assured by at least two consultants that no one is to blame, although Bronwen's age is a factor.

We think it is best for the girls if we speak very little of this. They know their mother is safe and that the baby is not well enough to come home. That is as far as we have gone in explaining to them the situation. I am firmly of the opinion that it is a question of least said, soonest mended.

We will continue to take advice from the doctors as to the care the child will obviously need but as I am sure you will appreciate, there are many decisions in front of us and I trust you will accept it when I respectfully ask you to please stay out of them all.

For the moment, Bronwen is staying in hospital for feeding purposes until the child is strong enough to take his nourishment from a bottle. When that day comes, the likelihood is that he will be placed with a team of people who have the knowledge and experience to look after him.

If you have any urgent questions, I would prefer that you direct them to me and leave Bronwen to recover from the trauma of both the birth and its tragic outcome without adding to her stress. Do not labour under any misconception that you can do anything to help. He will not amount to anything.

My best wishes,
Rex

Douglas let the letter fall into his lap, breathless with disgust.

'I can't believe you've kept something so worthy of the bin for so long,' he said eventually.

'Isn't it abhorrent?'

'It's such an offensive letter that I wonder

why you didn't destroy it there and then.'

'I am surprised to hear you say that,' Lottie replied, a little put out at the implied criticism. In truth, she had often wondered the same herself. 'I would have thought the journalist in you...'

'Oh no, this isn't a story for the masses,' Douglas said, 'this is too personal.'

'Perhaps I wanted to keep it as evidence.'

'Of his bad character? To use against him?'

'That may have been my intention at first, of course. I was so furious at him not letting me know sooner, and even crosser at being told to stay away, that I think I thought I might show it to Bron one day, to prove what a pig she had married.'

'And did you?'

'There was no need. She already knew, but she wasn't the sort to leave him.'

'So you got on the next train of course, and went straight to her, despite this cold-hearted request that you stay away?'

'I did,' Lottie said, her brimming eyes ablaze with ancient defiance. Even from a distance of fifty years, the stand seemed daring. Rex had been a man who inspired fear, in her, in his wife and his daughters. The thought of facing up to him suddenly made her very tired.

Douglas held the letter an inch from his glasses, scanning for a particular phrase.

'Mongolian idiocy?' he said incredulously.

'That's what they called it back then.'

'Mongols,' he nodded. 'We all did. Outrageous when you think of it.' He folded the paper and put it back in its envelope. 'So why *did* you keep it?'

'I suppose I wanted proof that the child was born. I must have realized how quickly he was to disappear. He was written right out of the story, you know.'

She sighed a big sigh. 'There.'

The secret was finally out. Bronwen and Rex Barton had had a son, but they had given him away. Now she wasn't the only living soul who knew that. Lottie wanted to reach out and touch Douglas, to put her hand on his, to thank him for finally relieving her of the burden but tears were too close.

'No room for a Mongolian idiot,' Douglas said, shaking his head.

'It wasn't called Down's Syndrome until the 1960s...'

Lottie knew these things. The condition had loomed large for her for half a century, articles leaping from the page, programmes shouting to be watched from the TV pages. Her words were beginning to slur as she felt herself falling into a nap.

'...after the man who first invented...'

'Diagnosed,' Douglas corrected.

'Thank you...'

He watched her head fall against the wing of the chair, waiting for her jaw to drop slightly and for her breathing to even out before he put his hands on the pushrims of his wheelchair and went to find them both a cup of tea.

Eighteen

'And this then is the south-facing back garden...'

Already, the shiny young couple trailing after the estate agent were the enemy. They had spent the last hour poking forensically around Maggie's home, and now she was going to have to listen to them sizing up Jamie's lawn-mowing skills.

The agent's unctuous voice seeped through the gaps in the timber of the Wendy house where she had been lurking since their arrival. It was typical that her first viewers should book an appointment on the very day she needed no distractions. Her first instinct had been to postpone but then she had thought of Rob in Indonesia, Jamie and Ben in Southampton and all those empty rooms upstairs and she had heard herself saying of course, that's fine, any time.

'As you can see, there is plenty of scope for an extension...'

She bobbed beneath the window of Arthur's outhouse and pretended to be sorting the washing, not wanting to be discovered sitting in an old deckchair among the rusting tools and discarded seed packets writing a list of

questions on the back of a cereal packet pulled from the recycling bin.

Did I come into the world gently?
What did I look like?
Did Bronwen feed me?
Did she ever talk about me?

'We would have to get rid of that old shed.'
Through a slit, Maggie could see the woman's
pale calves and pink moccasins.

'It's an eyesore.'

'I understand the planning permission for a
laundry room and conservatory is still live...'

'Why didn't they go ahead?'

'Let's just say there was a change of circumstances.'

'I could tell when I walked in that it wasn't
a happy house...'

Their insensitive drivel trailed away as they
wandered towards the shrubbery under
which two cats and three hamsters were
buried. 'Don't even dare think you can dig up
the escallonia!' she wanted to shout after
them.

A wash load of nylon tights were hanging
out of the tumble-dryer door like entrails and
she caught a few static crackles as she pulled
them out and flicked them apart. She was
feeling a little electrical herself – the flash of
unbidden energy with which she'd greeted
the viewing couple had unnerved her, she
didn't want to be the sort of vendor to lick
prospective purchasers' boots in return for a
morsel of positive feedback. But her sparks
were actually nothing to do with the sale of

her home at all. Since receiving Lottie's letter, self-discovery was breathing down her neck and she and the elusive truth were rubbing up against each other at last, creating a lovely friction.

'You're burning particularly bright tonight,' Stefan had said in the pub yesterday. 'Is this the new Maggie?'

Maybe it was, she thought as the old wooden door behind her creaked open and she span round to deliver her spiel.

'The shed is not include— Oh, Don!'

Standing in the doorway was her ex-husband, wearing a brown linen shirt he must have had for at least seven years. She could remember trying to iron it and tossing it back on the pile in frustration.

'I thought you were going to be the people looking round the house...'

'Come to make you an offer you can't refuse?'

'It would have to be a good one – they're *so* rude.'

'I've just seen them shaking the rotten fence post,' he said, picking up an old hose connector that had never worked. 'Don't you ever throw anything away?'

'Not if I can help it.'

He ran a finger up a stack of plastic flowerpots and inhaled the familiar air which smelt – had always smelt – of dusty bulbs, Daz and trapped sunshine. When the boys were young, they used to spend Arthur's pocket money on something called Space Dust which exploded in their mouths like tiny fireworks, and he could hear the echo of some going off now.

'Well, you never know when you might need it again, do you?' she said.

'There is that...'

Maggie shifted the laundry basket with her foot.

'Anyway, if you've come to see how I feel about Jamie and Ben living with you...'

'I haven't. I know you're fine...'

He tapped a paintbrush with rock-hard red bristles against a jam jar.

'Good, because I really am. I think it's right for all of us.'

'Actually, I was going to suggest—'

'I wish they'd hurry up,' Maggie interrupted, peering through the grubby glass.

'Leave them to it. The longer they stay, the more likely they are to buy.'

'But I'm meeting someone this afternoon.'

Disappointment wiped the hope from Don's face and she enjoyed depriving him of the comfort of knowing the someone was a ninety-year-old woman. He scraped the moss growing along the bottom of the window frame.

'So how did you know I was in here?' she asked.

'Powers of deduction.'

'Am I that predictable?'

'In some ways, you haven't changed at all,' he said, fiddling with a peg from the small wooden table before posting it into its faded cloth basket, 'but in others, you're—'

'I'll take that as a compliment,' she said, running a pair of tights up her arm to check for ladders.

'It was going to be one.'

Maggie threw the knotted tights into a box of rubbish.

'Has Jamie sent you to pick something up?'

'No.'

'What does bring you here then?'

'You do,' he said.

'Colin!'

It was the weave of Len Hedges' knitted scarf that finally brought it back to Lottie. She regurgitated the name in the middle of a silence that, although entirely companionable, had been going on just a little too long.

'Colin?' Douglas asked. 'Who's Colin?'

The three of them were sitting on the terrace in front of Douglas's bedroom window, watching a gardener dead-head the climbing white rose bush that covered the iron pergola over the path. A game of draughts, set up twenty minutes ago, sat untouched on the table between them.

'Rex and Bronwen's son,' Lottie said in a tone implying 'who else?'. 'Len, how long have you had that scarf?'

Len Hedges, ten years Lottie's junior but her senior in terms of mental deterioration, wobbled his head as if to loosen gummed-up thoughts, reminding Lottie of the way she had to rattle her tin of travel sweets if she hadn't opened it for a while.

'This scarf?'

Len took off the floppy knitted length and held it up as if seeing it for the first time. Lottie doubted you could still buy wool in such a colour. Once, Air Force blue had been everywhere.

'What would you need to know that for?'

'I don't *need* to know, I was just wondering if it was...'

'1957?' Douglas suggested.

'Was it really?' Len said, tipping back his head in amazement. 'Well, I never. I wouldn't have been able to put a date on it myself but...'

'No, Len, that was a guess,' Douglas explained. 'How would I know how long you've had that scarf for?'

'Well it was a very good one then, very good indeed I should think.'

'So *was* it about then?'

'Was what?'

Lottie and Douglas swapped their 'God help us!' look.

'Can I see it?' she asked.

Len passed it over. On the way back, his hand hovered over the draughts board and moved a black counter.

'Your go, Douglas,' he said, leaning back with satisfaction. And so the game between the two men finally began.

Lottie sat there fingering the scarf's furled edges. The gaps between the stitches were big enough to poke a tiny finger through. Perhaps Len's late wife had once been a hospital visitor because it could have been knitted on the very same needles, with the very same batch of wool, as that peculiar little vest Colin had been wearing when she and Bronwen had visited him on his first birthday...

'Where are you taking me?' Bronwen asks, settling her pregnant bulk into the front seat of Lottie's MG Magnette Varitone. She is back in the dreaded royal-blue maternity two-piece again. Its round neck with the line of smocking above the breasts makes her look like she is wearing a tent. No wonder she is depressed, Lottie thinks, living in that. Bronwen has never gone for the chic approach – their styles are very different – but nor has out-and-out frumpy ever been her way.

'I'm not telling you yet,' Lottie says, pressing the starter button, suddenly wishing she didn't look quite so trim in her yellow cap-sleeved dress with its fitted top and bell-shaped skirt. It was supposed to have an encouraging effect, a party dress, to make the day feel special. Instead, it just highlights Bron's mental state. They all know the significance of August the eleventh but no one is prepared to come out with it.

The map to the hospital is in the glove compartment, along with a selection of wrapped presents – a rattle, a cloth book, a green felt rabbit, a white cotton vest with powder blue piping. When she'd tied the ribbon around them back in London, Lottie had been sure she was doing the right thing. Now, the risk of the whole idea backfiring is looming much larger. But, she tells herself as she takes the walnut gearstick knob in her hand, it is worth a try. Someone has to confront the denial of the last eleven months.

They drive away from the rambling family home which has become so full of clutter during the last year that Lottie feels sure it would make *anyone* gloomy, and she gives two farewell hoots of the horn. Rex and the four girls are already out of sight, which doesn't surprise her. The children have no doubt returned to their brunch – the only meal they ever seem to eat – and Rex's impatience to see the back of them all was written all over his stony face.

'You didn't have to do this, you know,' Bronwen says weedily. 'I'm all right, really I am.'

She isn't all right. She hasn't been all right since the day she abandoned her baby son to the authorities, and this latest pregnancy has so far been a disaster for her spirits, not to mention her blood pressure.

'I know I didn't have to,' Lottie replies cheerily, 'but I *want* to.'

Her miserable friend says exactly the same thing an hour later, as they leave the maternity wear section of a large department store. Bronwen's step – although clearly the gait of a woman nearing the end of another tiring confinement – seems lighter now that she is wearing clothes that at least *try* to put on a show. The butter-coloured rayon of the skirt

301

falls in more flattering folds, and the crisp sailor neckline of the cream blouse gives her summer complexion a lift that the royal blue had not.

'I thought you could do with a boost.'

'But I shouldn't have let you spend so much on an outfit that will only be worn for a few weeks,' Bronwen frets.

'Nonsense! You look gorgeous.'

'I hardly think so.'

'Well, you can always wear it next time round!'

It is meant to be a joke but Bronwen has forgotten how to laugh.

'This is the very last baby I shall be having, I assure you.'

A shop assistant hovering by a glass cabinet full of Spirella corsets shoots Lottie a look, but Lottie shoots it straight back, return to sender.

'You deserve it,' Lottie tells her as they turn from the shop floor into the stairwell.

'I don't. I've been worse than useless, not just to you, but to the girls and Rex and...'

'Cut yourself some slack, Bron, you're too hard on yourself. Anyway, you'll thank me for it this afternoon.'

It is a deliberately tantalizing comment and she waits to be quizzed further. Apart from that one question when she'd first got in the car, Bronwen has asked nothing about this mystery tour. In fact, she hasn't instigated any conversation at all.

'I said you'll thank me for it this afternoon.'

'I know where you're taking me,' Bronwen says quietly as they emerge back into the hustle and bustle of the haberdashery department. 'I'd just rather pretend I didn't.'

The hospital where Colin has spent his first year is a grand-scale Victorian institution set in its own grounds that Lottie feels sure would once have had 'Lunatic Asylum' cast across its high, forbidding iron gates. These days, it is called Tor Vale and the gates are open as they turn in. A friendly security man writes down their names and gives them directions for parking and as Lottie drives the Magnette up the wide drive, she is relieved to see all manner of people – albeit some in their dressing gowns – wandering freely around the lawns. A little further away, an exercise class of sorts is going on under a tree. No children though, she notices with unease...

Bronwen has been silent for the last mile.

'It's much nicer than I...' Lottie says, by way of encouragement. 'I was imagining something more...'

'They said he would need constant supervision,' Bronwen interrupts in a sudden fusillade of words, 'and even then, he won't ever achieve anything. They said he would get too big to handle and we wouldn't be able to cope. They don't know their own strength.'

'You don't know *yours*,' Lottie challenges.

'This would finish things between you and Rex if he ever found out,' Bronwen blurts back. Her voice is tense and cross, and Lottie squeezes the steering wheel to stop herself saying something she might regret.

'Are you *really* still thinking of Rex?'

'The last time we were here, it was him at the wheel...'

Yes, driving in the other direction, Lottie wants to say.

'Do you want me to turn around?'

'No,' Bronwen answers almost inaudibly.

Lottie slows down for a man in a pair of trousers that are too short for him to cross their path, but he stops in front of the car and puts his hand up like a traffic control policeman.

'What do we do now?' Lottie asks, amused, but still Bronwen doesn't look up. Her eyes have been firmly fixed on her lap – or what used to be her lap – ever since they came through the gates.

'Drive on,' she says quickly, sounding frightened.

'I can't. I'll run him over.'

Lottie pulls on the handbrake and opens her door but before she can talk to him, the man stands back and ushers them on.

'Thank you!' she calls gaily to him out of the open window. He slams his hand down hard on the roof of the car and Bronwen jumps.

'He's harmless,' Lottie reassures her, wondering if he has lived here all his life and then realizing she doesn't want to think about it if he has.

They are silent as they park the car, skirt around the grey brick walls and walk up the wide steps to the main entrance. Lottie tries to see through the ground-floor windows, which have bars across them like all the others, but despite it being a summer's afternoon the curtains are as tightly drawn as the expression on Bronwen's face.

They are met in the cavernous reception by a uniformed nurse with wiry grey hair and tortoiseshell spectacles who manages to take Lottie, with her barely contained expression of impatience, for the mother. She directs all conversation her way as if Bronwen is invisible. But when Lottie opens her mouth to correct her, Bronwen grabs her arm and shakes her head.

They follow the nurse's efficient footsteps down corridor after corridor – left through double doors, right through a single one, straight on at the stairs. The hospital is an echoing labyrinth and they are being led to their treasure. Each time they turn a corner, there is a lift behind an ornate ironwork cage, but they take none of them.

'Wait here, please,' the nurse says at the entrance to a ward. As the swing doors open and a blast of infant noise shatters the reverberating silence, Lottie catches sight of a row of cots – twenty maybe – lining the right-hand wall. She counts at least three children standing up, holding on to the bars. Bronwen does not look.

'Would you like to see in?' Lottie asks her. 'I'm sure if we asked, we could see where he—'

'No,' Bronwen answers, and starts walking in a small agitated circle, wringing her hands.

The doors swing open again, the same nurse comes out, gives them a tight unfriendly smile and tells them someone will be out to see them in a minute.

After what seems at least ten, a large black pram pushed by a younger woman emerges. The hood is down and the flattened back of its infant passenger's head with the little low-set ears poking just above the supporting pillow makes Bronwen gasp. She recognizes even this, and puts one hand over her mouth. The other goes straight to the small hand clutching the cloth rim.

She keeps hold of the hand as if it were a lifeline. The nurse trundles down another corridor, not hearing the shrieks and the reprimands, the clatters and the bangs and the comforting noise of a baby bawling at top volume coming from the other side of the doors they pass. Lottie walks behind the three of them, catching shaves of Colin's face, an eye here, a rosy cheek there, as the nurse's body sways from side to side to reveal him in tantalizing glimpses.

Outside an open door to a vast room, empty save for a few lost armchairs, the pram comes to a halt and the young nurse says, 'There we are! If you want to take baby for a walk, there is a ramp to the garden just beyond those doors. I'll come and collect...'

She hesitates.

'Him,' Bronwen says sharply. 'He's a boy.

His name is Colin.'

'Oh, we know that, don't we, Colin?' the nurse says brightly, lifting him out, blanket and all. He looks like he knows her, trusts her, loves her even. His legs swing in the air redundantly, and when Bronwen reaches out her arms to take him, he reaches out his too.

'Come on,' she utters tenderly, 'come to...'

As the nurse hands him over, the blanket falls away to reveal a square but wilted little body, dressed only in a towelling nappy and a blue short-sleeved woollen vest.

'Will he be cold?'

'Not if you cuddle him!'

Inside the bare room, they sit themselves down in the chairs, Colin resting against Bronwen's large pregnant bump. She is touching him all over as if to remember him by Braille. Her hands instinctively massage his unclothed arms and legs, trying to stroke life into his floppy limbs. He rewards her with a fleeting smile and she melts. For a split second, as she unwraps his presents and shows them to him, Lottie sees sheer joy cross her friend's face again.

'Let's take this funny old thing off, shall we?' Bronwen says to her son. She pulls his arms expertly through the holes and, with one easy movement, the knitted garment is lying on the arm of the chair. Colin's naked tummy is too much to resist and she bends her lips to kiss its warmth. He smells just like all her other children and she will never forget that. When he is dressed in his new vest with the powder blue piping, Bronwen kisses him again. Keeping him safe with one arm around his slender body, she does something she prefers Lottie not to draw attention to. She picks up the Air Force blue woolly vest and with a deft flick, tucks it under her blouse and into the straining waistband of her skirt.

'Shall we prop him in cushions on the floor?' she suggests.

They try, between them, to sit him up, but he keeps falling sideways.

'Put him on his tummy,' Bronwen says, too large to get down with him. 'See if he will roll over?'

But he just lies there, pulling his head off the floor and smiling as if he knows what a stolen delight he is.

Lottie thinks of the book she has borrowed from the library, the one she had been intending to pass on to Bronwen until she had read it herself and thought better of it. The depressing chapters hold out precious little help for the future. Children like Colin, it claims, are 'ineducable', 'incapable of being toilet-trained', 'unable to learn more than a few simple words'. She doesn't believe it. She has seen plenty of children like Colin before now, being walked through the streets by their elderly parents, looking happy and alert, placid but affectionate, evoking kindness wherever they go. The book's footnote is the meanest shock of all, adding quite incidentally that these children seldom live beyond their teens, usually succumbing to chest infections or a weak heart. The horrible thought of it makes her shake her head.

Colin shakes his back.

'Did you see that?' Bronwen laughs.

She is transfixed by her beautiful son. And so she should be, thinks Lottie. It is impossible to imagine him growing into the kind of child that the abhorrent book describes – a squat imbecile with a long tongue lolling permanently out of a drooling mouth. She will burn it when she gets back to London, and pay whatever fine the library demands.

'Let's take him home,' she says impetuously before she can stop herself, and her clumsy outburst brings the snatched afternoon to an end long before it should.

'I win!' Douglas shouted from his wheelchair on the front terrace of Fir Lodge.

'Hmm?'

Lottie pushed her little finger through a hole in Len's scarf and looked up to see what was going on. Len was asleep, his mouth open and his arms folded across his sloping tummy. Douglas was stacking up the red counters and putting them back in the draughts box.

'Welcome back,' he said. 'Had a good trip?'

'How can you call that a victory?' she contested. 'Your opponent is asleep!'

'Oh, it's dog eat dog in the world of nonagenarian board games, you know.'

Lottie took a breath to laugh but the moment was whisked away, because there, standing in front of her, between the sleeping Len and a tub of geraniums, was Bronwen. She rubbed her wrinkled eyes – all this time travelling was playing with her mind – but the vision remained.

'Mrs Buchan-Jones?' the Bronwen mirage said. 'I do hope I'm not too early.'

A freckled hand – Bronwen's hand – came towards her.

'It's so nice to meet you. I'm Maggie Day.'

Nineteen

Stefan was picking tomatoes in the neglected greenhouse, wondering with each pull who would eat them now that Di wouldn't, when his unventilated peace was snatched from him.

'A *brother*?' he said incredulously into his brick of a mobile phone.

'I know,' Maggie replied, 'it's hard to take in, isn't it?'

He couldn't find the words to speak.

'Sorry, Stefan, I should have asked if this was a good time. I mean, were you doing anything?'

The fact that he was waiting for a call to come through about a bid he'd placed on eight nineteenth-century ladderback oak dining chairs was nothing. He pushed the Tupperware bowl full of his fat red harvest on to the slatted wood and ran a composty hand across his beaded brow.

'Rex and Bronwen had a son?' he repeated, wondering if he could possibly be misunderstanding. 'Di had a brother?'

'Not just Di...'

'Do you think she knew?'

'He was born the year before me, which is

why Bronwen gave me away, do you see?'

'Younger than Di then?'

'It all makes sense now, doesn't it? If you can't keep one baby, then how can you keep...'

'She never mentioned him...'

'Because she didn't know! I thought about ringing Amanda to see if—'

'Not yet, Maggie, not yet.'

Lottie's revelation was spinning round and round in Maggie's head like a clay figure on a potter's wheel – a baby boy called Colin, locked away and forgotten, then along comes another child, a healthy girl to taunt her parents with their original sin. Me, Maggie had to keep reminding herself, me! A birth so quick that Lottie herself had played midwife. She caught *me*! The faster the story span, the more distorted it became. Bits were flying off here, there and everywhere.

'When then?' she asked impatiently.

'Have you eaten?'

'No, but I...'

'I've got a nice bit of ham...'

Stefan walked out of the airless greenhouse and plonked himself on to a garden seat. He could hear Maggie's breathing, quick and shallow with the exertion of trying not to spew too much shock. So she had not been the first child her parents gave away. Bronwen and Rex had had a son the year before, a Down's Syndrome baby, the baby who didn't come home. Her story was not *the* story.

'Di ought to have known this,' he said when

he could.

Maggie wanted to say that Di was dead, that it was the ones who were left who mattered now. Instead, she murmured her agreement.

'Do we know where he's buried?'

Stefan's question came at Maggie through her stomach. A picture of an untended grave passed across her mind, a bee buzzing around wild honeysuckle, a plane flying overhead.

'Oh God, I can't believe I didn't even think to ask.'

'But we at least know when he died?'

Wind buffeted the line at Maggie's end.

'Perhaps you should give yourself a few days,' Stefan said into the void, 'and then go back and see Lottie again.'

'She had a letter from Rex saying the baby wouldn't make it to adulthood.'

'Well, I don't suppose it would be too hard to find out. We know his date of birth, do we?'

In the driver's seat of her layby-parked car, Maggie hit her chest with the flat of her free hand, remembering the slim leather-bound diary in Bronwen's box, with the word 'Birthdays' in gold on its red front. Three days down from Jamie's date, on August the eleventh, Bronwen had simply written the letter 'C'. Not Catastrophe or Calamity or Collusion then, but Colin.

'Bronwen's summer depressions ... that's why she hated August...'

Stefan picked up the bowl of tomatoes and took a small plump one from the top. Its

313

seeds burst in relief against his teeth. They always got a glut of them about now and Di used to make chutney with the surfeit.

'Come when you're ready,' he said to Maggie. There was a jar of it from last year still in the larder. They could have some with the ham.

It wasn't an entirely conscious decision of Maggie's to go to Bronwen's grave next, but that is where she ended up. All along the brief stint of motorway, for the entire twenty miles of the dual carriageway and for the remaining half hour of winding country lanes, she mulled over Lottie's advice.

'I wonder if you might now perhaps be able to forgive your mother her transgressions?' the old woman had asked as they'd embraced each other goodbye, her silvery head of hair barely reaching the younger one's bosom. The hug came easily, which made such sweet sense once she'd learned that Lottie's touch was the first she had ever felt.

'Had I hair? Was I large? Did I cry?' she'd asked, ravenous for detail after half a century of starvation.

'You came to me as quiet as a mouse,' Lottie had told her. 'And you were no noisier the few times I saw you as a child. Meek and mild Maggie. That's how I thought of you.'

Transgressions! Maggie drank in the word as she drove. To hear Bronwen's lifelong friend admit the wrongdoing was a piece of magic really. She could so easily, out of

314

loyalty, have adopted a least-said-soonest-mended approach. Because after all, what did it matter to her? But no, the wonderful, tiny, shimmering Lottie Buchan-Jones had had her say at last. Everything about her had glistened as she spoke – her frill-edged powder blue cardigan with its argent thread, her lick of peachy lipstick, the glass brooch at the neck of her luminous silk blouse.

'Bron should never have let Rex rule her the way she did. I fell out with her over it more than once. The way she let her babies go – I can't say it didn't make me feel differently about her...'

Lottie's hypnotic story had flashed with so much candid opinion that Maggie had found herself in the unusual position of becoming Bronwen's chief apologist. How clever was that?

'But she had no choice! She had four other children to raise. What else could she have done?'

'What hundreds of other women in her position did, of course. Stand up to him, do what she knew was right!'

'But there was so little help for children like Colin in those days.'

'In those days? Dear girl, it was nearly the sixties! There was plenty of help, if she'd only looked for it!'

'Did you say these things to her too?'

'I speak as I find,' the diminutive nonagenarian had said sincerely, 'and if I were you, I would start doing the same.'

My fairy godmother, Maggie decided as she drove through the village where Bronwen had lived and died. She caught me once, and now she's catching me again, or at least she's showing me where the safety net is.

Keeping her head down (for this was Amanda territory), she crossed the pub car park and slipped surreptitiously through the side gate to the churchyard. She had to cast her mind years back to Bronwen's funeral to get her bearings. Which way out of the porch had they followed the coffin for the interment? She walked quickly down the path that ran along the yew tree lined wall – if anyone had spotted her, they might have thought she was on a secret rendezvous, a private assignation with someone she'd rather not be seen with. Which in a way, of course, she was.

In Don's kitchen, Jamie was concentrating so hard on standing his ground that he didn't realize Jess had already conceded it. He was so intent on having his say that he had barely noticed her new hair, cropped like a pixie's. Student hair, she called it, her schoolgirl tresses swept up by a trainee from the salon floor.

On the table between them was a University of Southampton prospectus, a printed page from a horticultural college website, a bus timetable, a brochure from Happy Days Nursery and a projected Timetable of Care, written in his own hand.

'A degree from Southampton puts you in

the top rank of UK graduates,' he was telling her, putting into practice a pitch he'd been preparing for days. 'You need three B's to do the four-year BSc Chemistry with foundation year course, and you've already got your maths. I've been guaranteed a place on the NVQ One and Two Horticulture course which I can do over two or four years depending on how fast I want to go. A bus to and from Southampton stops at the bottom of this lane three times a day and—'

'I agree...' Jess said.

'There's a childcare grant available, based on eighty-five per cent of your income, and your student loan should be about four and a half thousand quid so that should cover the nursery fees. I've booked an appointment for you to see it at eleven. It's in the village, it's got a little garden and—'

'OK...'

'And Dad has offered me some work. It'll just be some basic sanding and undercoating at first but I reckon I could earn a couple of hundred quid a week like that and still fit in my course work. He's saying he doesn't want any rent and that I should look at it as his way of making up for the last five years. Which I've told him isn't possible, just in case you think I'm being bought, but—'

'Hey, Jamie, I said OK...'

The last discussion Jess wanted to venture into was the absent parent one, so it was a relief when the whole point of their conversation suddenly appeared in the open doorway, crying. Derek Morley was hovering behind his grandson, apologizing.

'He won't stay with us, I'm afraid, and Anne is developing a headache.'

Jess swooped Ben up and wiped his cheek but the child swung his upper torso away from her and stretched his arms out to his father.

'He's not sure about your hair,' Jamie laughed quickly, taking Ben and putting him on the floor. The child hid behind his daddy's legs and wrapped an arm round each of his thighs.

'He'll get used to it.'

'I like it.'

'Why don't you and Mum come in?' Jess suggested to her father. 'There's no need to sit in the car.'

'Cup of tea?' Jamie offered.

'No, we're all right,' Derek answered, already disappearing. 'We've brought our own thermos.'

Jess shook her head at the empty doorway.

'They're driving me insane.'

'So I'm still the bad boy, am I?'

Jamie opened a cupboard and took out a bag of sultanas. He chose an apple from the fruit basket and a knife from the drawer and began cutting the fruit into chunky slices on the built-in marble block. Jess shrugged.

'I can cope with that,' he said, 'but what I've really been trying to say, Jess, is that I'm not prepared to give Ben up.'

'I know you're not.'

'But I *do* know I have to let you go...'

He scooped the apple and sultanas into a plastic bowl and put it on the table with the flourish of a cocktail waiter offering a complimentary dish of nuts. Ben wriggled from his hideout and climbed on to a chair to eat.

'Us aside, Jess, I've seen what happens to part-time fathers and I'm not going to let that happen to me. I won't have less and less to do with Ben until I barely count.'

'I don't want that any more than you do.'

'And whilst you're at college, it makes sense for him to live with me...'

'I agree.'

Jamie tossed the square apple core across the unit into the compost bin and missed.

'You do?'

'If it's what you want.'

'Is it what *you* want?'

Jess ran a hand through her new short hair.

'It's not like I'm giving him away, is it? I'll always be his mum, I'll always be here for him. And if you want to be with him...'

'I really do.'

'Then that's how it should be.'

'But?' Jamie said, his voice right on the very edge. 'Go on, say it.'

'Say what?'

'I can hear a "but"...'

'No, there is no but,' she told him, 'not this time.'

Amanda Barton had long had difficulties with the fact that her father was not buried in

319

the same area of the churchyard as her mother. Her over-developed sense of loyalty towards her parents meant that whenever she felt the frequent urge to visit Bronwen's grave, which was in a sunny corner plot close to open countryside, she was also obliged to visit Rex's on the north-facing side, which was overlooked by a pub car park. The dilemma never posed itself the other way around because she always went to Bronwen's first.

Turning the stiff outside tap on the wall of the neighbouring church hall had left an imprint on the fleshy pad of her left palm, but her right hand was carrying a tin jug full of water and she couldn't rub away the soreness like she wanted to. Instead, she pressed it against her lips and sucked.

From a distance, Maggie – volcanic with enlightenment since her visit to Lottie – misinterpreted the movement. She jumped to the conclusion that Amanda's hand over her mouth was a gesture of dismay, but for once the imagined sisterly shortfall didn't hurt her. She hadn't come here to talk to Amanda, she'd come to make her peace with Bronwen. Her mistake still managed, however, to get their chance meeting off on entirely the wrong footing.

'What are *you* doing here?' Amanda asked pleasantly. It was a rare bonus if another family member turned up to share with her the lonely task of grave tending. 'Did Peter tell you where I was?'

'I ... er ... no, I haven't been to the house...'

Maggie always referred to Amanda's home (which used to be Bronwen's and Rex's home, which before that used to be Judy's, Diana's and Jane's home too) as 'the house'. Everyone else called it, quite naturally, 'home', but she couldn't, since it had never *been* her home.

'Just a clever guess then?' Amanda quizzed, pouring water from the jug through the holes of the grave's circular flower holder. It was an intensely familiar scene and yet Maggie could not remember the last time she had been part of anything like it. The memorial vase and the green glass chippings made her shudder and she was suddenly grateful that this grim duty wasn't hers, that Arthur had chosen to have his ashes scattered in his favourite wood, that really, she had escaped all sorts of obligations.

'I wasn't actually looking for you ... I came here to ... I was going to come and see you later but I...'

'Oh, I always come on a Friday. The flowers don't last much longer than a week in this weather and if I didn't do it, I don't know who would...'

Speak as you find, Maggie, came Lottie's voice, but the words were still just a tremor inside her.

Amanda picked up the heap of dead foliage and hauled herself up.

'Sorry, darling, do you want a few minutes on your own? Why don't I go and do Daddy while you and Mummy...'

It might have been the combination of

condescension and twee euphemism that did it, but before Maggie could stop herself, she was saying what she had intended *not* to say until she was absolutely sure she was ready. And she was so not ready.

'I've got something to tell you,' she spat out.

Amanda put her hand on the granite headstone, gripping its curlicue end. 'You're going to say you're ill, aren't you?'

'No...'

'Oh, thank God.'

But Amanda's face had barely had time to relax before it twisted back into confusion.

'I've been to see Lottie, Bronwen's school friend,' Maggie said, as if that was all the information her sister needed.

'Lottie? But she's dead!'

'Not at all. She's actually very much alive in a retirement home near Winchester. Di went to see her only last Christmas in fact...'

'But Daddy told me...'

'Yes, well, Rex told you lots of things.'

Amanda really did put her hand to her mouth then.

'Not here, Maggie,' she said through her fingers. 'If you're going to cause unpleasantness, I'd rather it was somewhere else.'

'It's not unpleasant,' Maggie told her. 'Lottie told me something that—'

'NO!' Amanda shouted across the grave. 'I don't want to know what Lottie—'

Nearly fifty years of unspoken injustice bubbled up like hot lava inside Maggie. 'You will, when you hear what—'

Her sister turned away.

'Amanda, listen...'

'*No...*'

'But it changes everything!'

'I don't want everything changed! I like it how it is!'

And then, all over the churchyard that hadn't heard a raised voice since last December's bride threw her bouquet to the wrong friend, Maggie's choler finally erupted.

'We had a brother!' she shouted at her sister's retreating back. 'Bronwen and Rex had a son!'

Amanda started to run, the sharp stones of the gravelled path pressing into the thin foam soles of her cheap canvas pumps.

'You've no idea what we've all missed out on!' Maggie screeched into the still pastoral air, before letting herself drop on to the grassy blanket under which her mother's bones lay.

The next day, Maggie phoned Jane in Madrid.

'Don't you think you should verify this old woman's story first?' Jane asked. 'She could be making the whole thing up.'

'She's not.'

'She could be.'

'But I've got Rex's letter.'

'If I were you, I'd want some other proof that the birth actually took place.'

'What about *you*? Don't *you* want proof?'

'To be honest, I'm not fussed, Maggie.'

'You're not fussed about your own brother?'

'My sense of family isn't as developed as yours.'

In the background, Maggie heard a horn honking. 'Should I have another go at talking to Amanda?'

'Why not ask Judy that one?' Jane replied, and then said she really had to go because she was meeting a girlfriend in a café in the Puerta del Sol or something.

Maggie did ask Judy, one afternoon early the following week, by which time her lava was less molten, if not yet quite rock.

'Amanda may of course already know,' her second eldest sister said slowly in the over-grown garden of her university mews house that was full of cats and books but oddly devoid of photographs or spare beds. 'I've been doing some sums since your telephone call and she would have been nearly six by then. I would have been only four, you see, so my recollection is—'

'No one is in the dock, Judy...'

'No, of course not...'

'But Amanda was the one who coined the phrase "the baby who didn't come home", wasn't she?' Maggie said, reaching for a biscuit. As she had not eaten for days, Judy's polite offering of stem ginger cookies and weak tea was manna from heaven.

'We thought that was *you*, of course,' Judy said. 'Mummy went into hospital to have what I thought was going to be another little sister for me but she came back without one.

She hid in her room for what seemed like months, then when she finally got up, I remember I wasn't allowed to sit on her lap.'

'That could have been me *or* Colin...'

'She must have come home without a baby *twice* then.'

The sisters shook their heads in unison as they tried to rewrite their past, an effort similar to the sensation of watching the film of a much loved book, all that self-created imagery overridden by someone else's interpretation. Already, they were struggling to remember the original version.

'It's no wonder the ripples caused by my adoption never really reached the edge of the family pond, is it?' Maggie said. 'My pebble wasn't the big one.'

'Are you thinking now that maybe you were the lucky one?'

'I don't know about lucky, but my adoption certainly didn't have anything to do with Bronwen's age, or puerperal fever or their financial position or Grace's misery or any of the other reasons I've spent my whole life trying to be convinced by...'

'So you think Mum couldn't allow herself to love a perfect baby when she hadn't been allowed to love an imperfect one?'

'It makes more sense than anything else ever did.'

'How else could she have given you up?'

The two of them sat in an atmosphere closer to friendship than they had ever breathed together before.

'At least I had you lot eventually,' Maggie said after a while.

'Oh, sisters are just people, finding their way just like anyone else,' Judy said, lifting her sunglasses and resting them on her velvet hair band.

'No "just" about it.'

'He'd be fifty next month. Do you think he's still out there somewhere?'

'No, do you?'

'No.'

And they both cried then, weeping separately in their garden chairs until the older one remembered what to do, and got up to put her arm around the younger.

Epilogue

Thirteen months later

Apart from the large and rather ugly 1970s-built redbrick Percy House, Elworth Close consisted of whitewashed bungalows keeping themselves to themselves behind high conifer hedges. Economical cars sat patiently on drives, their retired owners only seen on days dry enough to mow the neat rectangular verges of grass that ran along the fronts of their properties, or repaint the metal gates or wash their vehicles or whatever other front-of-house maintenance programme brought them every now and again to the attention of the more unconventional occupants of the purpose-built residence over the road.

To Colin Barton, these lesser spotted neighbours were only as real as the little wooden figures who popped in and out of the little wooden house on the wall of the kitchen where Sandy or Tina or Dave cooked and served him his meals. What the bungalow people of Elworth Close – or the little wooden figures, come to that – did when they retreated into their homes didn't occur to Colin. He just enjoyed them for the time they were available to him, and when they disappeared he found something else to enjoy. Today, he stood in the big picture window of Percy House, absorbed by the removal of supermarket carriers from the boot of a silver car opposite. It was a bonus that the place he had lived in for the last five years had no conifer hedge screening it from the world. His last placement, which had lasted a record seven and a half years if you didn't count his first twenty-two, had had a high stone wall around it, but Percy House didn't even have a fence. Anyone could look in and wave to him if they wanted to, which sometimes they did and sometimes they didn't. He liked the after-breakfast man who raised his newspaper at him best.

From the pocket of his loose beige trousers, Colin pulled out a black leather purse and brandished it through the safety glass at the female owner of the silver car. He wanted her to know that he sometimes went food shopping too but she scurried behind her boundary without looking up.

'Money bags!' Tina teased as she passed him, dragging the vacuum cleaner across the new green carpet that none of the staff liked. It was too hard on stockinged feet and reminded them of office flooring. She was going to say as much at the next area meeting.

'Aah.'

Colin, his tongue pressed in concentration against his upper lip, nodded and put his purse back in his pocket. When he looked up, the red car that took him to the Day Centre and the chiropodist had parked on the hot tarmac directly in his view, so he tapped with one finger on the window and waggled it at Dave, the driver. Dave, smiling, tapped and waggled back, and put his arm through Jim's to help him walk to the door.

Colin Barton shuffled away to sit next to Pam on the wine-coloured velour sofa that they had shared for four years now. Before that, they had shared the green one. Two unwrapped presents, one in the shape of a shoe box, sat at his feet.

He picked up his colouring book from the low coffee table in front of him and cut out a page which he then put carefully on a pile of other cut-out pages. There were only two sheets in the book left now – a drawing of a mother duck and a baby duck, and one of a boy flying a kite. The pile was a tea mug high. None of the pages had been coloured in because it was the cutting out that Colin enjoyed.

Pam was knitting. Colin pointed to the wool hanging from her needles, nodded encouragingly and counted clumsily on his fingers. Upstairs in Pam's bedroom at the end of the corridor that had a fire door at each end were three plastic bags full of scarves for the children of Africa. Every now and again, a member of the Percy House care staff tried to persuade her to pack some up and send them off but Pam insisted she wasn't ready.

'I haven't got enough for all of them yet.'

'You can't knit a scarf for every child in Africa, Pam.'

'I can if I want,' she'd tell them.

'Put his teeth in,' Betty tutted from an enormous armchair on the other side of the room. She spoke without taking her eyes off the cookery programme on the wide-screen television which she watched by religiously following the movements of the chef's hands with her own. 'Put his teeth in.'

Colin bared his upper gums at her in a friendly taunt.

'Betty's right, you should really have your teeth in today,' his care worker Tina agreed. 'Don't you want your teeth in on your birthday?'

He shook his head.

'Not on his birthday,' Pam answered for him.

'Aren't you going to unwrap your presents?' Tina asked.

'Not on his birthday,' Pam repeated.

'But I'm going home in a minute. I want to see what you've got.'

'You bought them!' Betty shouted naughtily, still chopping imaginary herbs in mid-air.

Tina called through to the kitchen.

'Isn't Betty supposed to be doing her "supported living" session this morning?'

'She gave up!' a female voice called back. 'She didn't want to make biscuits, she wanted to make fishcakes.'

'Betty!' Tina admonished lightly. 'You don't

330

even like fish!'

Tina pulled the vacuum cleaner through the wide arch into a smaller space that the architects had originally intended to be a dining area but was far better used as Percy House's administrative hub.

'He won't open them,' she reported to her line manager Sandy, who sat at a cluttered desk trying to work out holiday rotas.

'He never does,' Sandy replied. 'Probably stems back to his early years...'

'When someone would have opened them for him?'

'Or told him he wasn't allowed to do it until after lunch or some other bloody stupid rule.'

'Bless him.'

'Unless he knows it's another pair of slippers of course and he just can't be arsed...'

Tina took Betty's personal file from a cabinet and in it wrote: *Restless night, hourly wandering. Sat with her from 2–3am, gave her milky drink, let her lie in. She's complaining of toothache so have made her dentist appointment for tomorrow 2pm. Uncooperative today.'* She put the file carefully back in its private place and then in a staff communications book – a battered spiral-bound notebook with a biro hanging from it by a piece of string – wrote *'DON'T FORGET TO WISH COLIN A HAPPY BIRTHDAY!'*

'I don't know what he's going to make of this afternoon's visit,' she said to Sandy.

'I don't know what to make of it myself,' Sandy said.

'Who are you going to say they are?'

Her pragmatic boss plonked the holiday folder into a tray. 'I suppose we just tell him the truth.'

'It'll confuse him...'

'Confuse *him*? It confuses *me*...'

Colin Barton was proud of his bedroom. The tiger poster on the wall over the sink pleased him very much, but he also liked the comforting boyish face of the children's TV presenter that he had cut out of a magazine and stuck above his bed. Even more reassuringly familiar were the two soft toys on his bed, one a stiff little rabbit made of green felt, the other a large teddy bear wearing an Air Force blue woolly vest. These two friends had been in his possession for as long as he could remember. Care workers and slippers came and went, but the rabbit and the teddy stayed. For a very long time no one had been allowed to touch them, but then Mamma Sister had arrived.

'No darling, I'm not your mamma,' Maggie had corrected him the first few times he'd called her this. 'I'm your sister.'

'Mamma Sister,' Colin had insisted, his articulate pointing finger moving between the two of them – his chest, her shoulder, his chest, her shoulder – to illustrate the significance he knew damn well was there.

To help him, Maggie had dug out and framed an old photograph of Bronwen, taken at a wedding, surrounded by her adult daughters.

'Mamma,' she'd say, touching Bronwen. Then, patting her own chest with one hand at the same time as touching her image on the photo, she'd say, 'Sister.'

'Mamma Sister,' Colin would nod, resting his head on her collarbone. He enjoyed the physical liberties she allowed him. Leave Maggie alone, Tina had tried to suggest in the early stages before Maggie was even a glimmer in the payroll's eye, but Maggie had put her right and said there was no need, she was quite happy with the contact. Now, even though the incessant hugging and stroking and patting crossed an unfair boundary as far as the other residents were concerned, it would have been both impossible and wrong to stop. Everyone knew they were simply making up for lost time. Maggie couldn't say his tangible conferral of approval didn't give her a little thrill. 'Amanda,' she'd show him loyally, 'and Judy, and Diana and Jane ... all Colin's sisters.'

But he would simply waggle his expressive finger in her face, before repeating the chest and shoulder pointing routine again. In the end, it was Tina who came up with the solution.

'You're just going to have to be them all!'

Downstairs, the three women were having the kind of tea-break conversation that would never have made it past the first question in the staff room at Melwood School.

'Do you think it's possible that we recognize

333

our own kin, even if we're complete strangers? If you hadn't told Colin who you were, for example, would he still want to touch you so much?'

'You think there's a genetic smell or something?'

'Why not? I was walking my collie along the old railway track the other day and we met at least four other dogs, but the only one she sniffed was another collie.'

'There can't be. I had no idea my sisters were my sisters until I was ten. I thought they were my cousins.'

'But that's still a genetic connection...'

'True. Have you got sisters, Sandy?'

'Not so's you'd notice.'

'What about you, Tina?'

'Two.'

'And how do they smell?'

'One good, one bad...'

At the noise of a parking vehicle, their heads turned towards the picture window. Two women got out of a blue car. The one without her hair pulled off her face by a velvet headband was being ushered to the door by a tall man who had one hand on her back and the other behind his own.

'Ooh look, it's Prince Philip!' Sandy declared.

I've never been able to smell a thing, Maggie realized without minding. And yet into her head swept a vision of them all sitting around a table, sharing food and drink and having the sort of perfect time that families

334

all over the world sometimes but rarely pull off. Perhaps it would happen one day soon, just down the road, in the pre-war, slate-roofed, metal-windowed house she now called home. It needed a lot doing to it but it suited her well. It had a garden plenty big enough for Arthur's shed and a pets' corner should she need one, it had two spare bed-rooms for returning children and grand-children, and also very usefully, it had a large outhouse which was ideal for making beauti-ful but expensive kitchens in. That was what had sold it to her and Don in the end – that, and the fact that it was cheap enough not to have to sell Don's barn, which meant they'd been able to give Jamie a proper key for his twenty-first.

'Do you think Colin will understand who they are?' Tina asked quickly as the bell rang.

'What does it matter if he doesn't?' Maggie asked, before going to open the security door to let them in.